P9-BAW-750

BARELY MISSING EVERYTHING

BARELY MISSING EVERYTHING

MATT MENDEZ

A Caitlyn Dlouhy Book
NEW YORK LONDON TORONTO
SYDNEY NEW DELHI

FOR MARLO, ALWAYS.
AND CARLO PASSASEO,
WISH YOU WERE HERE.

An imprint of Simon & Schuster Children's Publishing Division + 1230 Avenue of the Americas, New York, New York 10020 + This book is a work of fiction. Any references to historical events, real people, or real places are used fictitiously. Other names, characters, places, and events are products of the author's imagination, and any resemblance to actual events or places or persons, living or dead, is entirely coincidental. + For information about special discounts for bulk purchases, please contact Simon & Schuster Special Sales at 1-866-506-1949 or business@simonandschuster.com. + The Simon & Schuster Speakers Bureau can bring authors to your live event. For more information or to book an event, contact the Simon & Schuster Speakers Bureau at 1-866-248-3049 or visit our website at www.simonspeakers.com. + The text for this book was set in Palatino LT. + Manufactured in the United States of America + First Edition + 10 9 8 7 6 5 4 3 2 1 + CIP data is available from the Library of Congress. + ISBN 978-1-5344-0445-8 (hc)+ ISBN 978-1-5344-0447-2 (eBook)

"THE WORLD WE LIVE IN IS A HOUSE ON FIRE AND THE PEOPLE WE LOVE ARE BURNING."

—SANDRA CISNEROS, A HOUSE OF MY OWN

BARELY MISSING EVERYTHING

BEFORE THE MISS

The lights take me right back to that night. To the game. I can almost hear coach yelling. Smell the stink of the gym. That night led to the house party, to a swarm of raiding uniforms and one pulling a gun on me. Everything in my life went crazy from there.

I'm blinded by the fluorescents and running as fast as I can. I hear the truck's engine idling. Shouting coming from behind the light.

I have to make it to the truck if I want to see my dad.

If I want to do anything good with my life.

I have to.

All I need to do is dig deep.

Show some heart.

CHAPTER JUAN
(CHAPTER ONE)

Juan Ramos was dead. His game stiff and clumsy from the jump. It was January, the season already beyond the half-way point, and every game had been part of a parade of embarrassments. The air inside the gym hung thick and sour, the ventilation system crapping out before tip-off and making each breath like swallowing a hard-boiled egg. Juan stood at the edge of the huddle as Coach Paul ripped the team for not playing smarter. The Austin Panthers' point guard stood doubled over and tried to catch his breath. He had plunged the team into a hole after only five minutes, turning the ball over twice in a row and going 0-for-5 from the field.

"Ramos, take a seat," Coach Paul yelled, mean mugging him from the middle of the huddle. "You're showing no heart out there."

"Whatever," Juan said as he took a seat on the bench.

Heart was never going to matter. The game had swirled down the toilet the moment Juan's mother, Fabi, and her boyfriend, Ruben, strolled inside the gym during layup drills, the clicking of Fabi's high heels echoing across the Panther Athletic Center—the PAC—and inside Juan's head, causing his attention to pinball from defensive assignments and running the offense to wondering why his má had showed at the game in the first place. A thing she never did.

Dressed in a pair of tight jeans and a too-small Austin Panthers T-shirt, her wrists spangled with bracelets, his mother pointed to a pair of empty seats behind the Panther bench, her fingernails long and glossy red. Like she'd wanted, Fabi had the attention of every man in the PAC, and once seated, the mesmerized men went from watching her to sizing up Ruben, collectively wondering how a goofy motherfucker like him had landed a woman like Fabi. He was shorter than Fabi by more than a few inches and wore a cowboy hat that dwarfed his head. His blue jeans had creases ironed down the middle of the legs, and he wore his Austin Panthers T-shirt over a long-sleeved, button-down shirt. Of course, Juan didn't have to wonder. Ruben only seemed like a sucker. He was the owner of EZ Motors, a used-car lot that made a killing selling shitty rides to Fort Bliss soldiers and people with even shittier credit. He was a predator, and unfortunately Fabi had "easy prey" written all over her.

The Panthers were also easy kills. All they had going

for them was Juan, the best player on the worst team in 4A Region 1, District 1. And with him playing like a scrub, they had no chance of winning. It was Juan's senior year, but it had begun without letters from college recruiters—even though he'd been All-District the past two seasons—leaving him to wonder just what exactly he was going to do after graduation, if he even made it that far. His grades were garbage, and Mr. Rosales, his guidance counselor, had told him before the start of the semester he'd be better off learning a trade than worrying about basketball or college.

With Juan on the bench, Derek Evans darted up and down the court, the EPHS Tigers' point guard extending the lead in two quick possessions. The score: 20–0. Juan had made the mistake of playing too aggressively against Evans. On defense he'd reached for steals, slapping Evans across the arms and earning a cheap foul. On offense Juan tried too much isolation, ignoring wide-open teammates and taking terrible shots. Evans was a senior, too; a guard with speed and court vision that had made recruiters take notice. Coach Paul told Juan before the game that Evans was peaking at just the right time. That timing was absolutely everything. Timing and not being a five-foot-eight Mexican.

The Panthers finally got on the board after almost ten minutes, junior guard Eddie Duran hitting a three in relief of Juan. Coach Paul walked to the end of the bench and sat beside Juan. Juan tried to watch the game but couldn't concentrate. The back doors to the gym had been propped open, but the cold breeze only made things worse. Able to smell his own sweat on his undershirt and damp uniform, he turned queasy. Coach Paul slapped him on the back and whispered, "Tell me when you're ready to quit acting like a spoiled diva and play some ball? That's all I'm asking." He strolled back to the head of the bench, raising his voice so anyone who wanted to hear him could. "Just give me a thumbs-up or something, Juanito. Pretend you have some pride."

Lack of pride wasn't Juan's problem. All the time he spent working on his game, the dribble and passing drills, running stadiums and wind sprints and suicides, hours working on his shot, his form and follow-through, endless weight lifting and push-ups and even yoga, were all done because of pride. There was a little over a month left in the season, and while riding the pine, the exact kind of trouble facing Juan was now becoming clear. With his last semester's grades as bad as the night's stat line, there was a chance he'd have to make up classes come summer—or worse, could miss graduation altogether. And what kind of gigs could he land *if* he even managed to graduate? Would the Border Patrol hire a Mexican who'd managed to fail Spanish? Who sucked at math and science *and* English? He hoped not, even if they paid like $52,000 a year to start. And *fuck* working for those ICE motherfuckers.

Ignoring Coach Paul, Juan headed to the scorer's table; he could hear Fabi cheering behind him: "You can do it, mijo. Show that pendejo coach what you're made of." Juan's belly felt like it was filling with air, sharp pains jabbing his sides. It was the same feeling he used to get before games his freshman year, right before he puked into trash cans. Back then Juan had been nervous about playing organized ball, worried his aggressive style wouldn't translate from the playground. Coach Paul was always in his ear, telling him he needed to understand the game, learn when to be aggressive and when to throttle back. To *manage* the game and not gamble on every play, but the Panthers didn't have enough game to manage. Wanting to win, Juan took his chances, going hard after every loose ball, trying every tight pass and gambling on every contested shot, hoping the ball would bounce his way.

Juan kneeled at the scorer's table. Coach Paul nodded at him and held three fingers in the air to remind Juan to play smart and not pick up another foul before the half; the game was not quite out of hand at 25–12. Juan understood, and checked in after Derek Evans had been fouled by Eddie Duran and was set to shoot free throws. Juan jogged onto center court as Eddie headed to the bench. Fabi leapt from her seat and waved her arms in the air. "Go, Juan! Beat some Tiger ass!" At a quick glance she could be mistaken for a student, her Panthers T-shirt knotted slightly above the waist, with more than a hint of exposed skin. The man sitting beside Fabi zeroed in on her chest, not caring that Ruben was staring him down or that Juan was now throwing up, doubled over and retching as everyone else watched, groaning and then laughing as he ran from the gym.

By the second half the PAC had almost cleared out. Only bored parents remained, talking and ignoring the game. The Tigers were destroying the Panthers 64–33, the Panthers' worst points beating of the year. So far the season had been mostly losses, the sole win coming on the road, in a tournament game played in Lubbock, Texas, against a team of gringos missing half their squad. Most of their starters had gone down with the shits before tip-off, a case of self-sabotage with bad mayo finding its way into their sandwiches before the game. Juan had scored twenty-five points in the first half alone, repeatedly blowing by an uncoordinated second-string point guard with nobody contesting him at the rim. The predominantly white crowd quickly turned hostile, chanting, *"Build the wall! Build the wall!"* before halftime. Coach Paul pulled Juan in the middle of the second half after noticing Juan being booed every time he touched the ball. He didn't care—he'd just balled the best game of his life, draining thirty-foot jumpers that whipped the bottom of the net and dominating on D, anticipating dribble patterns and picking the pocket of the opposing point, firing down the opposite side of the court for layup after layup.

The Panthers' bus was rocked after that game. Silhouettes emerged from behind the gymnasium, crashing rocks against the yellow siding, the hollow thunks echoing inside, the windows chipping and spiderwebbing across the purpled tint. The team huddled between the seats of the bus as it quickly escaped, silent when Coach Paul told them they wouldn't be staying for the rest of the tournament, Juan stunned that winning could feel so much worse than losing.

Now Juan stayed in the locker room as the Panthers took the court for the second half, telling Coach Paul he still felt sick even though he felt fine after spewing his guts—just, well, embarrassed. Fabi had been texting him, asking if he was okay, if he needed her, but Juan ignored the messages. The only reason Juan eventually returned to the bench was to keep Fabi from looking for him in the locker room. Coach Paul nodded approvingly as Juan took his seat, still dressed to play but having no intention of doing so. The ventilation at the PAC finally kicked on and he was able to breathe. Coach Paul probably thought Juan was showing some pride, braving his illness and supporting the team. Fabi had moved to the other end of the court, talking to the parents of the opposing squad, waving at him until he finally waved back.

Watching Má, looking like a forever teen over there, Juan began to wonder how life had been for her in high school. Fabi had also gone to Austin, at least until she became pregnant with him her sophomore year and dropped out. He imagined she'd been popular, but didn't know that for sure. She didn't have any best friends—at least none that he knew of. She was smart, getting her GED without taking any study classes, but maybe not that smart, seeing as she still worked at the same bar that had been her first job at seventeen. He'd always assumed his father had gone to school with her—he wished Fabi had been the type to keep yearbooks. She didn't hang photographs on the walls of the apartment or keep albums or have pictures on her phone aside from the cascade of selfies taken in front of the bathroom mirror. So many times Juan wanted to hold a yearbook in his hands, thumb through the glossy pages and maybe come across a familiar face. His own.

Whenever he brought up his father, though, she turned squirmy. When he'd been little, she'd tell him he didn't need a dad, that it was them versus the world. He used to love that idea, but as he grew older, and learned their world often included random boyfriends, he began wondering who his old man could be. Why these other dudes were in his life but not his father. But Fabi always dodged his questions with shifty answers. *It's really complicated, mijo. I'll tell you when you're older. When you'll understand.* Juan didn't get why she would hide this from him, like knowing a name would change the fact that he wasn't around. Still, he never pressed too hard, seeing how panicked she became whenever he asked—always changing the subject and raising her voice as she spoke real fast, going from English to Spanish. He rarely asked at all now.

A hard whistle blow brought Juan's attention back to the game. After spending the entire first half dominating, the Tigers now looked bored, even as they continued to dictate the game, setting down screens and crosscourt picks, nonchalantly finding the open cutter who cruised to the basket for easy scores. Juan was glad he didn't have to go back in—at least he got the chance to watch JD, his best friend since kindergarten, play.

JD Sanchez didn't play often. He wasn't the worst player on the team; considering how bad the team was, he could have taken any starting position, except for Juan's, and the Panthers still would have lost the games it had by the same margins. The reason JD didn't play was his attitude. He wasn't the eager underdog Coach Paul wanted or needed him to be, the guy with less talent but lots of heart. The rah-rah guy. Instead JD openly criticized Coach's play calling, renaming their offense the "Pick and Stroll," and refusing to cut his hair when Coach suggested they do so for team unity, arguing that his locks were freedom of speech. He once told Coach Paul the only reason he'd joined the team was because he wanted to soak up his parents' fair share of tax dollars, since he was sure none were being spent in the library—like he ever went. Juan knew JD was full of shit. He came to practice every day and spent almost as much time working on his game as Juan did. JD loved basketball, even if he hated the pressure of being on a team.

But tonight was the best JD had played all season. By Juan's count JD scored ten points and ripped five rebounds, moving with a confidence Juan didn't recognize. JD's usual rebel camouflage didn't work on the court. There was no amount of trash you could talk that would take the place of tough defense, no long hair to hide behind when you were afraid to shoot the ball. Something had changed him recently, JD was playing looser than usual, playing better because of it. Juan wondered if JD would tell him what was happening or stay the same secretive dude he always was.

"¡Mijo! ¡Oyes, Juan! ¡Mijo! We're going to meet you outside," Fabi screamed from the bleachers. "Novio wants a cigarito. This game's over anyways."

The game clock showed two minutes left as Juan buried his face in his hands, everyone turning to look at him. Fabi and Ruben stepped down the hollow steps of the bleachers, her clicking heels again loud and unbearable. Juan kept his face buried, not wanting to see his teammates or players from the other team, coaches or random dudes in the stands turn their attention from him to his mom, their eyes burning on her ass as she short-stepped from the gym. Them slapping each other on the arm as she breezed by and agreeing they'd all *smash that*.

Juan remembered some of his má's other "novios." The manager of a nightclub who promised Fabi club dates where she could perform with the house band but never delivered. Another who wanted her to model for his furniture store but hired a former Budweiser girl instead. The lawyer who hooked her up with a free will. All these vatos bought Fabi clothes or jewelry; one pendejo got her a truck, a Mazda B2600 she still drove. And now there was Ruben "King of the Deal" Gonzalez. Juan hated these novios, recognizing them for what they were: cheap nobodies wanting to use and make trash out of his má.

The buzzer blared, startling Juan. Final score: 75–40. Glad that the game was finally over, Juan followed his teammates onto the court and joined the single-file line to congratulate the winners, both teams high-fiving and muttering "good game" to one another. Juan said nothing, the whole after-game ritual fraudulent. The Tigers pretending there was anything "good" about the game was more humiliating than the beating itself, more humiliating to him than splattering his guts in front of the home crowd.

"It figures I get my best game in our worst loss," JD said, meeting Juan at midcourt, nodding at the spot where Juan had puked and grinning like an idiot. The rest of the Panther team, Coach Paul included, quickly disappeared into the locker room. "I won't even get to remember this shit fondly. All anyone is going to talk about is you puking. That was hilarious, by the way."

"Glad to contribute," Juan said. "I must have eaten something bad."

"Maybe those Trumputos put a curse on you," JD said. "They're probably still pissed at you for stealing that game from them—and their country. The whites are pissed about all that."

"We won that game! We didn't steal shit! Besides, you weren't even there!"

"I know. I'm just joking. Chill. I was sick."

"Well, I'm just sick of all this losing."

"It's just a game. It don't even matter."

This was classic JD, always missing the point. Juan was

sure JD took being the leading scorer on the losing side as some kind of moral victory, but Juan knew there was no such thing. Any performance, no matter how brilliant, got erased by losing. Every beatdown, every triple-double that came attached to an *L*, brought Juan one step closer to having his own *L* permanently stamped across his forehead. Or maybe it already had been, and that's why the recruiters failed to come. They knew what Juan knew deep down: He couldn't turn his team into a winner because he wasn't one.

Out the gym door Juan could see Ruben's neon-green H2 hogging two spaces at the end of the PAC parking lot. He and Fabi stood behind it. Fabi craned her neck as the team began filing from the locker room. Ruben stared into the small screen of his phone, swiping at it with his finger. Fabi had texted Juan three times now, saying she and Ruben were waiting for him. That Ruben was nice enough to want to take them to dinner. The Hummer had televisions molded in the leather headrests of each seat, underneath the monogram *El Rey* stitched across in neon-pink lettering. It's wheels were chrome and shiny as mirrors.

"Where you parked?" Juan asked JD, pulling him back from the door, stopping him before he strutted from the locker room, the post-game shower failing to wash away his ten-point swag like it failed to cleanse the loss from Juan. The team was already asking if Juan was going to make the "half-court heave" part of his regular game.

"Teacher's lot. I don't want my ride getting dented up by the kinds of assholes who come to high school basketball games. Except for your mom—she's not an asshole. . . . Why is she here, anyway?"

"I need you to pick me up at Cakes."

"For what?"

"I don't want my má and her pendejo boyfriend to see me leave. He wants to take me to dinner. No way."

"Ask if you can take a friend." JD threw his hands in the air, exasperated, his eyes wide. "I'm hungry."

"Let's just eat at Danny's."

"Is that why she came to the game? So *he* could take you to dinner? That sounds all right to me."

"I don't know why. And I don't care."

JD was shaking his head now, his hands on his hips like a disappointed teacher, before he suddenly stopped, a thought seeming to zap into his head.

"Maybe he wants to be your new daddy? He can get you the neon-green bike with TVs you've always wanted. You can be in his goofy commercials, be like the Prince of Payments or some shit like that. You two could work it out over some flan. C'mon, let's go get some free food."

"Why am I friends with you?"

"Because on the first day of kindergarten you wouldn't stop crying and I was the only kid who would sit next to you. You remember."

"Yes, *I'm a giant crybaby.*" He elbowed JD in the gut. "Now, go tell my má I left already. No seas cabrón."

"Bueno, pero I'm gonna need a hug first. For you being all mean to me."

"I'm not hugging you."

"Yes, you are. So I can get over your assholery. You only children got no social skills." JD stood waiting with outstretched arms. With no siblings and some cousins he was sure weren't really cousins, Juan counted JD as one of the few people on the planet he could say he loved. He hugged his brother from another mother, each slapping the other on the back before JD surprised Juan by gripping him tightly. "I'm proud of your emotional honesty, cabrón."

Juan felt a surge of relif as he watched Fabi and Ruben finally hop into the Hummer and peel away after a quick conversation with JD, tires squealing and the smell of burnt rubber lingering as Ruben cut through the emptying parking lot. Juan's phone buzzed. Fabi. He didn't answer. Once he was sure Fabi and Ruben had driven far enough away, he made his way behind McKee Stadium and the rest of the high school. Raking a discarded broom handle across the chain-link fence surrounding the perimeter, he imagined the fight Fabi and Ruben were having. Her apologizing for her asshole son and him making a bigger deal of Juan's ditching them than it actually was, trying his best to have an advantage over her.

Trash blew against the fence, trapping plastic grocery bags along the bottom, adding to the snarl of small tumbleweeds and candy wrappers. Before seeing Fabi at the game, Juan had planned to skip the party at Danny's. Come up with some excuse and head home, watch some old Jordan highlights on YouTube. He wasn't in the mood to party, but those plans were now out the window. Fabi would be looking for him, and the party at Danny's new house, way over on the East Side, would be a good place to escape to.

Cakes by Sonny—the small bakery on Stevens Street where they sold cheese fries, tortas, conchas, and loosies—was closed. *Damn.* Juan kept his hands shoved in his pockets as he waited for JD. He now wished he hadn't left his AHS sweatshirt balled up in his locker. That he owned a jacket. Someone, who probably owned both a sweater and jacket, was grilling. The greasy smell of carne asada made Juan's thoroughly emptied stomach ache.

Flashing his lights, JD sped across the bakery's three-space parking lot and slammed his brakes in front of Juan, the engine of his '88 Escort pinging as it idled, fan belt squeaking. The body of the hatchback had originally been blue but had bleached to an almost white—well, everything except for the red driver's-side door and front fender, junkyard parts JD's old man used to fix a wreck JD had been in while learning to drive. The back passenger window had also been replaced, by duct tape and cardboard, after a break-in where the cassette deck—who was still listening to cassette tapes?—had been ripped from the dash. JD wrote on the cardboard in fat marker: *Some dick stole all my shit.* Perhaps he hoped no one else would feel the need to poke around the inside of his car and steal his loose change or the pinwheel he'd glued to the dash.

"Gimme a cigarette," JD said as Juan jumped inside.

"I don't have any, and you can see Cakes is closed."

"Always with excuses. Have some fucking pride."

"Let's go to Danny's already. He'll have frajos. And beer."

"And weed?" JD said.

"Probably," Juan said. "It's a party."

"I bet he doesn't. He's at Cathedral now. The rich kids got him. I bet they're playing spin the calculator and doing homework."

"You kidding? Those dudes are way more fucked up than either of us. I bet Danny smokes bath salts now. "

"You really think so?" JD said, putting the car into gear. "Do you think it's hard to keep that uniform clean being addicted to hobo meat?"

"I'm sure the struggle is real," Juan said. "And being in the student illuminati is no joke, either."

"Catholics are assholes."

"Isn't your whole family like hardcore Catholic?"

"Just my mom and my sister and my old man and my brother, both nanas and my one tata who is still alive, all my tías. But *that's* it. Don't get it twisted."

"And you? You're not Catholic anymore?"

"I lost my faith when Father Maldonado dumped me for a younger altar boy."

"You're messed up."

"True," JD said, pulling away, a blast of white smoke clouding from the tailpipe. "For real, though, promise you won't be all salty. I can't deal with that tonight."

"That's *you*, homie," Juan said, adjusting the passenger seat. "You'll be the one hating on Danny's new peeps all night."

"Just the shitty ones."

The nerves Juan had felt since tip-off faded as JD drove, and he began to warm to the idea of a party, of heading toward something fun and with no drama, even if only for a night. It felt like a win.

THE PARTY
(CHAPTER TWO)

The East Side of El Paso sprawled beyond what Juan had once considered the boonies, Joe Battle Boulevard and Americas and into Horizon City. Developments with names like Montana Vista and Las Tierras were a new oasis in once-barren patches of cactus, rock, and weeds. Builders had speedily cleared the landscape before anyone seemed to notice, much less complain about, the vanishing desert. Single-family homes had been slapped up and no one had wanted one more than Danny's father, a retired army master sergeant. According to Danny, his old man couldn't get out of Central fast enough, wanting away from the crappy part of El Paso and to get a piece of the good life his new plum job as a field service rep—whatever that was—with Lockheed Martin now offered him.

Danny lived in Cascade Point, a housing development

that looked just like the others they'd driven by, rows of shoebox buildings with big garage mouths, all painted either light brown or tan or khaki, some a creamy coffee shade with darker trim and well-matched peat gravel landscaping the front yards. The same desert plants that had been uprooted to make room were now neatly planted along the concrete driveways and walkways. Creosote bushes and mesquite trees, thorny cacti looking pretty as long as they were planted alongside rosebushes and colorful flowers Juan didn't know the names of.

"I can't believe Danny's even throwing a party," JD said. "They've only been in the house, like, what, a few months? I know his parents travel a bunch, but they're gonna notice if the place is trashed when they get back."

"Danny's crazy," Juan agreed. "But it ain't my chante." And he didn't think he was exaggerating when he called Danny crazy, either, at least not much. Danny had been expelled from Austin in November, right before Thanksgiving, after blasting the main hallway with pepper spray. Mr. Pokluda, the assistant principal, was trampled as students rushed to get outside. Danny was lucky the cops hadn't been called, that the Sarge, as his father liked to be referred to, had once donated uniforms to the entire football team and was padrino to Pokluda's oldest daughter.

Cascade Point was still under development; Danny Villanueva's house was completed and ready for a party. Silhouettes moved behind the lit windows of the house, muffled music sounding like a band performing underwater. To the left and right of the house were empty lots, construction markers poking from the flattened dirt like industrial weeds. Down the block the skeleton of a two-story home had been framed. Juan studied the bones; without the meat and skin of drywall and stucco the home seemed weak, destined to one day vanish as quickly as it was built. The apartment building Juan and his mother shared was made of brick. And even though the plumbing and electrical were bad, both uncovered in spots, the roof coming apart shingle by shingle, he never imagined the walls of the building completely vanishing. For better or worse the neighborhood, his neighborhood, was a permanent reality.

"You think we'll know anyone here?" JD asked, slowly approaching the house.

"I hope not," Juan said, wanting to be as far away from his current life as possible.

Juan could tell by the cars lining the sidewalk and clogging the driveway that no one from Austin was at the party. JD's Escort was glaringly out of place, like a cheap plastic button mistakenly dropped inside a jewelry box full of family heirlooms. Juan circled the cul-de-sac and parked at the other end of the block. Juan knew JD was embarrassed about being poor, always quick to turn his shame into jokes or politics, pretending the mismatched quarter panels and door of his ride were part of his personality. Being poor sucked, and Juan didn't see the point of pretending it didn't. For what?

“Sure you parked far enough away?” Juan asked.

“I don’t want to get it scratched,” JD said.

“Or stolen,” Juan said, playfully slapping JD on the shoulder as he cut the engine. “This thing is a classic.”

“True. They probably made a million of these, but still . . . a classic.” They looked at the almost full block they needed to walk to reach Danny’s, laughed, and got out of the car.

“We can move it another block down. I bet your Escort is the last one running.”

“You’re probably right about that.” Slamming the doors shut, JD and Juan headed toward the party.

“Promise you’ll drink the free beer and have a good time?” Juan had his doubts.

“Yeah, yeah, yeah. I’m good.” And JD seemed good, not even twitching at the sound of the poppy indie-light music coming from Danny’s as they got closer, some acoustic or banjo band with too many singers and spastic clapping.

Danny stood in the open doorway, a bottle of beer in his hand. He’d been waiting for them. “Heard you puked all over the court. ¿Qué pasó, güey?”

“¿Quién dijo eso?” Juan wanted to forget about the game, about losing, about puking. About Fabi and Ruben and whatever them coming to the game could’ve meant.

“Is that shit on YouTube already?” JD said.

“No way,” Juan said. “No one watches those games, never mind records them.”

“Lucky for you,” JD said.

“Maybe not so lucky,” Danny said. “My dad, *the Sarge,*

said Coach Paul should be recording all those games for film study and sending tapes to recruiters. He said Paul can't coach or manage a goddamn thing. That's why he got fired from his last gig, and why nobody's recruiting you."

"I always thought it was because you're Mexican," JD said.

"I don't care," Juan said, a total lie, thinking Danny was probably more right than JD, but only by a little.

"At least that Eddie Duran dude will get his chance next year. The Sarge said he was gonna record his games for him."

"Why?"

"The Sarge goes to church with his dad."

"You don't go?"

"Nope."

"Desgraciado," JD interrupted, laughing, the word rolling off his tongue like the villain of a telenovela.

Thinking of the Sarge recording Eddie's future games was too crappy to deal with, so Juan turned his attention to Danny's new place. The living room walls were bright white and unblemished, no blackened fingerprints on light switches or doorframes, no holes busted in them. The carpet was freshly vacuumed, neat lines running down the entire length. An odor from the carpet overpowered the room, a chemical smell revealing its newness. Juan loved it. The party was in the backyard and kitchen; the silhouettes they'd seen in the windows were kids Danny had been giving the tour of his new chante to. Danny ran to the fridge and grabbed a couple of forties and a box of cold pizza for Juan and JD.

Juan cracked open the twist top of his and took a long pull before jamming a cold slice into his mouth.

The two-story house was massive, over three thousand square feet, Danny explained as they moved upstairs. Juan didn't care about exact measurements, instead understanding the size by the number of rooms: three bedrooms and three bathrooms, a loft, a living room, *and* a family room—not to mention the kitchen, with a nook and stainless steel appliances, and even a dining room. Danny's family had a three-car garage and a backyard bigger than the parking lot at Juan's apartment building. Danny's bedroom was still full of boxes, his parents' master bedroom locked. The third bedroom was the smallest but still bigger than Juan's, maybe bigger than Fabi's, too. Suitcases were on the bed, along with a neat pile of clothes laid on top. Some skirts and blouses, bras and panties.

"My prima's moving in with us," Danny said, shaking his head and not bothering to close the door or hide his cousin's chonies, pink-and-black numbers.

"Is she hot?" JD asked.

"Her parents are activists, took off to protest all the anti-immigration bullshit for a few months," Danny said. "My crazy dad said *they're* crazy, but what could we do? They're familia, so she can stay."

"Where are *your* parents?" Juan said.

"The Sarge is at some conference, and my mom dipped with my tió and tía to some protest in Arizona for the weekend. She only resists part-time."

"Is she here?" JD said. "Your prima?"

"*No*, man, and aren't you still in love with Melinda Camacho? 'Ay, mi linda Melinda. I still *love* you even though we only kissed once in seventh grade.'"

"I don't know why you guys keep bringing that shit up. And it was eighth grade."

"Because it's funny," Danny said. "And true, too. Ain't that right, Juanito?"

"Your house is sick," Juan said.

"Thanks?" Danny said, confused. "You fucked up already?"

"Uh-huh," Juan said, taking another drink from his forty. He imagined the room was his own, his family all living under one roof. Grampá in Danny's room and Fabi in the master bedroom. Being inside Danny's house had changed Juan's feelings about Cascade Point; the homes no longer seemed temporary and cheap. Juan knew how dumb it was to fantasize about a thing that would never happen; as a kid he daydreamed about his father one day appearing, taking him and Fabi away from their apartment to a new life. As Juan grew older the daydream changed into his search for his father, Juan having to decide what to do once he found him. Would he fight him? Forgive him? And then what?

Fabi called again; Juan already had two unheard voicemails and knew the next morning was probably ruined, him having to hear about how rude he'd been to her novio before being shipped off to Grampá's for day labor. He deleted the messages without listening to them.

Walking inside the cousin's room, JD said, "I'm taking a look."

"No, you're not," Danny said, quickly walking him back out. "What's wrong with you?"

"Cálmate, güey," JD said. "Besides, why'd you bring us here in the first place?"

"Shit, just to show off how big the house is and brag. That's it. I didn't know you'd get all creepy."

"Creepy? All I did was walk inside her room and look at her underwear and ask if she was hot. . . . Okay, that's totally creepy. My bad."

"I'm gonna get drunk now," Juan said, wrapping his arms around JD and Danny's shoulders, huddling them close, suddenly wanting to be done with the tour. His phone buzzing in his pocket again. "This *is* a party, right?"

"Claro que sí," Danny said. "Let's get back downstairs."

"Pos vamos," JD said.

The party was the same as every Austin High party Juan had been to, except everyone had nicer clothes and the music was terrible, the playlist a disaster of electronica and indie bands Juan was sure people only pretended to like. Couples made out in the darkened living room, sitting on the sofa and on the Sarge's leather recliner. Danny led Juan and JD through the kitchen, where dudes in letterman jackets kicked it around the counter taking shots of cheap tequila. He introduced them to some of his other friends. A couple of guys from the baseball team, Joaquín and Manolo, and two girls, Adelita and Carmen, who ran cross-country and went to the Loreto Academy, a private school for girls. Danny's new friends seemed okay, but Juan didn't do more than say "What's up" before taking a chug from his forty, not sure what else to do. Danny explained how Joaquín and Manolo were from Juárez. That Cathedral High School drew students all the way from New Mexico. That they were cool. That Cathedral was pretty cool.

"How much does it cost to go there?" Juan said, looking at Joaquín, thinking maybe, just for a second, that he could transfer schools.

"I heard my parents say it was like eight thousand for last year," Joaquín said. "Something like that."

"Holy shit." Juan looked at Danny, who was staring at the ground, suddenly uncomfortable and not wanting to look at him. "That's like buying a new car *every year* or something."

"Well, like a used car," Manolo said, putting his hand on Danny's shoulder. "Everything cool, Daniel? You don't look like yourself."

"Yeah, I'm good. Thanks."

"Shit, not as good as me," JD said, draining his beer and then slapping Danny on the back. "I just found out I'm wasting my education *for free*. Time to go outside. C'mon, Juan." They grabbed fresh tallboys from the fridge and made for the door.

Danny stayed inside with his new friends. Juan didn't

blame him. He shouldn't have asked about Cathedral's tuition and embarrassed him like that. Having money wasn't Danny's problem. It wasn't even a *problem*. Juan watched him from the backyard, through a window. Standing in the kitchen with Manolo and Joaquín, with Carmen and Adelita, he seemed to be having a good time. Laughing and drinking. He remembered when Danny used to live with his grandparents, in a tiny house with a leaky roof and only one bathroom.

The wind blew cold, but it didn't stop anyone from partying. Music blared from tiny speakers that looked like rocks placed along the concrete walkway leading to the patio, where pockets of kids Juan didn't recognize blobbed together. Another group hung by a chiminea in the middle of the yard, its open mouth glowing orange as the wooden logs popped and hissed inside, plumes of smoke rising from the slender neck. Nobody talked to Juan or JD.

Just as Juan was going to tell JD that they should go back inside, a slash of bluish light suddenly crossed Juan's chest. He jerked his head up. Other bluish beams zigzagged the inside of the house and the backyard. Conversations that had been humming only moments before abruptly stopped, all sound blanketed by the *whop whop whop* of helicopter blades. The ghetto bird buzzed overhead, a single wash of brutal light kicked on, drowning out the full moon that had been bright enough to light the party. This wasn't how parties were broken up in the movies, where a single cop warned the party's host to keep the music down and the bash kept going afterward, because in movies cops could be fucked with.

This was a raid. But who was raiding? Was it the cops? The sheriffs? Or was it ICE, there to hunt for "illegals"? Gangsters?

A half dozen uniformed men swarmed the backyard; a girl standing across from Juan erupted into tears as a light was shined in her face. "I'm sorry," she said to no one before doubling over and puking. The mix of preppy white kids and fresas suddenly seemed out of place; they were still in the middle of the desert, where having money meant nothing.

The *whop* of chopper blades clapping against the air grew louder.

Juan gave his head a shake, trying not to freak, wishing he hadn't downed that last forty, wishing he didn't already feel fucked up. He tossed his freshly opened can to the ground—stupid!—because the movement grabbed the attention of a lawman. Instantly drawing a gun, he approached Juan. He was an El Paso cop—not that it mattered, really; all law enforcement was designed to fuck with brown people. This wasn't the first time Juan had had a gun aimed at him. A gang of cholos from Central, dudes who relentlessly cruised a gray Cutlass, once peeked the double barrel of a shotgun at him after a game, the driver asking him if he thought he was faster than a speeding bullet. To run away so they could see. They seemed more interested in a laugh than actually shooting him, so he turned and ran, giving them the joke they wanted and hoping to get as far away as he could. But apparently there was no escaping from the cops, not even at Cascade Point.

Whatever. Juan was used to being hassled. Usually the chota wanted to take down names and snap pictures for the citywide gangbanger database, check for warrants and now, papers. Do their big-brother routine. If he played it cool, ate a little of the shit the police served, he could be on his way. But this time he wasn't going to get the chance to play it cool. The cop drawing on him suddenly holstered his weapon and yelled into the radio fastened to his shoulder, his attention drawn to something behind Juan.

Juan turned. It was JD, perched on the back wall of the yard. "Come on, Juan. Let's go!" JD yelled, then jumped. *Dude, what!?*

Juan glanced back at the cop, who was now eyeballing him. *Try it,* his eyes seemed to be begging. Juan could tell he was about to be taken to the ground and wrestled into handcuffs. About to be taken to jail and charged with some made-up shit. About to lose. The cop charged him, and Juan gambled, waiting for the cop to get close before pulling a hesitation on him. He stutter-stepped, and the cop, unsure of which direction Juan was going, lost balance. But unlike on the basketball court, where a speedy point guard could blow by an undisciplined defender without being touched, the cop grabbed the bottom of Juan's T-shirt as he zipped by, yanking Juan toward him and the ground. Juan planted his feet into the desert dirt and struggled to stay standing, his shirt ripping as he finally pulled away. The cop fell to the ground, landing flat on the beer can Juan had just tossed, booze splattering everywhere. Juan spun and raced for the wall.

He vaulted over it easy. Less easy was the ten-foot drop on the other side. He flailed for a second before collapsing to the ground, his left ankle rolling underneath him. It began to throb immediately. *Run through it. It's nothing. Just run through it.* He tried to gather himself, figure out where he'd landed, expecting to be in an alleyway like the ones in Central. Juan was used to using the alleys for escape; he once ditched those same cabrones from the Cutlass—only then they were chasing him on foot—who had planned on jumping him, pissed he'd said no to their invitation to join Los Fatherless. But now, as Juan realized he was in another backyard, he had no idea what to do. The yard was similar to Danny's, only smaller and with a slab of concrete alongside the house, the premade footers and rebar poking through, ready for a cheap wooden patio like Danny's to be built.

"This way!" JD hissed just as a voice came from the other side of the wall: "Two went over."

JD bolted across the yard and over the far wall. Juan limped as he ran, his ankle hot with pain.

As he leapt the second wall, Juan found himself in yet another backyard. A pair of floodlights flashed on. Footsteps pounded behind him. How many identical backyards would he have to jump through before he found a pawnshop or bar or bakery or auto shop, even a dumpster to hide inside? He hustled to catch up with JD—cursing his burning ankle. He would be lucky to be able to play with this injury. To just be able to walk on the court and be slow and have no vertical would be a miracle.

His ankle went numb as he finally caught up with and passed JD in their fifth backyard. Adrenaline pumping, Juan sprang up and pulled himself to the top of what turned out to be the final wall in their way, a ten-footer at the end of the development. Juan caught his breath and watched as JD tried to make the jump. From on top Juan could see the broken-up party: police cars surrounding Danny's, partygoers spilling into the front yard and being directed to leave. *Of course.* None of *them* had guns pointed at their chests. None of *them* were going to be handcuffed. None of *them* were going to jail. If only Fabi hadn't come to his game, he thought furiously—she never came!

"JD, come on!" he barked.

JD struggled to make the jump, only managing to slap his chest against the wall before collapsing to the ground, breathing hard. Two cops entered the far end of the yard. Damn. Juan jumped back down. The same blinding bluish lights that had slashed through the party were now on him as he prepared to give JD the boost he needed. JD wasn't used to this, to being on his game when shit really mattered. To crunch time. Juan lifted and pushed JD over the wall.

"Stop right there!"

Nope. Juan was over the wall a second later, the cops

screaming for them to stop, to get their bellies on the ground and give it up. On the other side of the wall a steep dirt hill sloped toward a construction site with tracts of half-built homes and empty plots. That's where they needed to go. Where they could hide until morning.

As they sprinted down the remainder of the hill, Juan worried about what was beyond the development. If there was nothing but more desert, endless dirt and rock and bullshit cactus, then they could be running toward nothing. The cops could surround them. They could already be waiting. And where did that helicopter go?

"Man, why'd you run?" Juan yelled, struggling to keep ahead of JD, losing steam himself.

"Because . . . I don't know, fuck!" JD said, panting.

A chain-link fence surrounded the development at the bottom of the hill. Juan heaved himself onto the webbing and pulled himself over the fence, narrowly missing the crisscross points on top but landing on the same ankle, hard. This time it seemed seriously fucked, the pain sharp and pulsating up and down his leg, unable to hold his weight. Behind him JD tripped on his own feet and stumbled into the fence, his face planting hard into a support post. He dropped instantly to the ground, disappearing into the shadows.

"JD . . . JD . . . Shit," Juan whispered from the other side. He limped over to where he'd thought he heard the thud, but he could also hear the cops coming, the rubbing and squeaking of their leather gun holsters and shoes pounding the hardening ground. The gamble wasn't going to pay off.

"Fuck, man, why'd you run?" he cried out again. Then he limped as fast as he could through the construction sites, across the empty lots and through the unfinished houses. Wooden frames, beams and joints and exposed electrical wires turned out to be no place to hide. The bright desert moonlight illuminated everything. Juan made his way toward the only unit that had some interior walls up. He was pretty sure JD was busted but wanted to text him anyway. To check on him. He hoped the fence post hadn't fucked him up too badly, that the cops didn't when they found him.

He spied a box of tile inside the house and sat on it, trying to regulate his breathing. He was surprised by how drained he felt, like he just finished playing an entire game. He looked around; the roof of the house had yet to be mounted onto the frame, the back walls were still unfinished. He was now totally exposed. And he'd been right about there being nothing but desert beyond the development. Nothing but mesquite trees and yucca and hills with rocks and hard dirt. There was no place for him to hide, no place to run to.

Juan's phone buzzed. It was a text from Danny:

Why you clowns run?
Sooooo ghetto! WTF?

He was about to respond when he heard the *whop whop whop* of the police helicopter overhead. *Fuck.* He slid his phone back inside his pocket.

Down the street, a motorcycle cop was carefully cruising toward him, his spotlight cutting from one side of the site to the other, red and blue lights silently flashing. The guts of the half-built homes glowed as the light passed through them. The light then cut across Juan, and the motorcycle stopped. He thought about running toward the desert, but then what?

Juan limped from the unfinished house, hands in the air. The spotlight from the helicopter flooded on, Juan instantly in a swirl of light and dust, chopper blades thudding loudly as police sirens called from the distance. For the second time tonight Juan knew he was going to lose big. At least this time he'd run his hardest, and through injury. He'd shown some fucking heart.

JD DON'T KNOW
(CHAPTER THREE)

Juan Diego sat on his bed and watched as his amá tore his room apart, tossed socks and underwear from his dresser, dug into the closet he shared with his younger brother, Tomásito. JD's shoes were dumped in the middle of the room after being checked for any contraband stuffed inside. Tomásito, who'd been sent outside to play, spied from the backyard through their cracked bedroom window as their mother, still clutching the box of condoms she'd found hidden in JD's dresser, began pulling his collection of bootleg DVDs off the shelves. JD had arranged them alphabetically, by director and genre. Mostly B-movie horror, classics and zombies. Some kung fu and Hong Kong and Samurai. Cine Mexicano, American indie, and a growing documentary collection. Outside, Tomásito tried to pretend he wasn't snooping, occasionally tossing a basketball in the air and trying to catch it whenever Amá looked out the window. He was nowhere near the portable hoop, so there was no obvious game the little pain could be playing.

"What kind of drugs are you on?" Amá asked.

"The none kind," JD answered.

She'd dumped his movie collection on the bed, his Taratinos now mixed with his del Toros, his Eastwoods and Ed Woods and Cuaróns and Gondrys all in a meaningless pile. Now taking a seat beside him, Amá tried looking JD in the eye, but he wasn't down with that and stared at the floor instead, his head throbbing. He had a bump on the middle of his forehead, dried blood around his nostrils. All he wanted was a shower, to sleep and then skip the awkward conversation his amá seemed intent on having.

"Where did you get these things?" She held out the open box; six were remaining from the original twelve.

"I bought them," JD said, trying to sound casual, like she was holding sticks of gum and not evidence of an affair. Truth? He'd found the condoms on Christmas Eve, hidden under the driver's seat of his old man's truck. He'd been looking for the small screwdriver set his old man usually kept there, wanting to take apart an old Super 8 camera he'd lifted from a garage sale—a Russian model with a clockwork drive—when he found the box stashed in a paper bag.

"Why won't you look at me?" Amá asked.

He couldn't because he knew that when Tomásito was born Amá had had her tubes tied, had lost a lot of blood during labor and almost died—her or Pops always told the story on Tomásito's birthday. It was the worst! So he knew that the condoms were for Pops and his sidepiece. That Amá had no idea. And no way was *he* telling her.

"I just want to shower and go to bed. *Por favor*, Amá." Amá grabbed JD by the chin and examined his face. The way she looked at him, like if she wasn't physically touching him she couldn't be sure he was real, freaked him out. He turned away, thinking he might cry if he looked directly at her.

"Tell me again what happened to you." Amá's expression was like it always was: part worried, part pissed off.

"I fell."

He fucking fell, all right. The night was a blur, especially the part after he face-planted into the fence post, the blow dropping him into a trench along the bottom of the fence. The cops who'd been chasing him and Juan must have leapt right over him without bothering to look down. When JD came to, everything was quiet and dark; he was alone, the moon blanketed by clouds.

Amá pressed. "I texted you. I called you, and you never answered. What else am I supposed to think? You have to be on drugs, right? I mean, look at you." She let go of him and waved her hand at the pile of movies on his bed. "Look at the stuff you're into."

"There's nothing wrong with this stuff. They're just mov—"

"I never know where you are," Amá interrupted. "You're

always coming and going as you please." She was in her church clothes, a neatly ironed black button-down shirt and black slacks. Her hair was pulled back in a tight bun.

"I broke my phone," JD argued. True, his phone had been smashed when he fell, the small screen a spiderweb of broken glass. But she wasn't having it. Amá's face was sharp and hard and brown, like his own. Both of them were blasted from the same mountain rock. The black clothes were her Sunday uniform and not too different from the brown scrubs she wore to the State Center, where she worked the swing shift as a caretaker.

"Ay Dios, mijo. Are you sure you're not on drugs?"

"I'm sure," JD said. Smoking weed every once in a while was *not* the same thing as being "on drugs," not in JD's book.

"What about sex?"

"No one wants to have sex with me," JD said, afraid that was true, then thinking he shouldn't be talking sex with his amá. *Fuck, I am dumb.*

"Then why are there condoms missing? You're *lying* to me."

What could he say? *You're right, Amá. These belong to Pops. I guess he's not having as much trouble getting laid as I am.*

"And where's your car? Tell me that." Staring at the mess in the room, JD had the thought that Amá should've been a homicide detective. She held the box of condoms like it was the murder weapon in a crime she'd just solved.

"It wouldn't start. I walked home last night." Her eyes

drilled into him, searching for proof he wasn't full of mentiras. Then, suddenly, she dropped the box between them on the bed. It split open, and the six remaining condoms spilled out. Her shoulders fell as she stared past him, her lips pinching tight.

"You're a bad liar," Amá said, sounding like she might cry. "Or, actually, you're really good at it. I'm just finally catching on."

"I'm sorry, Amá," JD said at last, slowly realizing they weren't only talking about last night. Not only about him.

"Tell me about the condoms. Tell me the truth, for once in your life."

JD remembered the brown paper bag he'd found them in, the same type of bags they used at Jasmine's, the liquor store he bought forties at without ID. "I'm sorry I have them."

"*Why* do you have them?" She squeezed her bun, loosening it and then letting her hair down.

"I don't know." Not completely lying. "But I'm sorry." When he took them from the truck he wasn't sure what else to do. He planned to tell his sister about Pops stepping out, knowing Alma would go straight to Amá and everything would blow up, but he hadn't yet. Having the condoms meant JD could keep his life the way it was, keep the fantasy of a normal family—even if that fantasy, come to think of it, wasn't even a good one.

Amá shook her head in disappointment. "Not as sorry as your apá was when he saw me with these this morning.

He said I had no right to be snooping in his truck. He tried to make *me* the bad person. Can you *believe* that? And I know you're hiding more secrets in here. I'm not stupid, me entiendes?"

"Yes, y lo siento," JD said again. His eyes were watery. She already busted Pops. Probably already threw him out, knowing Amá. Fantasy over. Shit.

Amá stood up. Straightened her shoulders. Her thick brown hair still without any gray. "I need you out too. Right now," she said decidedly. "You need to leave."

"*Leave?* Where am I supposed to go?" His eyes went wide as he tried hard not to cry. He imagined Amá tossing Pops out, then continuing the search of his room, still looking for proof he was on drugs or that he was somehow helping his old man cheat. Her now ready to believe the worst about him.

"Go to Mass. Go to confession. Go anywhere but here. You don't get to hide your father's lies and stay living with me."

"I *wasn't* lying for him!"

"Then what were you doing?"

"I don't know. But not that."

JD promised Amá he'd go to Mass and confession, and she promised he could come back. Twenty minutes later, making his way up Piedras Street, he walked past Gussie's Tamales & Bakery. There was a line out the door, old ladies and groups of kids from the neighborhood holding empty pots for menudo to be poured into. He could smell the pan dulce as he went by. He was starving but had no cash for an empanada or marranito. Man, he loved those gingerbread pigs when they were soft and fresh from the oven, a glob of butter on the top. He crossed the street. Our Lady of Guadalupe was at the top of the hill, but before making his way all the way up, he decided to stop at Melinda Camacho's and take a break under her mulberry tree.

Sitting in the shade of her front yard, he wondered if Melinda was home. JD had been stupid for Melinda since he was a little kid, and he hated himself for being the longing-after type, a dude who pined after a girl who probably didn't give a shit about him. He'd had one girlfriend since Melinda, a couple of hookups, but nothing coming close to what he felt for her. It was pathetic.

Melinda's parents were presumido types, college grads who moved back to the neighborhood a few months ago after years of West Side life. They were "reinvesting in a historic neighborhood" by buying and fixing up an old house—the only two-story on the block—and living in the barrio. *What a joke.* Melinda, who like most of his family, called him Juan Diego, had briefly explained this the last time they spoke, during a chance meeting at Gussie's. She'd been dressed like someone going on a job interview, her dress long but form-fitting, a white-and-black number that only hinted at how banging she was. Her shiny black hair was neat, flowing down her back. Of course *he* had looked terrible—ratty basketball shorts and a stained white tee. He'd had wicked bedhead and worse morning breath. He was the dictionary definition of a dirtball.

They'd met as chamacos. Her grandparents were neighbors with his grandmá. Now Melinda was a senior at Loreto Academy, a private school she'd been going to since kindergarten. JD had crushed on Melinda from the first time they met. She had oddly pale skin for a Mexican, was athletic and confident and sensitive. She couldn't speak a word of Spanish, but spoke English like an adult; conversations she had with her parents sailed over his head. She couldn't play outside very long because she would sunburn—JD could go all day in the sun, turning more and more prieto but never hurting because of it. Melinda wasn't like anyone else in the neighborhood, and because of that the other kids either ignored her or hated her guts. To JD, though, she was irresistible.

She was his first kiss, when both of them were in eighth grade. It had happened on her grandparents' porch, on an evening about to turn to night, them sitting quietly after she'd road-rashed her knees during a game of stickball. JD had pulled Melinda to her feet and walked her home, the game continuing without them. Melinda hadn't said a word, hadn't disappeared inside the safety of her grandparents' home, and instead sat on the porch swing. JD sat next to her, also silently. He remembered the smell of water from running hoses evaporating on the concrete sidewalk. Hearing dogs barking and soft television coming from inside the house. Melinda put her hand inside his, and he turned to look at her, her skin shiny with sweat as she brought her lips to his.

After that day they spent a whole summer meeting by the light post on the corner of Memphis and San Marcial, taking walks through the neighborhood, holding hands, and kissing like crazy. JD grew comfortable with making the first move, leaning his head and lips toward hers. JD didn't tell anyone about Melinda, not even Juan. He liked having a secret.

Still, news of their walks made it around the block, and eventually Melinda's papa caught them making out in the alley behind JD's nana's house. He yelled at Melinda to get away from that loser kid. Actually used the words "loser kid," even though he knew JD's name, his family. Melinda had looked into JD's eyes, her expression going from startled to embarrassed before she turned and ran away. JD had had no idea that would be the last time they would be alone together—not counting their run-in at Gussie's.

Nobody seemed to be home at Melinda's now, and JD began to feel like a sucker-ass stalker. Anyway, what could they possibly have in common anymore? He didn't have good grades, wasn't in the National Honor Society or running the student government like she probably was. He didn't belong to any clubs except for the basketball team, and he was barely a part of that. He was a story from her past, a memory turned into whatever shady image her father had created for her—another hood rat who would derail all the plans he had for her. The fucker was probably right.

He was stupid for still thinking about Melinda at all. He hopped up and quickly walked the rest of the way to Our Lady of Guadalupe. Then he stopped. He didn't mind going to the church like Amá had asked, but confession wasn't going to happen. It wasn't because he had anything against the idea of spilling his guts to a stranger—what did he care? But what did it matter if a god forgave your mistakes if no one else did? So he pulled out a cigarette. If he wasted enough time, he could head back home, Amá would think he'd been to confession, and he could get some sleep.

After his smoke, he went inside and sat in the back pew. The place was empty, Masses already over for the day. At least now he could tell Amá he *went* to church. Sunlight cut through stained glass windows, causing images of saints and crosses, chalices floating above them, to glow. On the walls were paintings of more saints. The Archangel Michael spearing the Devil, and John the Baptist standing in a river, arms extended over a bent body ready to be baptized; La Virgen presenting herself to Juan Diego, him clutching a shroud with her image. JD had been named after the saint, and he guessed he was lucky he hadn't been born on the feast of Guadalupe a few days later; his life was every bit the motherfucker without having to go through it with a girl's name.

He rubbed his forehead tiredly, feeling the bump, and remembered planting his head into a fence post. He wondered if Juan had been able to get away from the cops and was now afraid he hadn't. It would be his fault for running, for calling Juan to follow. *Shit!*

• • •

Back home, JD looked around his room. It was a disaster—DVDs everywhere, his clothes and movie equipment dumped like garbage. Seeing all those old camcorders and cameras, bought or stolen from Salvation Armies and garage sales, cheap stands and floodlights he planned to one day use for lighting, yanked from the back of his closet and still never used, was . . . embarrassing. He had the feeling—like Juan not-so-secretly wanting to play pro ball—that trying to be a filmmaker was a born fucked idea. He'd been hoarding secondhand equipment for years, wanting to create Guillermo del Toro monsters or Robert Rodriguez action, but he wasn't sure how to do anything beyond stockpiling old stuff. Because, shit, he had no idea where to start. Or how. And even if he tried, anything he made from junk, stayed junk.

Picking up a slim, pocket-size video camera, a Panasonic HM-TA1 he found at a thrift store for twenty bucks and the only digital one in the group, he'd surveyed his room through the viewfinder. From behind the lens the room seemed like it belonged to someone else. JD had never shot anything more than a few test shots with any of his cameras, but staring at his stripped bed and the pile of clothes on the floor, the opened drawers and emptied shelves, he decided, *What the hell.* He flipped on the camera, which surprisingly had 10-percent battery life, and panned across the room. "This morning Amá found the condoms in my dresser, the ones Pops had been hiding under the front seat of his truck.

I hid them after finding them on Christmas Eve. And now my old man has left. Or, actually, Amá kicked him out." JD filmed across the room and stopped on the note Amá had taped to the mirror. He zoomed in on her writing, wondering how he sounded on film. Probably like an idiot. He continued narrating anyway. "'Your father will pick you up at 6 to get your car. Don't let him in the house.' Well, I'm pretty sure I ruined the family. . . . Cut."

Neither JD nor his father said a word as they pulled onto I-10 and drove toward Danny's. His old man was still dressed from work, sleeves rolled to his forearms, his black tattoo, Amá's name written in Old English lettering—Estela—partially exposed. JD dreamed of covering his own body with tattoos, though none as tacky as a name—even if it was Amá's. The cabin of the truck smelled of sweat and metal. In the bed his old man's toolboxes, a pair of jumper cables, and loose nuts and bolts slid from side to side as they changed lanes and hammered down the highway, exhaust blasting behind them.

The radio was on KLAQ, the official shitty classic-rock station of Chuco, and barely audible. JD struggled to hear the song playing but couldn't quite make it out. It was either Poison or Mötley Crüe, some overproduced hair metal bullshit that was as bad as the overproduced indie garbage hipsters liked. JD wondered what his father had been into when he'd been his age. Metal or alternative? Hip-hop? Norteño or mariachi? Maybe he hated music, wished he could live in the town from *Footloose*. Whatever the old man liked, JD wondered why he had never thought to ask before. Why he didn't know anything about his old man except the one thing he *didn't* want to know.

Rolling down the window, JD stuck his arm out; he liked feeling the resistance against it as the cabin filled with the sound of rushing air. He could sense his old man staring at him and rolled the window back up.

"Don't tell me your friend lives past the Americas. I just spent all day over there."

"They just moved. His dad got some big-timer job after retiring from the army," JD said. "They think they're all good now."

"No seas pendejo. I should've done that, been a lifer. I'd be an E-9 by now. Actually, probably retired, too, but still."

"Why'd you leave, then? What's an E-9?" JD adjusted himself, wanting his old man to talk into the camera he was hiding under his jacket. Pops only talked army whenever JD failed to clean the yard to his specs or needed a haircut, whenever JD really pissed him off.

"Because your amá was pregnant with Alma," he said. "Your amá didn't want to leave nana and her family. I got out for"—he tilted his head slightly, clenched his jaw—"for *her*." His face looked like he was trying to keep from puking his regrets all over the truck's cabin. "Our life could've been way different."

"And an E-9?"

"Goddamn it!" Pumping hard on the brakes, Pops

slapped the dashboard with the palm of his hand as a black Honda cut in front of them to exit the highway. His entire body was tense, arms flexed and bent, his left hand gripping the wheel and the right fist suspended in midair, wanting to strike. JD knew his father wasn't really pissed at the Honda driver or at having to drive to the East Side. These were the types of things he was going to yell about instead of stolen condoms or being kicked out of the house. "Being an E-9 is being the boss," Pops said, calming down. "One stripe better than your little buddy's dad got to be, by the way."

As far as JD knew, his old man had always been in charge of himself. He'd been a plumber for as long as JD could remember, but that wasn't all he did. He hung drywall and installed flooring and roofs and could fix almost anything on a car. He worked all the time, but he never seemed to have a boss or a regular schedule—he never seemed to have a lot of money, either.

"What were you doing up here?"

"What do you think?"

"Plumbing job?" JD asked, looking straight ahead at the open road. The radio station cut to static as they exited the highway and drove along a two-lane road with no lights until they reached Cascade Point.

"They're building tract homes like crazy out here. It's better money than clearing drains and septics all day."

"Oh," JD said. "These houses are nice, though." He fingered the camera in his jacket pocket, the back smooth and warm. He had no idea what he hoped to get, but maybe Pops would say something important, something to make him feel better about what was happening and then he'd have it. Instead Pops snorted.

"Shit, they're building them too fast. Besides, they're nothing but chicken wire and stucco. They're no good."

"I thought these houses were for richy-riches."

"Some are, but even those are built exactly the same. Most of the places out here don't cost nothing. People from Central and the Lower Valley are moving this way. All the new soldiers coming to Fort Bliss. It'll turn shitty in a few years. Your little friend's daddy just traded one ghetto for another. . . . Is that your car?"

Pops didn't waste time, pulling up to the Escort and going for his toolbox, waving for the keys before opening the door and popping the hood. For the first time all day he looked relaxed. Comfortable. JD didn't know if *he* ever looked like that doing anything. Probably not even when he slept. Without a word his old man looked over the engine bay, not touching anything. JD wanted to know what Pops was looking at, to know how his car worked—but Pops had never showed him how, not really, always too busy or explaining things too fast when he did.

"Try it," Pops said, tossing the keys back to JD, who fumbled them, barely out of the truck himself. He took his seat behind the wheel, took a breath, and turned the key, wanting, somehow, for the car not to start. Of course the motor wheezed to life, just like he knew it would. Pops appeared suddenly through the windshield as he closed the hood. "It seems good now."

"Thanks, Pops." JD looked at his father. Pops must've known JD was full of shit, the car abandoned for reasons that had nothing to do with a bad starter or a dead battery, but he didn't want answers or an explanation, instead tossing his tools in the bed of his truck, okay with the lie. Was JD wrong for wanting answers from his old man? To know why Pops was seeing another woman? To know who she was? He felt like a total hypocrite.

"Go straight home," Pops said, not bothering to look at him. "And put some ice on that chichón. Your head looks lumpy."

"I swear . . . I swear it didn't start," JD stumbled. "I'm not lying."

"Straight home," Pops said as he cranked the truck's engine. He pulled into the street as JD retrieved his camera from his pocket to record his father driving away. But the camera was now cool, the battery dead.

FABI AND HER CARIÑO (CHAPTER FOUR)

Fabi sat on the toilet and peed, holding the thin plastic stick between her legs. After freaking out all weekend about Juan, she had wondered how bad the week was going to be, and now Monday morning was starting off this way. This was her third pregnancy test in three hours. The first showed a positive, a blue plus sign in the test window; the second was unclear—a pair of parallel lines meant to signify positive or negative but instead looking like a blob of pink. Her period was a month late, and she'd been off birth control for way longer than that—she hadn't been with anyone in forever, and getting pregnant wasn't something she worried about, not even after meeting Ruben.

When she finished she placed the stick on the toilet tank, next to a dusty basket of potpourri. The overhead fluorescent light buzzed and flickered like it always did.

The flooring needed to be redone, mildew seeming to have replaced the grout between the cracked and mismatched tiles. The faucet dripped nonstop. Complaining to the landlady, an obese woman name Flor Ramirez, would be a waste of time. Juan called her Jabba the Slut—*awful*. But she *was* lazy. Flor still hadn't fixed the window in her bedroom that had slipped from its frame, or looked into the leak stain forming on the ceiling above her bed. It had started small, just a swirl, but grew into a flared, brown hurricane.

Fabi washed her hands and sat back on the toilet, waiting for the digital test—*stupid* expensive—to spell things out for her. If positive, the word PREGNANT would appear across the viewfinder.

Meanwhile Ruben and Juan sat in the living room, awkwardly watching TV together. Of course, Juanito *hated* Ruben. He'd hated all her boyfriends. Fabi always thought Juan was just being territorial, but now she wasn't so sure. After watching his power struggle with his coach the other night, it was possible he thought all men, except his Grampá, were sketchy. Maybe he hated all of them. Still, Ruben was oddly patient, putting up with him. It had been his idea to watch Juanito's basketball game, and then he'd been okay with Juanito skipping out on them afterward, telling her not to worry about it. Like he got ditched all the time.

Then this morning Fabi had had to pick Juanito up at county jail. His bond had been set at $1,000, but a bond company—Get Free!— took $300 to get him out. Nothing *free* about that. There had been plenty of times when Fabi felt like a shit mom, but picking him up from jail and him not even looking happy to see her when he got released, that was the shittiest. Her life was some kind of a ghetto sitcom. She peeked at the pregnancy test.

The little white stick read PREGNANT, and Fabi felt like her bones had been replaced by steel rods. She couldn't move from the toilet seat, so she just cupped her hands around her face and cried. She'd been in her father's bathroom when she'd learned about Juanito almost eighteen years earlier, reading a similar stick covered in pee. She remembered how the room smelled like his aftershave, Aqua Velva or was it Brut? Her mother had just died, her sister about to disappear to college. At least this time she didn't puke all over the sink.

After a minute she told herself, *Start over.* She took another shower, and after brushing her teeth she slipped on some fresh clothes, did her hair, and put on her face before making her way back to the living room, still not quite ready to deal with either Juanito or Ruben.

"What took you so long?" Juan asked, pointing at his left ankle as Fabi joined him and Ruben in the living room. "I think this thing is broke." His ankle was purple and blue around the joint and to the toes, tiger-striping up the middle of his calf. Fabi moved to sit by her son on the couch; Ruben leaned forward on the mismatched chair facing them. Juan had been fine after the game, minus the upset stomach, and Fabi wondered just how he'd hurt himself so badly. Whether the police had anything to do with it. She reached out to touch his ankle, but Juan pulled away, wincing as he did.

"Would you like a ride to the hospital?" Ruben asked Fabi, ignoring Juan. "It's no problem."

"No." Juan shut him down before Fabi could answer. "Why don't you leave already? Don't you have *deals* to make?" He slumped down in his seat, crossed his arms, looking every bit the angry teen.

"C'mon, Juan," Fabi said. "You're being rude, to both of us."

"You two are an 'us' now? I get it." Juan was trying to make her feel worse than the worst mother on the planet. It was working.

"I don't want to bother you," Fabi said to Ruben, trying to ignore Juan. Ruben half stood, like he wanted to join them on the couch, but she motioned for him to sit his ass back down.

"It's no problem," Ruben persisted, readjusting in his seat.

"*I* think it's a problem," Juan said. "But no one ever wants my opinion around here."

"Shut up already!" Fabi felt like the rope in a game of tug-of-war. "You are in enough trouble! And Ruben, thank you for the offer, mi cariño." She immediately wished she hadn't called him that, him smiling the same toothy smile he did at the end of one of his cheesy used-car commercials.

That smile. Would he smile the same way at the news of

her being pregnant? Would he turn noble, talk about being there for her and the baby and possibly mean it? Would she find out Ruben had other baby mamas, a track record of knocking women up and then leaving, never to be heard from again? The simple possibility of that stunned her, and what stunned her even more was realizing she didn't know Ruben well enough to guess what he'd do. But all that would have to wait until after dealing with Juanito's ankle. "I'll call you later tonight. Okay?" she said to Ruben. "I've got my hands full today."

"Okay . . . bueno pues," Ruben said, still smiling as he sprung up to leave. Juan exhaled loudly, in that way teenagers do when they don't have the words to express how stupid they find everything, and zeroed in on the television, suddenly interested in a cooking show where a woman was wrapping seemingly everything she was making in bacon.

Without insurance, urgent care cost $120 for the visit and extra $30 for the air cast the doctor fitted on Juan's ankle—not to mention a day without pay and the hell Fabi would get from her man-boy boss, the twenty-five-year-old who went by Chuchi and dropped out of UTEP after one semester as a business major. The entire morning had a price tag of $450, more than Fabi had. The cost seemed steep for Juan, too; she could tell by the way he was staring at his ankle like his foot had been amputated.

"At least it's not broken," Fabi said as she drove home.

"Doc said a month or so and you should be good. It's just a sprain."

"With ligament damage. How am I gonna explain this to Coach?"

"It's not the end of the world. You can focus on your grades instead of basketball."

"It's too late for focusing on grades to do me any good," Juan said. "Besides, I'm already failing."

"You're failing?" Fabi asked. How was he failing?

"What a shock that you didn't know." Juan stared out the passenger window, his reflection in the glass looking like it was floating outside, looking a world away.

"Why do you gotta keep giving me shit? I didn't do anything. *You* just got out of jail. *You're* the one in trouble, not me. ¿Entiendes?" She pressed hard on the gas of her old truck, the engine revving higher and her quickly changing gears, sending the black Mazda flying down the street.

"*I* didn't even do anything."

"*Tell me you understand*, Juan."

"Yes, already. I get it."

"They don't put people in jail for nothing." Fabi squeezed the steering wheel, her knuckles turning white.

"Well they did me, but whatever." He shifted in his seat. Turned his body away from her, like she was radioactive.

"Don't say another word, cabrón. I'm trying to think about what I'm gonna do with you." Her hands looked like two ugly knots. Like they didn't belong to her.

In a few weeks Juan would have an arraignment

hearing—so he would need a lawyer, and even an okay one would cost more than Fabi could afford. How bad would it be if they went with a public defender? How big a deal could evading arrest be? And then there was the baby. *Pregnant!* How many weeks was she? Four weeks? Eight? *¡Ay Dios!*

Fabi sped through a four-way stop without taking her foot off the accelerator.

"Mom! What the hell?" Juan braced himself for an impact, grunting as he banged his ankle against the passenger floorboard.

She glanced at her speedometer—60 MPH—and took her foot off the gas. Her knuckles ached from how hard she'd been squeezing the wheel. She loosened her grip, her hands now trembling.

"What is wrong with you?" Juan asked, gingerly holding his ankle. "Where are we even going? We passed the house already." The color had drained from his face, his lips dry and grayish pink, eyes bloodshot.

Fabi's heart thumped hard in her chest.

Juan was staring at her. "Má, what's wrong with you?" he said. "We could've been T-boned!"

"I'm taking you to Grampá's," Fabi said, the idea coming to her as she was saying it. "You'll be fine there." She decided she couldn't wait to see the doctor. She would find one today, say it was an emergency and not leave the office until she knew all she needed to about the pregnancy. She would figure out the cost later.

• • •

Grampá was sitting on the porch, drinking a tallboy and wearing, as always, his blue Dickies coveralls. A bandanna collected sweat from his forehead; at his feet lay an open toolbox and an AM/FM radio with the antenna pulled all the way out, static-filled Oldies vibrating through the cracked speakers. The yard, which used to have grass—as a little girl Fabi remembered taking off her shoes so she could feel the soft green blades between her toes—was now a hard dirt lot with junky cars stalled on it, waiting for his attention.

Her dad didn't move when he saw Fabi and Juan pull up. Fabi wondered if he'd heard about Juan's trip to county. News like arrests, unplanned babies, divorces, and deaths spread quickly, Hollywood paparazzi not having shit on the metiches in Central. Fabi killed the engine and remained seated as it coughed to a stop; she wasn't quite ready to make her way to the porch. Since he retired from twenty years with the city as an electrician, her daddy made extra cash fixing cars or working on busted washing machines—anything, really, him the neighborhood Mr. Fix It—and when he was done working for the day, he spent his time relaxing in the backyard, patiently tinkering on an old Chrysler she was sure he'd never finish. It had probably been there since she was Juan's age. He stood as she hopped from the truck at last, watching her, suspicious as always.

"Hi, Daddy," Fabi said, taking a deep breath and then

climbing the stairs to join him. "Is it okay if Juan stays here for a while?"

Taking a sip from his beer, her father craned his neck in order to see Juan still sitting stonily inside the truck. "Is it okay with *him*, Fabiola? He looks like *he's* the one who minds."

"He's *fine*," Fabi sighed. "He hurt his ankle and I don't want to leave him alone at the house."

"At the apartment?"

"*Yes*, the apartment." Grampá nodded, his usual know-it-all nod. "They gave Juan meds at the doctor, and I don't want him alone while he's on them."

"You mean drugs? What'd they give him, acid? Mota? Pinches doctors are worse than narcos."

"It's just ibuprofen. For the swelling."

"What kind of drugs are you really on, mijo?!" he yelled down to Juan. "Are you gonna flip out or something? Eat my face? Should I chain you in the yard?" Juan stared back.

"He's not gonna flip out," Fabi said, not wanting to argue, at least not yet. "Can I leave him here or is that going to be too big a deal for you?"

She could tell she was pissing him off; he was rubbing his face and then giving her the same look he used to give her as a teenager. Fixed scowl. Squinty eyes. The lines around his eyes were deeper now, though, the spots on his cheeks darker. "So where did he hurt it?"

"You ask him. He'll tell you, and then maybe *you* can tell me exactly what the hell happened."

"You working tonight?" Grampá was standing close enough to hug Fabi but hadn't. She hadn't moved in to hug him either. Every moment between them was like this, an *almost*-something moment. *Almost* a fight. *Almost* a cease-fire. *Almost* the apocalypse.

"If it's gonna be a big deal, then forget it. I was thinking of what was best for Juan. Your grandson."

"I didn't say no. Don't be so grosera . . . and come give your jefe a hug, for God's sake. You want favors but won't even ask nice."

Why did he have to be such an ass? Fabi motioned for Juan to join them. Juan at last hobbled from the truck and limped up the stairs, Grampá saying to Juan, "I've got crutches somewhere in the yard."

"Thanks, Dad," Fabi said. "I'll be back to get him tonight. I just have some things that need my attention."

"Like going to work?"

"That too." Fabi sighed. "Entonces, tomorrow. I'll get him in the morning."

Fabi kissed Juan on the forehead and told him she'd drive him to school the next day, no arguments, then she headed straight for the truck. She drove off in the direction of Project Vida, the free clinic, deciding she had more time than money. She called Ruben, listened to his Ringback song, some cheesy reggaeton she didn't recognize that sounded awful. Ruben didn't answer, his voicemail instructing her to leave a message and he'd call back. Fabi had dated men like Ruben before, flashy types. Macho types. Ruben was nicer than the others. But Fabi knew being nice wasn't the same thing as being good. They were only related. Nice was like Good's cousin, cool but sometimes shady. Still, Fabi decided she would tell Ruben about being pregnant—she was not going to make *that* mistake again—but not until she knew what she was going to do about it. She hung up without saying a word.

In the waiting room Fabi tried to keep from freaking out by going through her bills; her mail was still stuffed inside her purse from the day before, when Flor tried to corner her at the mailboxes and Fabi rushed to get away. Of course looking at bills didn't help. The credit card she'd thought maybe she could put a lawyer on was almost maxed. The payday loan, used to buy a new transmission when the one in her crappy truck died, was coming due. Flor's overdue rent.

A muted TV hung on the wall, mostly ignored by the other pregnant women in the room, most of them half Fabi's age. They seemed busy reading pamphlets or thumbing through pregnancy magazines. Staring blankly at their phones. The television played one of Ruben's cheesy commercials. The one with him dressed like a soldier, fighting the "war on prices." God, those were corny.

Fabi thought about the years ahead of the soon-to-be mothers. Not just the moments after their babies were born—the sleepless nights and feeding schedules, thinking you might be messing everything up—but motherhood after the beginning. The part where you *were* messing everything up. Someone had forgotten their sonogram on the table beside her. She remembered her first one, the little blob on the screen, the flicker emanating from somewhere inside it. Juan's heartbeat. That had been the moment she'd realized she would keep him, thinking before that she wouldn't.

Fabi came across the last envelope in her pile, the corners bent and soft. Like they'd been rubbed. Fabi recognized the name on the return address immediately: Armando Aranda, 999178, Polunsky Unit, 3872 FM 350, South Livingston, TX 77351.

Throw it away, was her first thought. *Do anything but read it.* Armando Aranda. He'd been her boyfriend from a lifetime ago. Her cariño. She hadn't thought of Mando in years and now had the strangest sensation, as if she were traveling in some sort of time machine—a fucked-up time machine that was dragging her back to the worst moments of her life. She stared at the address. Why now?

She'd never responded to a single letter after his sentencing. It was one of the ways she'd planned to get on with her life; for a long time Fabi blamed him for her missing Mamá's final moments. Eventually, the letters stopped. And now she didn't know what to expect after cutting him off so completely. Anger? Hatred? Maybe, but Fabi sensed that wasn't why he'd written. Something else had to be happening. Something dramatic. She rubbed at those bent corners of the envelope. Damn. She was already on the verge of crying. The Mando Fabi remembered wasn't smooth but could talk, was smart but didn't know it—like Juanito—and was hopelessly honest. Now she wondered, what kind of man did Mando become on death row? And with a fierce tear, she opened the letter.

Fabi,

I've been wanting to write you for a long time, and it's been hard not to. At first it was because I didn't want to bother you. Not again. I know you have a son, maybe more kids, an entire family. A life. I've spent more than seventeen years in this place. More time than I could have imagined. But I'm out of time now. I have a date for the gurney. It's next month. Valentine's Day.

You're the one person in my whole life that I loved all the way. I only had my jefe in my life before you. He was a hard motherfucker to even like, us always getting into fights, him beating my ass, so being a good son, one that loved him no matter what, was too much for me. I never had to try with you. Everything was always easy—at least it was until I fucked everything up. It would be good if you could write to me before my time runs out.

Mando

Armando Aranda, 999178
Polunsky Unit
3872 FM 350 South
Livingston, TX 77351

MORE THAN YOU CAN HANDLE (CHAPTER FIVE)

"You'll get through this, Juan. God doesn't give anyone more than they can handle," Eddie was saying. Zero and first period practice was just about over. JD and Eddie had gravitated toward Juan, who was pedaling away on an exercise bike planted for him on the sideline of the PAC. Grampá had woken up early and driven him in Má's truck. She'd come to get him at Grampá's but fell asleep on the sofa, and Grampá decided to be cool for once, not wanting him to walk with a "gamey" ankle.

"Except when he gives you too much AIDS," JD countered. "Or cancer."

"That's not what I mean," Eddie said. "He's challenging you, Juan."

Juan didn't feel like being inspired by the backup point guard, the guy now taking his spot in the starting lineup and who Coach Paul told to stay by his side.

"Right, like he's challenged everyone who's ever committed suicide?" JD said, turning to Juan. "What is up with this dude?"

"I get what you're saying, Eddie," Juan said, wishing they'd both shut up. "JD is just being . . . JD." All Juan wanted to do was get the day over with, go home, and apologize to Má for getting arrested, for costing them money he knew they didn't have. To keep rehabbing his ankle.

JD gave Juan a confused look. "You can't be buying this Ultimate Jesus Challenge garbage. You don't even go to church. . . ." Coach Paul watched them from center court. JD and Eddie were holding basketballs instead of doing their cooldowns—a tired session of shoot-arounds done after practice. Juan kept pumping away on the bike's pedals as the rest of the team heaved buckets, the sound of the balls clanging against the rim and ricocheting across the gym floor constant. This would end badly for JD and Eddie; chitchat always pissed Coach Paul off.

"Maybe this is God's way of reaching out to you, Juan," Eddie said. "He works in mysterious ways."

"That's *even more* garbage. People only say that when they can't explain why shitty things happened," JD argued. "Look, man, I'm sorry you fucked your ankle up. I guess you shouldn't have followed me, but if you think about it, cops and walls are the real problems. Not me."

"I'm trying to concentrate here," Juan said, wanting to

ignore both of them. JD loved talking crazy, his arms now flailing, his mouth flapping like a hummingbird's wings. His crazy was no different than Eddie's.

Eddie leaned toward Juan. "With God, there is always hope, a way," he said, almost at a whisper. "Put your faith in Him." Eddie would be the perfect recruit the following year. With Danny's dad recording and editing his games, him talking God to recruiters and coaches, he was sure to score a scholarship at some small school or Christian university, even with a game half as good as Juan's.

"Are you two morons done talking?" Coach Paul yelled from across the gym. "Everyone line it up. If you have enough energy to chitchat, then you have enough to run." Coach Paul blew his whistle and the Panthers groaned as they stopped the cooldown session and lined up across the baseline. Juan wished he were on the court, able to run as hard as he could. In six weeks the season—his season—would be over. It was killing him to think he could never play for a team again.

Juan pedaled harder, his ankle taped and stuffed inside a loosely laced tennis shoe. Numb. The doctor at urgent care told him it would take four to six weeks to heal, but there was a chance he could come back early—if he rehabbed. Juan had never been hurt before, and the sight of his ankle—at one point looking like a purple alien head was growing from the side of his foot—had freaked him out. Knowing the most important part of rehab was to lessen the swelling, he'd started a steady diet of ibuprofen and ankle exercises. The doctor had told him to take it easy for a few days, but there wasn't time for fucking around. He was already putting weight on it, aiming to be back on the court in half the time. So, what the hell—maybe Eddie was onto something. A little prayer couldn't hurt, even if Juan had never prayed before.

Sneakers squeaked as the team ran from the baseline to the foul line and back, then to half court and back, until each player made the trip from end to end. JD was solidly in the middle of the pack. No limping for him. No crazy, life-ruining events happening to *him*. At the very least JD should have owned running from the cops, *and* he should have asked Juan about being booked—getting finger-printed and having his mug shot taken. Asked about the charges and bail—Juan himself was still kind of clueless about the charges, but still. JD should have given a shit.

"Too damn slow," Coach Paul yelled. "Against the Tigers we were always late. Late on our assignments. Late on our weak side help. Late to every loose ball." He blew his whistle and the team collectively groaned again, as they lined up once more along the baseline. "The boys from Irvin run and gun. Speed was supposed to be our advantage. A team of Mexicans can't afford to be short *and* slow, at least not on the court. We only got till Thursday to get this right. The game's Friday." As Juan pedaled, Coach Paul made his way over to him and studied him without saying a word. Juan kept pedaling, staring straight ahead. "I got a job for you," the coach finally said. "See me in my office after practice." The coach didn't wait for Juan to respond, just walked away as the team continued to run, Juan pedaling as hard as he could.

Coach Paul's office smelled like the weight room, like moldy leather and sweat. Juan liked the musty odor; it somehow put him at ease. The office walls were lined with trophies and old newspaper clippings of past Panther fame, each neatly folded inside frames that looked like wood but were plastic. There were also pictures of a young Coach Paul and his 1997 University of Arizona National Championship Team behind his desk. A collection of coffee cups and stacks of paper and folders cluttered the top. Juan had always felt lucky to be playing for Coach, grateful he'd been called to varsity his freshman year, making him the first freshman brought up midseason in school history. He'd replaced a senior, no less—the starting guard had been kicked off the team after getting busted for driving with weed in his car.

Coach Paul hurried into the office and dropped into the seat behind his desk. "You're not going to prison, are you?" He considered Juan for a moment, then tipped each coffee cup before finding one with at least one sip left. "You're not driving around your neighborhood selling drugs, right?"

"No," Juan said. "I was only running from the cops. Following JD. That's all."

"That was a mistake. That kid's a little asshole. Look, as long as the police don't come and drag you away, we're good. The bigger problem is that you're about to become ineligible. You're failing algebra." He drummed his fingers against the coffee cup. "Well? What do you have to say about that? After all I've done for you, I expected better. Shit. You barely passed Spanish last semester."

"I've been working harder," Juan said, trying to remember where his algebra book even was.

"Bullshit. Mrs. Hill says you solve for *x* like illegals pay taxes. You don't go to tutoring, either."

"Tutoring is during practice," Juan protested. Mrs. Hill held tutoring during zero period, between the morning hours of way-too-early and I-got-shit-to-do. "When am I supposed to go?"

"You trying to tell me you can't find some smart kid who'll tutor you? I bet the popular basketball star can find *someone*."

"I guess." Like always, Coach didn't get it, mistaking talent for popularity like he mistook constant running around on the basketball court for a good offense. Like he mistook his shitty jokes for funny. Juan had no idea who could school him up in algebra. JD was worse at math than he was. Danny was smart but probably wasn't the tutoring type. Those were Juan's only friends.

"So good. We got two problems out of the way. Last one. Are you gonna be able to make it back this season?" Coach leaned forward in his chair. This was obviously the most important problem to him.

"Yes," Juan said, beginning to rotate his ankle clockwise

for ten rotations and then counter, trying not to grimace. "The doctor said no problem." He closed his eyes and tried to concentrate, visualizing the swelling in his ankle going down, the bruising fading away.

"That's good," Coach Paul said, nodding. "Because I have a friend who coaches in Arizona, and I was thinking of having him come and take a look at you. I've been talking you up."

"At the University of Arizona?" Juan straightened himself. "That would be sick . . . I mean, a good opportunity." He knew letting his imagination loose was a mistake, but he couldn't help himself—*college ball*!

"Settle down, moo-cha-cho. I said *in* Arizona. My buddy coaches at the junior college in Tucson, Pima Community College. Where *I* used to coach. Everything I told him about you was before this trouble you've gotten yourself into. Before your grades took a total shit and now your ankle injury. I'm close to calling the whole thing off, honestly. Look, I'm putting myself on the line for you. I can't risk my reputation on you, can I?"

"All I did was run from the cops. I wasn't doing nothing wrong."

"Anything. You weren't doing *anything* wrong. And since when do innocent people run from the cops?" Coach Paul exhaled loudly, rolling his eyes. "Mrs. Hill says you have a big exam coming up, so here's the deal: if you don't pass, I'll call the whole thing off. You'll end up a breaker for sure."

Coach Paul liked to categorize the students at Austin High as either "rock breakers" or "yard rakers." *JD talks too much trash; he'll be a rock breaker. Duran is a good Christian kid but has shit for brains. He's a yard raker.* Until now Juan hadn't realized he too had been dumped into a category—or was about to be.

"I can pass her stupid test."

"Good. I don't want to waste my buddy's time. You know I got the junior, Duran, in your spot now. You think he can handle the position till you get back?"

"The Bible-thumper? I might suck at algebra, but at least I know how to run an offense. Eddie'd be starting next to me if he didn't freeze and blow all his assignments every time he went on the court. He's worse than JD." Juan felt bad for talking shit about Eddie; the dude was always cool with him, but he *was* a turnover machine.

"That's why I need your help while you're getting yourself together, assuming you *can*. I need you to work with Duran. Get him to understand the plays. If you can do that, then I'll let my friend know what a multitalented point guard I have. That he's got to come down and see you for himself. He won't pony up a scholarship on just my word. But once he sees you, I can get him to offer you one, no problem."

And there it was, what Coach had really wanted to talk about all along: next season. Juan should have seen it awkwardly coming, just like all the other plays Coach designed.

"Can I think about it?" Juan said, trying to channel his inner JD and be nonchalant.

"You gotta be kidding me," Coach Paul said, glaring. Juan wondered if there was the slightest chance Coach Paul wasn't full of shit. He wrestled his imagination from going wild, to keep from thinking of the players who'd gone from Division II to Division I and then, miraculously, to the NBA. Players like Avery Johnson, Sam Cassell, and John Starks.

Coach Paul leaned back in his chair, slouching like he sometimes did during time-outs, when the opposing team was going on a run. "Fine, have it your way. You know we got a game Friday. If you're not at open gym after school today, then I know what your answer is. You got that? I hope that's enough time for you."

The bell rang and Juan quickly nodded before leaving the office. He kept nodding to himself as he limped straight to algebra—no skipping class to smoke a cigarette on the bleachers or buy cheese fries at Cakes. He pushed the idea of the NBA out of his head, of a big university, but he kept the thought of playing at a juco. Pima Community College could be *real*.

Juan only had a couple of bucks for lunch so he decided to skip eating and pocket the money. As he'd sat through algebra, he'd realized he was probably doomed come test time. So after class he hobbled to the quad to think. The equations Mrs. Hill had scribbled across the chalkboard seemed an impossible language of letters and numbers. His homework was to graph quadratic equations using the expensive graphing calculator he didn't have, but Danny was sure to have one, and he probably knew how to use it too. He would text Danny after school and ask for help, maybe ask to go to his new chante.

Sitting on a bench, Juan watched as a girl he'd never seen before strode across the courtyard looking straight ahead and with a hop in her step. She wasn't trying to look Hollywood sexy or chola badass, which of course made her kind of both. Immediately Juan wanted to impress her. She stopped in front of the library, checking her phone.

"What are you looking for?" Juan yelled across the quadrangle. "What building?"

"The registrar's office," the girl called back, turning toward him. "I need to pick up my cousin's records. Apparently, he's been banned from campus."

"It's hard to find," Juan lied, propping himself up from the bench and hobbling toward her. "But I can take you, if you want."

The girl smiled, shaking her head in disbelief. "Looks to me like you can barely move. I'll find it myself, thanks." Her teeth were perfect, which made him embarrassed of his own crooked grill.

Juan hopped around on one leg, wanting to see more of her smile. "I can move. In fact, I got some pretty sweet moves. Ask anybody around here." Juan knew how stupid he sounded but couldn't help himself. "I'm Juan Ramos, starting point guard."

The girl's smile disappeared, replaced by a smirk.

"Roxanne, and I hope you're better at bouncing balls than you are at talking to people."

"What's *that* supposed to mean?" Damn. Why didn't he just laugh that off? Now even her smirk was gone.

"Wow," Roxanne said. She had thick, curly, black hair that bounced to her shoulders, and dark brown eyes. "You sound pretty defensive. Sensitive, even."

"I'm not sensitive," Juan snapped back, sounding totally sensitive.

"Right . . . I'm going now. Nice to meet you, Julio." She gave him a quick wink, then turned to leave.

"Juan," Juan said, now really digging this Roxanne chingona. "And the registrar's office is right near the panther statue. You can't miss it."

"Thanks for lying to me earlier," Roxanne said without looking back.

It was evening when Juan got home from school; he'd taken Coach's offer and met Eddie for open gym. JD and Danny were waiting for him behind the apartment, sitting on two overturned milk crates, like usual. A waist-high tangle of weeds, dead and yellow, hid them from sight, but Juan could hear them talking, laughing. Dogs barked, but more out of boredom than aggression. The neighbor across the alley was watching TV and drinking a forty, like he did almost every evening. Juan's ankle was throbbing after walking home.

"Really, fuckers?" Juan said, limping over. "Why are

you here?" The sun was starting to dip behind the Franklin mountains, and Juan hoped he could shame them away. "You shouldn't be hanging around the chante without me here. Jabba gets all pissed off."

"Don't be like that." Danny pulled a wrinkled sandwich bag with a thin layer of weed at the bottom from his backpack. He unfurled it and began rolling a joint. "I'm beginning to believe all the shit JD's been talking."

"What shit?" JD said, turning to Danny. "I wasn't talking shit."

"It's still basketball season," Juan said, shaking his head at the joint.

"You said he was ready to join a religious cult this morning." Danny kept rolling the joint, his forehead furrowed with concentration. "I gotta say, you both have been acting weird lately."

"Dude, I just got out of county. I think I got court in a few weeks. I ain't smoking shit." A judge had read the charges to him through a TV monitor while he sat in a small room, handcuffed, with an armed guard beside him. The judge asked if Juan understood the charges and Juan lied when he said he did, trying so hard not to cry that he had trouble listening. All Juan really remembered was to expect a summons in the mail re-explaining everything.

"You were only in the annex, and there's plenty of time to get this out of your system," Danny argued. He looked over at JD, who was staring at the screen of his video camera. "Put that shit away. Why would you record *this*?"

JD held the camera right up in Danny's face. "I told you, I'm making a documentary. I'm trying to record what happens to us."

"What the fuck are you even talking about?" Juan said, not actually wanting to know. He wished he'd gone home by the front of the building, risked the confrontation with Jabba the Slut about late rent or loud music or whatever she wanted to bitch about. She was always giving him shit, even when he was a little kid hanging alone when his má was at work, always telling him to stay away from the flowers. To stop feeding the stray cats and dogs. To quit popping beer bottles in the alley with rocks. (Juan loved the sound.) If he'd gone by the front, he would've avoided these two.

"He's been talking about 'scenes' and needing footage. Hasn't shut up about it until you showed up. It's sad, really," Danny said. He held up the freshly rolled joint for Juan to see. "You wanna hit this first?"

"No!" Juan kept standing, not wanting to get comfortable. Wanting them to leave.

"It's not sad!" JD said, sounding desperate to be taken seriously. "I want to make a documentary. After this year, who knows what's gonna happen to us?"

"Sounds to me like you're just taking videos like a sad mom," Danny scoffed.

"And what makes you the expert? Your pretty school uniform?"

"I'm an artist, man." Danny laughed. "And I'm going to college next year." Danny lit the joint and took a long drag.

"You drew one comic book. Kick back, Stan Lee. And not all of us have Fort Bliss daddy money," JD said.

"Or a daddy," Danny said, grinning at Juan before inhaling again. "Right, Juanito?" Danny blew a thick puff of smoke into the air, which slowly enveloped Juan.

Juan waved the cloud away. Danny could be such an ass. Did secondhand smoke pop up in piss tests? JD finally looked up from the screen.

"Eat shit," Juan said, moving away from Danny.

"You and Juan will probably go. But what about me? I'm screwed," JD said.

Juan pointed to his ankle. "*You're* screwed? How am I gonna get to college? Limp there? I'll be lucky to make it back on the court before the end of the season. No scout on earth is gonna want me. I'm fucking done." But on the slim chance that he wasn't, Juan *had* gone straight to Coach Paul's office after school, where Coach had tossed him the playbook and then opened the gym. He and Eddie immediately got to work, sticking to the diagrams Coach had drawn up—some easy motion stuff, read and react, zone attacks, the same uninspiring bullshit the team always ran, Eddie pretty much unable to grasp any of it.

"I feel real bad about that shit," JD said now, pointing at Juan's ankle.

Man, Juan needed to get his ankle in some ice and take some ibuprofen. The throbbing was spreading to his head. "Didn't sound like it this morning, cabrón. You and Eddie talking all that God stuff."

"I was just tired of hearing Eddie's nonsense. I do feel shitty, seriously," JD said, looking Juan in the eyes.

"You *should* feel like shit. It's your fault," Danny agreed. He was playing with his Zippo lighter, snapping the lid open and closed, the metal hinge making a satisfying clinking sound. He took another huge drag, examining the plume of smoke rolling off the cherry before offering it to JD. "You ran like a scared bitch. And now you don't have a phone. Maybe out a friend, too."

JD took the joint and turned to Juan. "How was I supposed to know you'd fuck up your ankle? I didn't get away clean, either. Shit at home is all fucked up now."

Juan stared him down. "What? You get put in time-out? Grounded? You got more church to do?"

"I did get sent to confession," JD said, now holding the joint in one hand and his camera in the other, recording the lines of smoke twisting off the end.

"Did you tell the priest how much you whack off?" Danny asked.

"Nah. I didn't want him to think I was bragging," JD said, taking a drag.

"Or flirting," Danny added.

"So you're not in any kind of actual trouble?" Juan said, not in the mood for jokes. "Look, I got real shit to deal with. All you got is some church. Who gives a fuck? And why did you run, anyway? We never run from the cops."

JD took a moment before answering, passing the joint to Danny, waiting for it to come back.

"I don't know," JD said finally. "I just did."

"He's a bitch," Danny said, laughing. Stoned. "We just covered this." Normally Juan would be smoking out. Getting out of his head. And even though now seemed like the perfect time to do just that, watching Danny in his uniform, with his crisp white shirt tucked into khaki pants, his dark blue blazer, his red tie still knotted and looking dramatically out of place among the weeds—out of place next to him and JD—made Juan not want to be outside of his mind ever again.

JD took another drag and held it in before coughing up the smoke. "First, fuck you, Danny. And second, *Juanito*, maybe take some responsibility for yourself. You didn't have to run. Besides, you only spent a day in county. It couldn't have been *that* bad."

Not that bad. Right. The cops had only wrestled him to the unfinished ground of the living room as he'd tried to give himself up, hands in the air. They only dog-piled on top of him, only stepped on his face and kneed him in the back as they twisted his arms into a pair of handcuffs closed tight around his wrists, only punched the back of his head. He'd smelled the bags of thin-set for the new flooring stacked around the room, breathed in the dust through his nose and mouth. Now he could feel the fear from that moment roaring back, bubbling inside his chest. Juan slapped the joint out of JD's hand and stomped it out.

"What the fuck!" Danny said.

Juan glared at JD, his eyes narrowed. "Don't say shit about things you don't know nothing about."

He hadn't been able to sleep in county. Some of the men in his cell were as old as Grampá, so frail and gray that he wondered what they could've possibly done. They never said a word. The majority were loud drunks, slurring their words and complaining how it was bullshit that they were pulled over in the first place. But the reason Juan didn't sleep was the Monster, a dude who looked like he'd been arrested in a nightmare, who came in just after Juan with a bloodied face, T-shirt, and knuckles. He had *monster* tattooed across his neck. The Monster spent most of the night trying to make eye contact with Juan and then laughing when Juan looked away, everyone else in the room pretending it wasn't happening.

"Now who's being a bitch?" JD snapped. "Come at me again and see what happens."

"What's gonna happen?" Juan hovered over JD. "We both know you run when you're scared."

"Is that right?" JD said, popping up from the milk crate, camera still in his hands. "This ain't the basketball court, motherfucker. And you're not a gang of cops."

"You're disrespecting my house," Juan said, now standing face-to-face with JD. "You need to go." The pitch of his own voice surprised him, how pleading it sounded.

JD smirked. "You don't own this place. You don't own shit."

That's when Juan swung hard, a quick right, crunching

JD's cheek. The camera dropped as Juan put JD to the ground with another shot, this one a left, landing on the side of his head. Then Juan pounced, connecting quick punches to JD's ear and the back of his neck. His blood felt like razors tearing through his veins, his muscles soaked in hot anger, but JD squirmed away and scrambled to his feet. He stomped on Juan's ankle, striking just above it, at the shin. White pain seared through him. JD threw wild punches as Juan tried to stagger to his feet, landing two blows to the head that took Juan back to the ground. Juan's ankle was wrecked, he couldn't get up, and with JD on top of him, raining down blows, Juan knew he was in trouble. JD was stronger than Juan expected, angrier. He could feel his nose runny with blood, the taste of metal coating his tongue, and he was forced to curl into a ball, trying to protect his ankle. So he didn't see Danny digging through his backpack. Didn't see Danny retrieving the gun. Neither did JD, whose punches landed wildly against Juan's back and arms. But they both froze the instant they heard the gunshot. *BLAM!* The sound paralyzed them.

Danny dropped the gun after firing straight into the air. JD quickly sprang away, his face red, his eyes searching. Juan uncurled slowly. On the ground beside him was the weapon, the barrel still smoking. He could smell the burning residue of gunpowder, the chemicals and lubricants Danny's old man used to clean the weapon. Blood from his nose dripped down the back of his throat as he swallowed.

"What the fuck, Danny?" he yelled as JD picked his stupid video camera back up.

"What the fuck *you*," Danny yelled back.

"Where the fuck did you get a gun?" Juan already knew the answer. At Danny's old house in Central his father had had a small arsenal; Danny once showed him the three shotguns and the collection of handguns his dad had stashed in a gym bag inside his closet. Juan closed his eyes and tried to breathe normally, but his heart was pounding, his skin buzzing like tiny lines of electricity were zipping across it.

"*Why* do you have a gun?" JD asked, lowering his voice.

"It's my dad's," Danny confirmed. "I've been carrying it for a while now."

"Why the fuck are you shooting it? Are you crazy?" Juan asked.

"I don't know." Danny's body was pure panic, face and neck turning red, his breath coming hard. "It seemed like something that would happen in a movie. Some dramatic shit to get you two to stop fighting."

From behind Danny, Jabba was storming toward them, a phone in one hand, shouting. Juan imagined the cops already following behind her like an angry army, the fat, old hag leading them like a bloodthirsty general happy to finally be in the shit.

"Cut!" JD was yelling. "Cut, cut, cut. Mrs. Ramirez blew the shot. She's in my frame." JD held his camera on the scene for a moment before dropping it to his side. "How many blanks do we have left? Tell me we have some left."

"¿Qué babosadas están pasando aquí?" Jabba demanded, eyeballing the boys. Her bare arms and face were slicked with sweat, her sweatpants cut off into shorts. Mrs. Ramirez had been living alone in the first apartment in Juan's hallway for as long as he could remember—a widow, his má had told him. Juan never believed the story about how her husband was kidnapped and killed in Juárez, leaving her the apartment building to run alone. The dude probably wanted to disappear and booked on her. Jabba was a slumlord who read tenants' mail and raised rents without notice. No way did anyone ever love her.

"Estamos haciendo un vídeo. It's for school," JD said, holding the camera up for Jabba to see. "Se llama 'Mexican Fight Club.' La pistola es una réplica."

Juan clued in immediately and picked up the gun. He waved it around as if it were a toy, though it felt like anything but—more like a hammer or a brick. "It's not real. It shoots blanks," he added, hoping he sounded as casual as JD. Beginning to wonder if maybe JD wasn't onto something with at least looking like he never gave a fuck.

"¿Y tus drogas? Are those for a movie too?" The baggie of weed was on the ground, but all Juan could really concentrate on was the smell of the gun. Danny slowly walked over and put the baggie in his backpack.

"Por supuesto," JD said. "¡Somos artistas! Don't worry, we're professionals."

"Lárguense, cabrones," Jabba said before turning to Juan. "Hablaré con tu mamá, don't *you* worry. I'm a professional *too*."

• • •

Fabi wasn't home, so Juan guessed Jabba would have to wait before telling her about the gun and weed, though she must have bought the movie story, otherwise the cops would be taking him back to county right about now. Damn, that was close. Jabba had threatened to kick them out before, but Fabi had convinced her not to—as her longest tenant, she seemed to have some kind of pull, even if Jabba hated Juan. Now his má would have to do it again.

The sun was fading, the thin curtains blocking the remaining light as Juan sat in the living room and thrust his ankle into a bucket of ice. *Shit*, that burned. He dug into his pocket for his phone, but of course the battery was dead. He didn't want to interrupt his treatment to charge his phone, but that also meant not cruising the Wi-Fi Jabba never password-protected while his foot froze. Juan moved a stack of mail piled on the table beside him, looking for the television remote, and when he didn't find it, began sifting absentmindedly through the envelopes. Bills stacked on bills. *Poor Má.* Then he came to a letter with a name he didn't recognize, not to mention the return address. *A prison address?*

Prison. Shit, that's probably where he'd have ended up if Jabba had called the cops. That pinche gun—what the fuck, Danny? He didn't want to think about algebra and how he didn't remember to ask Danny for help, didn't want to think about his ankle or the fight with JD. About Eddie Duran and his deal with Coach. Court. Jail. He held the opened letter in his hand and wondered if he should read it, betting Má hadn't meant to leave the letter out. He read the name on the envelope again: *Armando Aranda, 999178.* Juan had been ruining his life with so much ease, it scared the shit out of him. *How bad do you have to fuck up before your name gets a number attached to it?* Juan decided to read the letter, wondering if the answer could be inside.

THE CUTLASS
(CHAPTER SIX)

Tomásito jumped on JD's bed, collapsing the center and rattling the box spring under his feet. Making a ton of noise. He laughed and jumped harder, reaching his arms toward the low popcorn ceiling. His part of the room was a straight mess, toys dumped on the floor and discarded underneath his bed, his dresser a disaster of dirty clothes piled on top and restuffed into drawers alongside the clean ones. Crayon scribbles covered the wall beside his bed along with drawings he'd pinned up. They weren't the typical nine-year-old bullshit—houses and depictions of family smiling and waving. These were monsters: a giant octopus with knives instead of tentacles, swallowing a cow; a shark with mouths at both ends and a fin on each side so it never had to sleep and could always attack and eat everyone all the time; a lion, with horns and legs like a horse, that breathed fire and attacked anyone who was mean to Tomásito. Of course JD often appeared in the work, either being burned or eaten or speared right in the belly and bleeding out. JD's share of the room was squared away, his movies back in order—now by release date and genre—and his bed neatly made.

"You're gonna fall, you dumb shit," JD said, packing his game uniform into his gym bag.

"You said 'shit,'" Tomásito said. "I'm gonna tell. I'm gonna tell. I'm gonna tell."

"You said it too."

"That doesn't count," Tomásito said as he stopped jumping. "I was just saying what you said."

"Do you think God cares why you said it? You said a bad word. That's all he cares about. Sin is pointless like that. At least I can go confess, but you haven't made your first Holy Communion yet. If you died right now, the devil would drag you to hell and you'd burn forever and ever. Those are the rules. Ask Amá. You better hope I don't kill you right now."

Tomásito cocked his head the same way Amá always did, a raised eyebrow and sideways glance, trying to determine if JD was lying or not. Of course JD didn't care if Tomásito told about the cussing. Since she booted his old man out, Amá had barely left her room—except to go to work. Alma was the only one to talk to her—she'd been home a lot more, which was a relief. She had graduated from Austin a few years earlier, worked at the mall, and was saving money, talking about going to college or maybe joining the army. Before Pops was booted she'd moved in with her boyfriend and spent most of her time with him, but now her old bed had piles of folded laundry on it along with her makeup bag and brush and hair dryer and all sorts of other girl crap. Seeing his sister's things made JD realize how much he'd missed her—even if her being back and sharing their room meant it woud be crowded as fuck again. Tomásito squatted down and leapt straight into the air, swiping his hand toward the ceiling.

"You're not gonna kill me," Tomásito said as he took flight from JD's bed yet again and ran his hand across the popcorned texture of the ceiling, scraping off the hardened plaster with the palm of his hand before crashing to the floor, his head thudding against stained carpet.

The tears were immediate and so was the blood from his nose. Rushing over, JD sat his brother up and squeezed his nose. Tomásito screamed. Once, in eighth grade, JD had had a basketball thrown at his face when he wasn't looking by Roman Alvarado; his coach had squeezed his nose in just the same way immediately after. He remembered how it hurt, how he wanted the coach to let go, but in the end the bleeding stopped. With his free hand, JD reached for his camera, now fully charged. This was a moment. The past few days—the truck ride with Pops, the fight with Juan—had been filled with moments like this, which he'd failed to fully capture on video, but where his life felt like it was changing. He wondered how many instants like these he'd ignored in the past, not thinking of them as important or as part of some kind of larger story. His heart was racing, just as he was sure Tomásito's was. Still squeezing his brother's nose, he flipped his camera on and pointed it at him.

"I know it hurts," JD said, trying to sound soothing. "I've done this before. Try to calm down."

"I want Amá!" Tomásito said, squirming like crazy. "Let go; you're hurting me!"

"I'm trying to help you."

"Stop it!"

"Fine." JD let go but kept the camera on his brother, now a mess of snot, tears, and blood. Tomásito gulped for air like he was drowning. JD was so fixated on the scene in front of him that he hadn't noticed that Alma was at the doorway. She swept into the room and took Tomásito in her arms, glaring at JD.

"¿Qué está pasando aquí, Juan Diego?"

"Nada . . . Tu sabes como eres." It was true; Alma had to know how much fakery Tomás always conjured up. JD turned the camera on her.

"¿Y como *es* su hermano? He's only *nine*! And I know how *you* can be. Why the hell are you recording all this instead of helping? It's like you're always hiding from all of us. Always out, disappearing from your family. Now behind a camera. Why is that?"

"I'm making a movie."

"A *movie*? Settle down, Spielberg." She was rubbing

Tomásito's back, calming him. She held the bottom of his shirt to his nose and instructed JD to put the stupid camera down and help her. He did as she asked, killed the camera. *Spielberg?* That motherfucker hadn't made a decent movie since *The Sugarland Express*.

Now, washing his brother's face and hand in the bathroom, JD explained how Tomásito jumped off the bed, how it wasn't really his fault. Alma shook her head, meaning *of course it was*. Being the oldest in the room meant JD was responsible, and now he was making excuses and not taking responsibility for his family. Like someone else she knew.

"You *are* a lot like Apá. I come in the room to find Tomásito bloody and crying and you filming him instead of helping him, being a brother. That's your *job*."

"*He* jumped off the bed," JD said, now thinking back to his conversation with Pops. Him wishing he could've stayed in the army, been an E-9, but instead getting out for Amá. Because she wanted him to, for family. "How is that my fault?"

"He's *nine*. *You* make him quit jumping."

"Whatever."

Once cleaned up, Tomásito bolted, like a caught animal released from a cage, leaving JD with his sister.

"And what is going on with you?" Alma said, taking a good look at him. "I mean, shit. Have you seen your own face lately? You're a mess."

"I don't know." JD shrugged. "I got into a fight with

Juan. It's almost healed." JD's face and body ached from the fight, but at least the chichón on his forehead was almost gone.

"What, Juan? Why?" She reached out as if to touch his bruised cheek and then pulled her hand back, like she'd been reaching out to touch a ghost and thought better of it. "Did you at least get some punches in?"

"More than some. I think I might have won that fight."

"Yeah, right. If you landed some punches it's because Juanito let you. Same reason he lets you score when you play ball—so you keep playing."

"I think I beat his ass," JD insisted as Alma laughed and suddenly wrapped him in a big sisterly hug, apparently no longer afraid of ghosts.

"No, you didn't, but that's okay. Are you guys, like, enemies now?"

"Nah. I messaged him. Everything's fine. I used your phone, by the way. Mine's busted." He'd been fucking things up, he knew it. He apologized for running from the cops, for always talking shit, for going hard at his ankle during the fight. Juan replied with an It's all good, and JD wondered if things actually were.

"Quit using my phone without asking," Alma said, annoyed. "Look, Amá wants to talk to you. You have a game today?" When JD nodded, she said, "Come home after the game. Spend some time with her. Can you do that?"

"I guess," JD said, knowing Alma wouldn't take no for

an answer. "I'll cancel all the fights I had scheduled for tonight."

Since he was sitting out injured, Juan had agreed to record the night's game for JD. His ankle was still messed up even though he'd said it was getting better. And while Juan said he no longer blamed him for the injury, JD knew he did, could understand why, even though not everything that had happened that night was his fault. Partying on the wrong side of town. With people they didn't know. In neighborhoods they hadn't figured out. Things were bound to be fucked up if something like cops happened.

"Make sure you get a mix of shots," JD explained as he handed Juan the camera. The Panthers and the Irvin Rockets were warming up behind them, both teams in shootarounds before falling into layup lines. "You want some close-ups. Get facial expressions. Shots going in. Stuff like that. You also want some medium shots. Like us running the half-court offense. Some ISO. Action. And you want some wide shots. Try to get as much of the gym as you can. The crowd. The game. That way I can edit everything together—"

"Dude," Juan interrupted, nodding toward the gym floor. "Coach looks pissed. You better get down there." Coach Paul was eyeballing JD, arms crossed as the horn buzzed and both teams returned to their benches. *Shit*.

"Get some B-roll, too!" JD yelled over his shoulder as he rushed down to the gym floor, not sure if Juan knew what B-roll was. "Coach said I was starting tonight. So get some footage of me at the jump, porfas." After two and a half days of filming, JD had downloaded his footage to his laptop—the one Danny sold him for a hundred bucks after his old man scored him a new one. He was surprised how little footage it actually had—only an hour—but he felt good, really good, to be doing it. To be getting out there with the camera.

The PAC was only partially filled; the season was already a bust, and no one really cared what happened in the last six games. The PA system crackled Run the Jewels's "Oh My Darling (Don't Cry)," JD's favorite song. So cool. He'd been playing well of late—somehow his má finding out about his old man's affair and what that meant for his family made basketball feel unimportant and easy to play—but he'd never started before. Never had the eyes of everyone in the gym on him all at once. He walked onto the court with the other starters feeling like a fake, like a cardboard cutout of a basketball player about to be propped up on the court and posed.

Shake it off, Sanchez! He held his head up, moving to an empty spot before turning to face center. An Irvin Rocket stood alone at center court, and Coach Paul began losing his mind. "For God's sake, Sanchez. You're jumping for ball!" JD rushed to the empty spot on the painted orange basketball with the brown *A*. The sound of laughter bubbled around him. He glanced out at the stands and found Juan holding the camera steady on him. "C'mon, Sanchez!"

Coach Paul shouted. "Get your head in the game!"

The Rockets' big man was easily six foot five and probably outweighed JD by thirty pounds. A beast. The ref tossed the ball into the air, and as JD jumped, the Rocket leapt over him and gently tapped the ball to his point guard. Plucking it from the air, the point guard made two swift dribbles downcourt before lobbing the ball toward the rim, where the Beast snatched it from the sky and flushed it down, with JD still planted at the *A*, watching. The Rockets were off to the races after that. It only took two more plays—JD turning the ball over on the Panthers' first offensive possession, the ref calling him for a travel and then another blown defensive assignment; then JD got caught in a pick and roll leading to another easy Beast stuff—for JD to find himself back on the bench, where he stayed for the remainder of the game. He tried to signal Juan to quit recording, but the jackass ignored him, instead hobbling around the PAC, shooting what looked like a variety of wide shots, mediums, and close-ups. As if *he* were motherfucking Spielberg. Maybe he and Juan weren't "all good" after all.

The blowout was worse than the El Paso High loss. Without Juan, the Panthers were unthinkably bad; the Rockets played their second and even third stringers before halftime. It hadn't occurred to JD before how hard it was being Juan, how brilliantly he played each and every minute of the game just to make every defeat less brutal, to leave a pocket of space for moral victories—like for his own double-doubles—and keep everyone believing that maybe the next game the outcome could be different.

JD wanted only a piece of that for himself. To be good at something and not always have to be the clown. He heard some of the other players talking shit about him, joking about the jump ball and getting dunked on. Juan, Eddie, and Coach Paul were standing by the coach's office when he got out of the shower.

"Boy, am I glad I started you," Coach Paul fumed. "You made me look clueless."

"Well, that's not hard to do," JD said. He should've gone back to his locker. He was fucking up. "You do most of the work on your own" came out of his mouth next. JD felt like a bomb errantly dropped from the sky, armed and free-falling. Unable to change course.

"Who do you think you are, talking to me like that?" Falling.

"You were talking shit first." Falling faster still, the speed blinding.

"Do you wanna stay on this team, Sanchez?" Out of time. Solid ground. Impact.

"Does everyone have to do your job for you?" *BOOM.*

"You know what? You're off the team. I'm gonna give a chance to someone who gives a shit from the freshman squad, just like I did with Juan. You're no good on a basketball court, and I'm pretty goddamn sure you're no good anywhere else. Pack your bag and leave. Report to PE for the rest of the semester."

"Whatever." JD couldn't look at Coach Paul, afraid he

might cry. He tried to make eye contact with Juan or even Eddie, but they were staring hard at the ground. No one acknowledged him at his locker; the few Panthers still changing pretended nothing had happened. Even though he knew they were probably not going to win any more games—and that Coach Paul was a racist dick—JD still wanted to be on the team. To not disappear from school life like he was from his home life. To not vanish.

Ten minutes later JD sat in his car, engine off, in the semi-dark of the PAC parking lot. He'd packed his things, leaving behind his dirty game uniform and warm-ups tied in knots and dumped on Coach Paul's desk. Everyone else was gone; he'd even watched as Coach Paul jumped into his lame-ass Jeep Wrangler, with its open cabin and sun-beaten interior, faded surfing stickers and balding tires. JD knew he needed to get home but didn't want to.

"Hey, dummy! Answer your texts," Juan yelled as he slapped the hood of the Escort. JD jumped in his seat.

"Jesus . . . I told you my phone is busted," he said, rolling down his window.

"I thought you were lying." Juan smirked. "You're always lying."

"Except when I'm not." JD got out of his car and dug into his pocket, retrieving the broken phone.

"Why are you still carrying it around?" Eddie asked. JD hadn't seen Eddie standing behind Juan. He was dressed in his warm-up gear, AUSTIN PANTHERS printed across his chest, looking ready to play another game. Eddie was a willing backup on the court; he could probably be one in life, too.

"Worthless people like worthless things," JD said.

"Stop being dramatic. I bet Danny has an old one he can give you. He never throws shit away. I'm sure he can swap some SIM cards out and get your phone working, no problem. He's like a Russian hacker."

"Maybe," JD said. "I do already have his laptop. As long as I keep landscaping during the summers and he stays a good consumer, I'll always have this kick-ass secondhand life."

"Who's Danny?" Eddie asked, leaning against the car. They were the only ones in the parking lot. The LED lights from the lampposts above cast bright rings across the empty spaces, harsh shadows layered around them.

"Our rich private-school friend," Juan said. "He's also the crazy one of the group." The neighborhood was quiet except for the sound of them talking. No music coming from the houses. No old people watching TV with their front doors open, the volume up way too loud.

"I don't know about that anymore," JD said slowly.

"Coach Paul is wrong for kicking you off the—" Eddie was saying when a primer-gray Cutlass with murdered-out windows and rolling 22s crept by the parking lot. The carload of dudes were each taking the time to stare them down. It was those fools from Los Fatherless who creeped Central El Paso. Eddie froze. JD returned their bullshit mugging all the way until the Cutlass turned the corner.

"Don't do that!" Juan said, slapping JD's arm.

"They ain't gonna do shit," JD said. "Coach Paul's harder than them."

"Yeah, sure," Juan said, but added, "Let's grab some forties and head to Scenic. Get the fuck out of here before those fools come back."

"I gotta head home. My amá wants to talk to me." JD hadn't seen Juan act this twitchy before, but getting drunk was exactly what JD felt like doing.

"Why?" Juan looked confused. "To talk about the condoms?"

"Yes. About the condoms."

"Fuck, man. Just tell her you don't even use them."

"No, man—"

"Wait, you're right. Don't say that. She'll think you're smashing all these randoms without any protection. Say you only have them in case you *need* to use them, but you won't need them because no one will get with you because you keep getting beat up and kicked off basketball teams and you're ugly and no one likes you and your breath stinks and girls have cooties anyway, so forget it. You don't even know why you have condoms."

JD looked at Juan, his face as blank as he could make it. Then he said, "Those condoms . . . were my *old man's*. I took them from his truck and stashed them in my room. My mom's tubes are tied, so I knew he was cheating on her." He took a couple of deep breaths through his nose.

"And I thought—oh, never mind. But then my amá found them when I didn't come home the night you went to jail. My pops basically confessed when he saw her holding them, thinking she found them in his truck, and now he's out of the house." JD shrugged his shoulders in defeat. "I think they're getting divorced. I'm pretty sure that's why she wants to talk to me."

"Shit," Juan said. "I didn't know, man." He turned to JD. "You never said anything."

JD thought about that. He probably should've earlier—he did feel better telling Juan.

"Nah, you're good," he told Juan, "unless you're the one my old man is hooking up with."

"It's cool. You don't gotta joke."

"I can joke about it now. My family is only ruined." The fact was JD couldn't stop himself from clowning. Having Juan and Eddie laughing was better than them feeling sorry for him. "You got my camera?" He should have been recording what had just happened, them shaking their heads and trying not to laugh. He wished he had recorded what had gone down with Coach Paul, too. These things were part of a story he kept forgetting to do, kept failing to capture but needed to. He looked out into the neighborhood of small block houses, most with lights on but some completely black, like a chaotic chessboard. He realized each space was like his, where a story was moving forward. He used to think that nothing ever happened in El Paso, that life never changed, but maybe there was *too* much happening, and the nothing he once felt was actually a defense against the constant flood of life-changing moments. Boredom the only way to keep from panicking.

Juan handed the camera to JD. "I got some good footage, by the way."

"Yeah, I saw," JD said. "You didn't have to record the entire game."

"I know, but I wanted to get some game film for Eddie. Show him some spots to improve. Hope you don't mind."

"Nah," JD said, relieved. At least his humiliation wasn't the reason Juan kept recording. Man, the night's shame never seemed to end. "You didn't happen to get any of Coach Paul losing his mind on me?"

"Sorry, man. The battery was dead by then."

Eddie proudly held up his phone. "He didn't, but I did. Juan told me you were making a movie. It sounds cool. It's just audio and the inside of my pocket, but maybe you can use it anyway."

"I love this guy," JD said, shoving Eddie on the shoulder. Eddie laughed, and, huh, he didn't seem like too bad a guy after all. "Let's go grab those forties."

"What about your mom?" Juan asked.

JD shrugged. "She's fine." But he knew she wasn't. Knew that the lights at his house were probably off.

"Yeah, she is," Juan said.

"Fuck off."

They burst out laughing and then stopped short when the Cutlass returned, this time rolling slower than before.

The driver leaned out the window like maybe he was about to say something but then didn't. Tattoos crawled up his neck and the side of his face. Then JD, Juan, and Eddie all saw it at once: the double barrel of a shotgun peeking out from the back passenger window. The inside of the cabin was too dark to see who was holding it, so the gun seemed to be aimed at them all on its own. The Cutlass came to a stop. JD couldn't move, couldn't pull his eyes from the barrels. They looked like flared nostrils of some starving animal about to attack, JD ready to feel its teeth tearing into him. Eddie didn't hesitate and sprinted into the darkness away from the parking lot as Juan dove to the ground. JD stood still, a statue. A target. The carload of cholos sped away.

GLORY ROAD
(CHAPTER SEVEN)

Cruising seemed the thing to do. Neither JD nor Juan wanted to be in any one spot after that shotgun shit. They sipped the forties they bought at Jasmine's. Juan talked about his ankle, how it was feeling better. Talked about how he found a rehab routine on YouTube and swore he'd be ready for Senior Day. About how Coach Paul promised that his friend from Arizona would be there to watch him as long as he helped Eddie—who'd just sprinted all the way home like a maniac. JD didn't believe any of that shit for a second but didn't say anything. Who knows, maybe something good *would* happen. Nothing good ever happened to him, but it had to for *someone*.

"Hit up Glory Road," Juan said as they approached Scenic Drive. "Let's check out what the college kids are up to." The view of the city from Scenic, a long winding road cutting through the mountains, where the lights of cars streaked along the curves of the highway below and neighborhood houses glowed like light bulbs twisted into the ground, was JD's favorite.

"Why? They're just binge drinking at bro bars," JD said. He felt drained after the run-in with the cholos.

"Just go, pues. What the hell else are we doing?" Juan said, then drained his forty.

"I guess you were right about those dudes. I should've looked away." He should've gone home, too, JD was realizing.

"Those dudes were just fucking with us. They weren't really gonna shoot. It's some kind of game to them . . . I bet." Juan rolled down his passenger window and birdied the empty, the bottle circling high in the air before crashing to pieces in the middle of the road. "And you better start catching up, lightweight." JD wasn't so sure. He couldn't stop imagining what would've happened if Danny had been there instead of Eddie. He remembered the sound of Danny's gun that day behind Juan's apartment. The clear, quick pop. Danny would have had his old man's gun out after the Cutlass's first cruise around the block. What kind of game would they have been playing then?

"All right," he said at last. "But just a real quick cruise."

Glory Road wasn't what JD expected, the short street crawling with nerdy dudes wearing skinny jeans, a sea of beards and glasses. He thought of Melinda. No doubt she was going to college—UTEP, only if she really wanted to. Still, JD could imagine her on this street or one just like it. Holding hands with one of these non–hood rats. They passed a sign declaring OPEN MIC NIGHT, ORGANIC CHAI TEA. He imagined her inside, studying or listening to some baboso in a wool knit hat strumming his guitar, shit that wasn't JD's deal. Waiting at a four-way stop, JD took a long pull from his forty. It had gone warm.

"Put that shit down," Juan hissed. "Are you insane? There are cops everywhere."

"*Now* I should slow down?"

With the forty back between his legs, JD made another pass down Glory. The whole scene looked like a movie set. The girls, the women, some dressed in the same style skinny jeans as the dudes but looking way better, and others in short skirts, high heels clacking as they crossed the busy street in packs, going from bar to bar. Everyone boozy and happy, confident. JD wanted this; as the malt liquor worked on him he knew he not only wanted to go to these places but also wanted to hang with these people, that he both hated and loved them, a thought that embarrassed him. He snuck another chug before looping around to the same four-way stop, this time watching a small group, two guys flanked by three girls, walking by.

"Holy shit! Look at that car!" the one wearing the suit jacket and button-down shirt said. "It's, like, literally patched together. It's like a quilt car." He stopped a few feet from their hood, pointing. "Are you guys seeing this?"

The rest of his group continued crossing as he stumbled after them. "Those Mexicans are driving a quilt car!"

It took all the control JD had not to jump from his seat and fight. He could just tell the motherfucker had never been punched in his life, had never been called useless or had a gun in his face. Probably the reason he talked shit to people he knew nothing about.

Instead, Juan smacked at his arm. "Hey, isn't that your old man's truck?" he asked, pointing just beyond the intersection at the continuing row of neon-lit bars farther down the road.

JD turned, and sure enough Pops, with a woman JD had never seen before in the passenger seat, was pulling out from a parking lot. With no other cars in the way, JD gunned it, swerving to miss the drunk "quilt car" guy—the pendejo still unhit. Still unafraid.

"So I guess we're following your old man," Juan remarked as they rode up directly behind the truck. "I mean, getting right on his ass in your totally recognizable Mexican-blanket car is probably what I would do. That's how they tail people in the movies."

"I wanted to kill that fucking gringo," JD fumed, scrunching down in his seat and lowering his speed, blending into traffic as they pulled away from Glory Road and turned onto Mesa Street. JD hoped Pops hadn't noticed him. "First of all, he called it a quilt car, which is stupid. If anything, it's a serape car."

"Shit! In that case you should have tried selling it to

him instead of driving away. You could've tossed some Halloween skeletons in the back and told him it was a Día de los Muertos car. He would have paid twice what it's worth," Juan said, laughing before taking a chug of his second forty.

"You think he would have had the twenty dollars on him?" JD asked with a laugh himself, sneaking another sip, the booze now going down easy. He followed his old man's truck back onto the freeway, zooming past downtown and then taking the 54 toward the Northeast. He kept close—not too close for him to notice but careful not to lose him. JD hadn't seen his pops since that night at Danny's—when he started his car—and didn't even know where he'd been living. He wondered if his father had tried to call. If Pops knew his phone was broken.

Getting off at Hondo Pass, they drove into a housing development. The houses were nicer than the ones in Central, at least from the outside. No busted cars on the lawns, no dirt yards, no graffiti on the walls. The ugliest things in the neighborhood seemed to be Pops's truck and JD's Escort.

When his old man pulled into a driveway, JD stopped two houses down and parked. He and Juan watched as Pops went to open the door for the woman and led her to the front door of the house. It was dark, but she looked to be around his old man's age, buried somewhere in her thirties. Did she know she was the *other woman*? Did she care?

JD reached into the back seat for his other forty. Cracking

the seal, he took a long drink. He kept watch as his old man was let inside, the living room light flicking on for a few moments before the house went dark again. *Damn.*

"Let me ask you a question," Juan said, thumping on his forty—already halfway done with it.

"Go for it," JD said, not actually wanting to answer shit. He felt oddly invisible watching his father living another life, like he and the rest of his family no longer existed. Like he was a ghost.

"What the fuck are we doing here?"

"Seeing what my old man is up to?"

"But . . . why? You've been so outside of your mind lately."

"Really?" JD wondered. 'Cuz he felt the opposite, like he'd been buried *inside* his own head. "How?"

Juan drummed harder. "Well, running from cops; staring down Los Fatherless, who were aiming a *shotgun* at us; and fucking with Coach until he had no choice but to kick you off the team. Those things."

JD took a second to think, and took another swig. He wanted to know who the woman was. He wanted to see what she looked like, but more than that, he wanted to know about her life, to find out what made her so special that his old man risked his *own* family—*everything*—for her. "Are you saying we shouldn't break into the house and take a look around?"

"We should not do that," Juan said, staring at him in disbelief. "That's not a thing, dude."

"You're right, we can do it later . . . and to answer your question, I just want to know why. Why my old man did what he did. He just left us, man. His family. It's hard to explain."

Juan slumped back in the passenger seat and they went quiet, each taking pulls from their forties. JD could feel the booze, felt suddenly tired and light-headed. Outside, the sky seemed massive and unbearably dark, the stars scattered across like spilled salt, tiny and insignificant. He thought about Glory Road, the sound of conversations and music that had poured out from each bar, and he wondered how trash like him could ever get to be the kind of person who belonged in places like those.

"I found a letter at my house," Juan said, his head now pressed against the passenger window, probably buzzing hard. "From a guy on death row."

"What? What are you talking about?"

"It was to my má. I guess he was her boyfriend or something."

"Well, that's fucking weird," JD said. "But I don't get what that has to do with my old man's sidepiece and him ditching me and the rest of the family."

Juan looked at JD. Both hands were clenched around the steering wheel. "Well, I'm beginning to think that death row inmate might be my father. They dated around the time my má got pregnant. He got locked up before I was born. It makes sense. The timeline. Why my má wouldn't tell me. So, I get a little of what you're talking about."

"Fuck. I'm sorry. I'm an asshole." JD took a long final chug, the warm and bitter beer glugging down his throat until the last foamy stream was gone. Of course Juan knew what JD had been going through. Having a father with another life had been his life story. "What are you gonna do? About this guy? Your *maybe* dad?"

"I don't know. I was thinking I want to go and, you know, see him. The dude's scheduled to be executed next month. On Valentine's Day."

"Fuck."

Juan was shifting in his seat, probably uncomfortable with everything he was saying. "What if he is? My dad, I mean. I just wanna know, you know?"

JD stared into the narrow opening of his empty forty, avoiding looking at his friend. Juan's face was desperate and pleading and exactly the way JD felt since leaving Glory Road. "Just ask her. What would be the point in hiding the truth from you now?"

Juan bounced his head against the headrest. "I don't *want* to ask her. If this guy is my father, he is also a murderer. It makes sense that she didn't want to tell me."

JD thought about that, about how terrible it must have been for Juan to have wondered all these years about who his father was, to have dreamt up all sorts of scenarios and reasons for why he was gone and how he could one day come back. No way did any of them include him being a murderer on death row. "Doesn't she owe you the truth, though?"

"No, not anymore . . . I think after everything I've done

lately, the least I owe her are her secrets. I can find the truth out on my own."

JD exhaled loudly. "Dude, again, I'm sorry about your ankle and you being arrested. I've been fucking up—"

Juan grabbed his arm. "Look, man, I said we were good. After finding out about this, I don't really care. But I need to ask you a favor. A big one. I need you to drive me to Livingston, Texas. I have to know if this guy is really my dad. I have to see his face and ask him."

"Right now?" JD cranked the engine and flicked on the lights. If Juan meant right now, then right now it would be. Juan had always had his back, and now was time to do the same. Even if it meant acting outside of his mind.

"No, not right now. Right now, let's go home. But before they kill him. No bullshit. You'll go. You'll drive me. You'll do this with me." A couple of revs of the engine sealed the deal.

JD nodded. "Yeah, man. I promise. We'll be like Thelma and Louise, just a couple of bitches on the road looking for answers."

"Man, sometimes I have no idea what the hell you're talking about."

Before leaving, JD placed their empty forties on the side piece's porch—Juan agreed the move classed the place up. JD maneuvered back through the neighborhood, trying to go back the exact way he came. The second forty was hitting, and barely minutes into the drive, Juan passed out. JD tightened his grip on the wheel, trying to focus on the blurring road ahead. The streets were empty, so all JD needed to do was get to the 54 and from there to Central—once in familiar territory, he could make it home without a problem.

Approaching a red light, JD cruised to a smooth stop and waited. He kept his eyes on the traffic signal, the bright light unchanging. He couldn't see any oncoming cars but knew taking the light was asking for the cops. So he waited. And he waited, and waited. He began hearing a faint rubbing sound, at first like a single grasshopper rubbing its legs, but the sound grew quickly, the rubbing transforming into a nightmarish swarm of locusts, the buzzing causing instant pain in JD's head. Lurching forward in his seat, JD realized he wasn't sitting at a red light. The car was speared into a cement-encased lamppost. He was now deathly sober, a rush of adrenaline surging. Shit! He must've fallen asleep at the wheel!

Juan unbuckled his seat belt.

"Fuck," Juan said. "You okay?"

"Yeah, fuck," JD said, doing the same and hopping out of the car.

The front wheels were propped on the curb, the front bumper was smashed, the hood was buckled up from the lamppost, and fluids were pouring from the radiator. The lamppost, at least, looked fine.

"What the hell happened?" Juan asked, rubbing his forehead.

"I guess I fell asleep," JD said in disbelief, trying to piece together what had happened.

They were in front of an air force recruiting office, the slogan, AIM HIGH, painted on the window.

"How do you feel?" JD said.

"All right, I guess," Juan said, looking at his hands for blood. None. At least there was no blood.

"Let's get this piece of shit off the curb, then."

JD and Juan heaved the Escort down from the curb, the heap settling on the asphalt. JD grabbed his insurance and registration from the glove compartment and gingerly picked up his video camera—it looking undamaged—before locking the doors. Even with the dented hood, when the fluids dried, the car would look like any other boring hooptie parked in a boring strip mall parking lot. No reason for anyone to panic about it being there.

JD looked at Juan's ankle.

"Can you walk?" JD asked.

"I've been doing it all day," Juan said.

"We don't want to be here if the cops come."

Juan hesitated. "What about your car?"

"The air force can have it."

LIVING THE DREAM (CHAPTER EIGHT)

Juan dreamt of the shotgun. Of the lowrider cruising by slowly and deliberately. Of a blast exploding from the barrels, fire and smoke and the smell of burning. In the dream he hadn't ducked, instead watching as the buckshot spread and sprayed across his chest, the metal pellets ripping into his skin and muscle. Smashing into his bones and knocking him to the sidewalk. He could feel the hole where his chest used to be with his hands, reaching inside the cavity of warm jelly and broken bone edges. There was another blast. JD dropped beside him, his face smeared away, as if wiped with a hot jagged rock. Blood quickly pooled, warm and sticky. Eddie hovered over them, praying, or maybe screaming, a terrified look on his face, eyes bulging. Blood continued pooling until it rose high enough to drown out sound. Then Juan woke up in a strange bedroom with bare white walls, and for the first time in his life, Juan prayed, not knowing any of the right words but begging to never see that Cutlass or those dudes again.

After praying, Juan looked around for JD and was both anxious and relieved that he wasn't in the room. He wanted to ask what happened the night before but was glad JD wasn't there to see him pray. It slowly dawned on him that he was in Danny's house—recognizing it from the first time they were there, from the tour. How he had ended up there? The last thing he remembered was sitting in a parking lot in JD's car—*did we crash?* His clothes reeked and the pounding in his head was relentless. His mouth was dry like desert dirt. *Water.* Juan decided to head downstairs.

"Dude, you are fucked up," Danny said as Juan poked his head into the kitchen. "First you don't text me about going out or nothing. Then you drunk call me to come get you at like one in the morning. What is up with that? I thought we were boys."

"We *are* boys," Juan said, embarrassed. "Where's JD?"

Danny glared at him. "Then how come all you can talk about is JD? He kicks your ass and now you're like his bitch or something. I should beat your ass too."

"He didn't kick my ass, and you haven't texted me since then, actually. I thought maybe you were busted for the party or shooting the gun. The Sarge might be a dick about either of those things."

"Yeah, my bad about that. That day was weird. The good

news is my dad is clueless about his guns, and I didn't even get a ticket or anything from the cops about the party. They thought we were squatting in the house, that nobody lived here. *That's* why they came in all hard. The Sarge has no idea, my mom, either. No harm done, really."

"Except me going to jail."

"Except for that."

There was no way the police thought they were squatting, Juan thought. The cops pulled this same move in Central all the time, conjuring up probable cause like shitty street magicians doing card tricks.

Danny waved him into the kitchen. "Have some cereal . . . and to answer your question, JD's looking for an old phone he can have. I'm like his personal Craigslist. He's also freaking out about his car."

"So what did happen last night, exactly?" Juan rubbed his face. Danny was sitting at a table in the nook; boxes of cereal, empty bowls, milk, and spoons were set out on the bar. Juan tried to imagine what it would feel like to wake up every day to a space like this, tried to think of a word to describe the feeling but couldn't, his head throbbing instead.

Danny recapped the rest of the night for him. JD had somehow managed to hit a lamppost in a strip mall parking lot, then JD and Juan abandoned the wreck and stumbled to a bus stop. Juan texted Danny, called about ten pinche times even though Danny had already agreed to come for them. When he got there, Danny explained how the car hadn't looked *all* that bad. Then Juan begged to go home, wanting his má. Crying. Danny texted Fabi—using Juan's phone—asking if it was okay to spend the night, apologizing for messaging so late. She responded with a smiley face ☺. JD had fallen asleep in the back seat, and they'd had to carry him from the car and dump him on the living room floor.

"Shit. How did I not remember this?" Juan asked.

"JD doesn't either. How much did you guys drink? Anyway, he wants me to take him to get his car this morning. It was dark, and I only cruised by—didn't want to get busted at the scene of an accident—but the car looked parked, like you two could have stopped there on purpose. I bet that thing starts right up."

Juan pressed his hands against his pounding head as Danny chugged orange juice from the carton. Danny had to be right—it wasn't a big deal, the accident. He didn't feel sore or like anything had happened at all. The only thing that hurt was the shittiest hangover ever. And his ankle, like always.

A minute later Juan changed his mind about that—maybe they *had* been in a serious accident, one with head trauma—because suddenly the badass girl who'd been talking shit to him at the Austin High School quad strolled into Danny's kitchen and took a seat at the bar. It was like he was hallucinating or something. She glanced at Juan, which immediately made him look at the ground like he was the world's most easily trainable dog.

"Toma esto, Roxanne," Danny said, holding the carton of juice out to her.

"You two are sad," the girl said, waving the juice away and looking bored out of her skull. "You make me feel sad."

Juan's brain scrambled to keep up. Was this the *prima*, Roxanne? "So—so—this is your cousin?" he stammered to Danny. The last time he'd seen Roxanne he couldn't put two words together, and now he was making the worst second impression imaginable. "I'm actually a pretty fun, happy guy," Juan pleaded. Ugh, even worse!

"Is that right." Roxanne reached for a box of Froot Loops and poured a bowl.

"No seas güey," Danny said. He raised an eyebrow at Juan. "Yes, this is my cousin. Which makes her a big nobody. I thought JD would be the one making an ass of himself, for reals."

"I already know her. That's all."

"You don't know me," Roxanne said, pouring milk over the cereal and eating a spoonful.

"I meant we met already." Juan's head was about to split open, which was good—the pain made it hard to talk and say anything more idiotic.

Then JD showed up, shirtless, and walked into the kitchen holding two smartphones in the air. "Can I keep one of these? I found them in your parents' room."

Danny swung around. "What were you doing in my parents' room? You can't just go looking through people's rooms. I said check *my* room."

"You said they might have some phones," JD said, looking confused. "Also, I looked up how to switch the SIMs on your computer. It's easy—"

Seeing JD with the smartphones reminded Juan—oh shit—of his upcoming algebra test. "Oh, man, you wouldn't happen to have an extra graphing calculator?" Panic swelled all of a sudden, so he plopped next to Roxanne at the bar and poured himself a bowl of cereal he had no intention of eating.

"What the fuck?" Danny said to JD, ignoring Juan. "And you want a ride all the way to the Northeast—"

"Look, man," Juan interrupted, sounding desperate, he could tell. "I got a test next week and if I don't pass, I'm kicked off the team. Also, I'm gonna need you to teach me algebra?" Which made him remember Eddie and his deal with Coach Paul. *Shit. Shit! Shit!!* He searched the room for a clock. He'd told Eddie to meet him at the PAC at nine a.m. The clock on the wall behind Roxanne gave him half an hour to change and be at the gym. He could still make it. "One more thing. Do you think I could borrow some basketball clothes . . . and maybe catch a ride to Austin? I promised Coach I'd help Eddie with the offense."

"You're the worst friends," Danny groaned and slid down in his seat, seeming to collapse in defeat. "You see this shit, Roxy? Not only am I Craigslist for these fuckers, but I'm Uber, too."

"Ándale. Ayuda sus amigos, Daniel. Mira qué tristes son. El tonto y el mendigo."

"Los dos son tontos y mendigos."

"¡Es más razón!"

"Fine! JD, I'll hook up your phone. Juan, I'll lend you some clothes and drive you all the way to Austin *and* lend you a graphing calculator, but Roxy can teach you algebra, since she's suddenly so caring."

"You sure it's not because you can't add either?" Roxanne said, raising her eyebrows at Danny and scooping another spoonful of cereal into her mouth.

"Hey, I can at least *add*," Juan told her, trying to be cool but finding himself sitting up straight and trying not to look as excited as he suddenly felt. He was pretty sure Roxanne, the girl from the quad, Roxanne the girl with amazing hair and perfect teeth—even if she barely smiled—had just (he hoped) agreed to tutor him.

"Thanks, D-boy," JD was saying. "Seriously." He handed Danny the phones and then moved to hug him. "Bring it in, Danny. . . . Can I still get that ride, though?"

"And I guess I can tutor this one," Roxanne said with a shrug, examining Juan. *Yes!* "I'll tell you what, primo, I'll even drive this one to his little basketball appointment—if he showers first."

They arrived an hour late, finding Eddie walking quickly through the neighborhood with his head down, away from the PAC. Juan rushed out of Roxanne's Honda and begged him to stay, begged him not to tell Coach Paul how he missed their training. Eddie didn't seem to care about Juan being late, just explained how he wanted to either be at home or inside the gym. Away from where the Cutlass, the shotgun, could find him, Juan could tell. Surprisingly Roxanne stayed in the bleachers as Juan ran Eddie through the offense, and after the practice she drove them both home. On the way to Five Points, where Eddie lived in a small brick home behind a set of railroad tracks on Pershing Drive, he explained how last night he ran the entire way, bolting through traffic and even jumping between the cars of a slow-moving train, paranoid that gangsters were after him. Juan watched how intently Roxanne listened, heard her explain how normal Eddie's response was. That he probably needed to talk to someone, a therapist.

From the back seat, Juan realized Roxanne's ride was new and that he'd never been in a new car before. The dash was curved and elegant, futuristic with bright blue LEDs and a giant touch screen. The smell of the cabin was absolutely perfect. After she dropped Eddie off, Juan turned nervous. His guts were churning, a blender hacking away at a handful of rocks.

Roxanne glanced at him as she drove. "You really need help with algebra?"

Juan looked ahead, trying to play it cool. "I got a test coming up."

"Right, but *algebra*? That's easy stuff."

"It's calculus to me." Juan stole a glance at Roxanne. Her hands were at ten and two and she sat straight—definitely not a chingona behind the wheel. She didn't even have the radio on. "If I pass, I get to keep playing basketball. I could get a scholarship."

"Huh." Roxanne looked confused, glancing back and forth between Juan and the road. "That seems ironic. I never understood *scholarships* for playing sports."

Basketball probably seemed silly to her, maybe stupid, but that was okay. Juan drummed lightly on the dashboard. "Lucky for me I plan to major in easy stuff." Juan smiled at her. "With a minor in bullshit. I'll probably need some algebra for that, and I have to learn what 'ironic' means."

Roxanne laughed—a no-shit belly laugh! "You can probably get a pretty good job with bullshit."

"I hope. What are you gonna study?"

"Public health!" Roxanne snapped her fingers and pointed at Juan. "I want to track diseases. Study different minority populations, see how things like smoking and poverty and fast food affect them. And I'm getting into politics. I'm going to be at least a senator."

"Cool," Juan said. Totally cool, he thought. She was *totally* cool. "So you'll help me, then, Senator?"

Roxanne pulled up to his apartment building. Behind the bank of mailboxes stood Fabi, reading a letter. Her face was pinched with concentration, or maybe confusion. Juan couldn't tell, but his nerves buzzed immediately. She glanced over at Juan and Roxanne, but he could tell she didn't recognize anyone in the car—the window tint too dark, the car unfamiliar.

"That letter has to be important," Roxanne said, nodding

at Fabi. "Otherwise why not read your mail inside like a normal person? I bet she's crazy."

"That's my mom," Juan said without taking his eyes off Má. She had to be reading another letter from Armando. The buzzing increased.

"I'm sorry," Roxanne said. "I sometimes say things—"

"Don't worry about it," Juan said. "She's reading letters from an old boyfriend. He's on death row." *Why did I say that?* He closed his eyes, not wanting to see Roxanne look embarrassed for him.

"Oh. Your mom is at the window."

"Fuck," Juan whispered, opening his eyes and rolling the window down. "Hey, má." She looked pissed, as if she'd heard him just shame the shit out of her.

"Hey, you," Fabi said. "That doesn't look like your little friend Danny. . . ."

"This is his cousin Roxanne," Juan said, wishing he could vanish. "She just gave me a ride home."

Fabi popped her head into Roxanne's car, looking over the dash and the bucket seats, the moonroof. "Nice car for such a young girl."

"Thank you?" Roxanne said.

"So it's yours? This car belongs to you?"

"Yes?"

"Huh, I never understood parents buying cars for their kids."

"*Okay*, Má." Juan opened the door and nudged his mom out of the way, moving out of the car. "Thank you for the ride," Juan said to Roxanne. "So, I'll see you for tutoring? My test is in like two weeks."

"I can do next Saturday," Roxanne said, and bolted as soon as the passenger door was closed.

Juan glimpsed the envelope in his má's hand, recognizing the handwriting on the corner and his father's name: *Armando Aranda, 999178.*

Fabi,

Being on death row is like having a disease no one wants you to get cured from. Everyone on the outside wants you to die and thinks every day you're left alive is a waste of everybody's time and money. Sometimes I feel like that too. But mostly I want to live, even though living is pain all the time. It's hard to explain how that makes any sense other than to say I don't want to kill myself. Not anymore.

To answer your other question, the truth is smaller than what was in the papers, on the news. Me and Carlo and Fernie robbed that Denny's, and I killed Clark Jones. That's true. What's also true was that my old man used to beat my ass so bad that he kept me locked in my room afterward, kept me hidden for weeks, until the bruises and bones healed. My body still hurts from being broke and never put back together right. But there are the smaller truths inside those bigger ones. Truths you can't see, like the tiny cells in your body that make up your bones and blood, the meat. I've been reading old science books from the library for years, thinking hard on what happened to me, why I did what I did. Then my old man died, and I figured it out. He'd only written twice, once to tell me to quit writing him and then again, years later, wanting to know if I could give him a kidney from prison. He never loved me, and I realized that for my whole life nobody ever did. Love wasn't in my blood, not in my bones or cells. Not until I met you. Your love was like a virus, an invader making my whole life crazy, still infecting me all these years later. I loved you more than I ever loved anyone, Fabi. And for a short time, you loved me. That's the smallest truth of everything.

Mando

PS You're on my list, in case you want to visit or come before that last day.

BOXING UP
(CHAPTER NINE)

Boxing up her room was easier than Fabi thought. She didn't have a lot of clothes—a few skirts and tops for work; some jeans that looked good with tennis shoes, flats, and heels; way too many T-shirts; and a small collection of jewelry but nothing too nice. Fabi rarely bought anything for herself. On her bed were rolls of film and stacks of pictures of her and Juan—most of them taken when he was little. She held up a photo of her washing a naked baby Juan in the kitchen sink. His mouth and eyes were pinched shut, balled fists beside his face, as if aware of how nervous Fabi had been during his first bath. She could see the fear in her own teenage face, not looking directly at the camera or at Juan, her mouth slightly open, sucking air to keep from going light-headed. Fabi remembered planning to have the photos framed and hung from the walls of the home she would one day buy. She'd been living in this dump of an apartment for almost seventeen years, and the walls were as bare as the day she moved in. Fabi boxed her shoes.

The eviction notice had been taped to the front door, citing illicit drug use and gang activity. A gun. When Fabi had gone to Jabba and asked her what the hell she was talking about, the landlady screamed at her, ranting about how Juan was dealing drugs behind the building, that he was making movies without a permit—whatever that meant. She told Fabi she was lucky she wasn't calling the cops, but if Fabi refused to leave the premises, she would. If she ever saw Juan near the apartment again, she would call the SWAT team.

Fabi knew Juan and his goofy friends liked to hang around the back and do guy talk. She sometimes smelled pot from her bedroom window, but hey, that's what teenagers did. She'd done much worse in her day—not only smoking pot but occasionally snorting coke and tripping on acid and ecstasy. Her past wasn't something she was proud of, but how could she tell Juan not to do the things she'd done herself? At least he didn't have to worry about getting pregnant.

Fabi knew she should be pissed at Juan. The eviction notice, the arrest—he could still be in serious trouble, and a court date *had* to be days away. But she couldn't dig up any real anger. The move was long overdue and needed to happen. For both of them. She did remind Juan that he needed to be on his best behavior, not doing drugs or pissing off an ignorant old woman, even if she *was* a complete bitch. And he did seem upset knowing they had to move because of him and his stupid friends. Even more upset that their only option had been to ask Grampá if they could live with him and by his motto: *My house, my rules*. A motto Fabi herself had never been able to stomach.

Fabi started on her photographs and the contents of a junk drawer—a ring of keys she had no use for, old tubes of lipstick and makeup, loose change—then sat on her bed. Her entire room, minus bedding, fit into three boxes she'd found behind the Vista Market Express. What she didn't pack in boxes were her two letters from Mando and the curled sonogram from Project Vida. Those went inside her purse, which went everywhere with her.

Her father was packing up the living room. He'd wanted to start in Juan's room—so he could snoop, she was sure—but Juan had already boxed everything he owned into a single Rubbermaid tub. The walls of his room had been covered with magazine cutouts of expensive cars parked under moonlight, mansions overlooking secluded beaches, and yachts gliding over perfectly still oceans. Fabi had never paid attention to the walls of her son's room before. Juan owned even fewer clothes than Fabi—he wore the same pairs of jeans two or three times a week and had maybe six or seven shirts. He owned a good pair of basketball shoes; Fabi made sure of that. She'd taken the glossies down before Grampá arrived, suddenly humiliated by the images. Juan had always refused her birthday gifts, never wanted a party, and usually didn't open Christmas presents until days later—often after she forced him to. Fabi had always thought of these gestures by Juan as humble or selfless, but what if they weren't? He seemed pretty comfortable cruising in that chavala's ride. What if he was embarrassed of where he came from? Humiliated by his own mother and feeling sorry for her?

Asking her father if she could move back home had been easier than Fabi thought, though she neglected to tell him about the eviction—why upset him? She explained to Grampá how Juan needed him, that him getting arrested had scared the shit out of her and now more than ever Juan needed a man in his life. These weren't exactly lies, after all.

Fabi stared at the water stain above her head one last time, examining the brown bubbles in the drywall and wondering how long the ceiling would hold. She realized she was lucky it never collapsed on her. Then she thought about the pregnancy. What was she going to do? She'd been a girl when she was pregnant with Juan, about the same age as the girl he'd been riding with. Why had she been so mean to her?

Maybe if Mamá had never gotten sick, things would be different. Gladi wouldn't have stayed home and played the good daughter, wouldn't have bathed and fed Mamá, changed her catheter and tried in vain to make her comfortable until she died and Gladi bailed to college. Fabi wouldn't have partied, too afraid of staying home and seeing the worst thing she would ever see. Her life now wouldn't always have to be hard. Maybe?

Fabi sighed and dug through her purse, looking for a pen. She grabbed her notepad from the drawer by her bed, the one she used to make grocery lists, though sometimes she made other lists too. Lists of other jobs she wanted. Places she wanted to one day live. People she wanted to be. She began to write.

Mando,

I got your second letter. I'm sorry to hear about your father, what he did to you. He sounds like he was a terrible person, and it's good that he's dead. I did love you, a lot, and we were something pretty great back in the day.

We were together the day my mama died. I had promised Papa I would take care of her that day. I had a feeling, in my soul, that she was going to die, and still I spent that afternoon with you. I regret that so much. After she died, I blamed you for me not being there to say goodbye. I blamed you for me having fun all those months while she suffered. I blamed you for me being too afraid to watch her die. When you were arrested, I was glad.

After Juanito was born, I moved

into my shitty apartment and started tending bar. I still live in that apartment and have the same job. It's hard not to think my life turned out this way because of that day. Because of you. I like your small truth idea, but I'm not sure that's how life works. Not sure that I can blame love for what I did. I fucked up, and I can't get that day with Mama back. But there are other mistakes I can fix. Things I can get right the second time. I'm pregnant again.

"We gotta talk about this thing." Fabi froze, pen in midair, as Grampá clomped into her bedroom and stood over her. He dangled a .22 pistol by her face, the handle pinched between his index finger and thumb like he was a cop who'd just discovered the key piece of evidence in some cheesy TV crime show. "Don't freak out, but I found a gun."

"*You* don't freak out. It's *my* gun."

"You can't have this in my house," Grampá said, lifting his chin. He held the gun closer. The gun—she'd almost forgotten about it. She'd gotten it years ago at a pawnshop. It was silver and black, a Smith & Wesson—the only brand Fabi had ever heard of, and so she bought it, thinking it a good idea. *Híjole.* The things she thought were good ideas back then hurt her brain.

"It's just for show," Fabi said. "I don't even have bullets for it."

"Ammo," Grampá corrected, wagging his finger. "And you shouldn't have this around Juan. Does he know you have it?"

Fabi shook her head in disbelief. "No, of course not."

"Do you even know how to use it?" Grampá was now pacing the room, no longer the cheesy TV show cop but instead the prosecutor, cross-examining an about-to-break witness.

"I took lessons. I decided later it was better for show."

"Dime cómo."

"Why bother." He wouldn't believe her even if she were to strip the weapon completely down and reassemble it, which she'd once been able to do, though it had been years since she had actually seen the pistol. It was hidden inside a never-used tamale steamer tucked away under the kitchen sink. Her father believed she was forever a liar and nothing was going to change that. "I'll keep it in my truck until I can sell it, okay?"

"I knew you didn't know how to use it. My house, my rules, sweetie." Grampá sat down beside her and patted her leg as he kept talking. "You better let your little criminal son know that too. I was talking to your landlady outside and she told me this apartment was for rent, if I was looking. She was just waiting for the little drug dealer and his prostitute mother to finally leave."

Fabi brushed his hand away. "Juan's not a drug dealer,

but she's right about me. All my johns pay in guns."

Grampá rolled his eyes. "Are you sure Juan's not into something? He's coming into my house. I'm just making sure."

"Ay Dios, Papá. That woman is crazy. I should have left here years ago." Fabi rubbed her eyes; they felt so heavy. Tired and hungry and not in the mood for any more questions, she stood up, wanting to leave but not sure where she'd go if she did.

"Mija," Grampá sighed. "Look, you don't always know when people close to you are *into* something. That's all I'm saying. Remember that murderer you dated?"

"You know what? Never mind. We can find another place to live. Don't worry about it." Fabi surveyed the room. She could fit everything in her truck. Put stuff in storage. Get a hotel for the night.

Grampá heaved himself up. He smelled like sweat and cheap aftershave, like he'd spent another night sleeping in the backyard. "That's not what I'm saying. I'm saying maybe you really don't know if he's on the wrong track. That's all. I *want* you both to come and live with me. I want to help."

Fabi considered her father for a moment. "All right, Papá." But she wouldn't fully unpack when they got to his house. She'd finish her letter to Mando, and then on the next page of her notepad begin a new list: apartments for rent.

"Honestly, we should have done this a long time ago, mija," her father was saying, leaving her room and walking into Juan's. Fabi followed, watching him stand in the middle of the room. The space was bare, the walls cracked where the support beams had buckled, the carpet soiled with dark splotches, burn marks around the electrical outlets. "I should never have let you stay here. I should have put my foot down."

"That's kinda why we were here in the first place," Fabi said. She stood side by side with her father. She was taller than he was, her frame built like his, but still strong, wiry.

Her father grimaced and then rubbed his face with the handkerchief he always kept in his back pocket and occasionally wore on his head. With his cheeks saggy and his balding head sweaty, he looked old. Frail.

"This place wasn't so bad," Fabi added quickly, wishing it were true. She wasn't sure why she wanted to make him feel better but found herself trying to.

"You were too hard for me to deal with all by myself, you and your sister."

"You didn't kick out *Gladi*," Fabi shot back. The urge to be kind was gone as quickly as it had appeared.

"Gladiola wasn't running away all the time," he said. "Gladiola didn't want to fight me every single day of her life."

"And she left you anyways." Fabi cupped her hand over her mouth, immediately regretting her words. *Why say that?*

"You're right about that," he said after a pause. His hands were shaking at his sides, slight flutters, his fingers permanently curled into partial fists. "I lost my wife and my girls one way or another."

"You know, I still needed you back then, Papá," Fabi said, feeling like she was shrinking.

"Who you needed was your mother," her father said, the shaking spread to his shoulders and head. "And she died on us." Her father looked even older, his hair thin and gray, the skin around his face creased.

Fabi put her arms around her papá. "I think this is gonna work out for the best, Papá. You're right."

"Me too, mija," Grampá said, scrunched in Fabi's arms. "Me too."

Fabi,

I remember the day your mother died. It had been the best of my life. I picked you up early that morning, before it happened, and we skipped school and cruised Memorial Park and hung out by our favorite tree. We chilled all day, from morning until night. Making love outside, in my ride. I thought we would be like that forever.

At the time I guess I didn't get it. At first I thought you needed time by yourself, but when you started hanging with that Martin dude, I got a little crazy. I get it now. I even get why you hooked up with Martin. Your mama going out with cancer, his dad the same. You two having to bury your parents on the same day. You didn't have to tell me, I just knew. You blame me for missing that last day with your mama, and I know you wish you had spent that day with her, but if that was the last day I was going to see you then I'm glad it went the way it did.

They called us "The Pulp Fiction Robbers" in the newspapers, which made us sound like a joke. And they'd treated us like one during the trial, making fun of our clothes and how the robbery went down, how we didn't wear masks. Even for choosing the Denny's near the airport, deciding that our idea that travelers would be carrying more cash than vatos from El Paso was stupid. Everything about us was a joke except for what happened to Sheriff Clark Jones. The prosecutor called him that during the trial. Over and over.

We'd snuck inside and took a booth by the entrance. We were stoned, having smoked the rest of our supply, and we decided that dealing the little pot we did wasn't bringing in enough money. I'd wanted to make more. To get enough to take you away, though I hadn't thought where or far enough ahead to make any real plans—I was thinking maybe Disneyland, Mickey Mouse and Goofy and roller coasters, would take your mind off of your mama dying. It sounds so stupid now, but I thought leaving, getting you out of your head, would somehow bring you back to me—make you love me again. Fernie and Carlo had .22s and I carried a sawed-off under my coat. Carlo was gonna do the talking and hit the register, Fernie was gonna collect the wallets—this was the "Pulp Fiction" part—and I was gonna guard the door, but the plan went to shit almost from the jump.

We ordered food, because the place was kind of empty and we hoped more people would come in, with more wallets and purses to take. Or at least that's what we told ourselves. I was scared, and I'm sure Carlo and Fernie were too. I still remember my eggs. How they were so runny, almost raw, the yolk spreading across the plate as soon as I cut into them. I didn't eat.

Instead I watched Carlo and Fernie grub on eggs, bacon, hash browns, pancakes, and toast. They had orange juice and water and coffee, even though I'm sure neither of them actually drank coffee. It was like their last meal.

When Carlo popped up and announced the robbery, a few people actually laughed. They must have thought he was quoting the movie or fucking around, him scrawny and pale and not too different from the dude in the movie, but when he jammed the pistol in our waitress's face as she brought our check, they realized we were serious. The waitress screamed as the stub of Carlo's gun pressed against her cheek. I puked all over our table.

Carlo looked pissed off at me as he dragged the waitress over to the register, and Fernie, partially covered in my throw-up, stood stiff as a statue. He just stared at me, like everyone else in the restaurant was doing. I know how stupid this sounds, like at the moment I should have been worried about other things, not caring about people making fun of me or what they thought, but that was all I could do. Like the people in the restaurant somehow knew how big a fuckup I really was. That I'd lost my girlfriend. Had dropped out of school. That I couldn't even rob a Denny's. I should've ran. We all should've run away.

Instead I jumped from the booth and pumped the shotgun and told everyone to get on the floor. When no one did I pointed the shotgun at Jones. He smiled when I did, like I'd just paid for his shitty Grand Slam. I told him to get on the floor and give me his wallet; he said he'd do no such thing. That if I had half a brain in my Mexican head I'd run home back to my mama. Better yet all the way back to Mexico. I could hear someone laughing behind me, and then shushing. No one was sure what to say or do. Especially me.

"You ain't gonna shoot me," Jones said.

"Fuck you," I said. "I'll blow your fucking head right off."

"I was a sheriff in Victoria,

Texas, for twenty-two years, and I can tell the difference between a man who does what he says he's gonna do and a lump of shit in a watermelon patch collecting flies. I could smell you and your amigos the second y'all walked through the door. Now hand me the shotgun and let these good folks get back to their food."

Jones moved toward me. At the time, I didn't know that Carlo and Fernie had already booked it (they're out now already, having served fifteen for armed robbery, at my trial testifying they heard me threaten to kill Jones). Jones was bigger than me, and even though I had the shotgun, and he was an old man, I was the one afraid. He'd blocked the only way out, and I knew the second I let him have the shotgun my life was over.

He grabbed the barrel and tried to pull it away from me, but I pulled back. We yanked back and forth; I could feel the stock slipping from my hands. I tried to tighten my grip, to keep the shotgun away from Jones, when I must've overreached and slapped my hand down hard on the receiver and trigger. The shotgun went off; the blast knocked me to the ground, broke two ribs when the stock slammed into my chest. I heard screaming, the restaurant emptying, as panic ballooned inside the room. It took a while for me to be able to sit up, to get my body to work, but when I did all I saw was blood; it covered me.

I didn't run. I waited outside for the cops. I didn't shoot Sheriff Clark Jones on purpose; I was just closing my eyes and pulling, same as him. Still, I do sometimes wonder if the prosecutors weren't right all along. If I didn't pull that trigger on purpose. If I'd wanted to kill Jones the second he had opened his mouth. Why do men like Jones always think that no matter what, everyone has to listen to them? That even when they have no reason to think they're in charge, they act like they are? That's the only reason he's dead.

I know when the day comes, the Jones family will come to see me die, and they'll tell themselves their being there is about justice. But maybe after they walk into that room, see me in the chamber, strapped to the gurney and the poisons pushed in, my body seizing to a stop, they'll get that what they are watching isn't justice. Or they'll get it later, when they start dreaming of my killing. Like on nights when I see Jones die, even after all these years, and it doesn't matter what I've told myself during the day. They'll know they picked wrong. That they picked never-ending death.

EDITING A NIGHTMARE (CHAPTER TEN)

JD waited for his sister on the front steps of Austin High like she told him to. And of course, Alma wanted to know more about what had happened as she drove. "Tell me again. I still can't quite picture it," she said as they arrived. They pulled up beside JD's Escort. The parking lot was full, except the space beside JD's car—still, the abandoned hooptie didn't stand out in a strip mall full of busted cars parked at Big Lots and Dollar Tree.

Alma was still pissed he'd blown off talking to Amá after Friday's game. And now she sounded like a reporter trying to catch a politician in a lie, wanting to know, in detail, how JD had managed to smash his Escort into a lamppost in an empty parking lot. Only, JD didn't bother lying. What was the point? The car was wrecked, and no number of imaginary dogs running into traffic or fantastical stories of being chased by road ragers, him swerving like a heroic racecar driver to escape them, was going to explain *that* desmadre.

"I was fucked up," JD explained. "One minute I was at a red light, the next I was smashed against this lamppost." Alma nodded, got out of her car, and squatted by the dented bumper. She examined where it had bent around the pole.

"Ay Dios. Have you told Apá?"

"Why would I do that?" JD said. "He's the reason I was up here. Why this happened in the first place."

"Because you followed him here?"

"Not to this exact spot. To a house just up the street. So yeah, that's right. I blame him."

Alma shot him a look, the same one Amá always gave him when he talked crazy: one raised eyebrow and her head slightly tilted. Eyes ready to roll if one more word escaped his mouth. "So you get none of the blame? No blame for not coming home after your game like you said you would? Like you promised?"

"You're missing the point. He's still cheating on Amá."

"So, Apá lying to Amá is the reason you wrecked your car and abandoned it, not telling anyone until this morning? That makes sense to you?"

"You don't have to make me sound so stupid." JD stared at the car. When he'd gone to get it with Danny, hoping the wreck wasn't as bad as he'd remembered, he found it was even worse. Not only was the radiator cracked and drained of antifreeze, but the oil pan was busted too. The engine certainly bone dry. "I'm not the one fucking everything up."

"You *are* fucking everything up. You've been avoiding Amá and the family. Your little brother thinks you're a bully. You get into fights with your friends. You wrecked your car while driving drunk and could've killed yourself or somebody else. And your entire explanation, for all of this, is *our* dad's affair. The thing that is happening to *all* of us."

JD thought about that. Pops's cheating had to be shitty for Tomásito, who was too little to understand why his father had to go. And for Amá, it had to feel like a life was ending. But Alma didn't really live in the house anymore. What was *her* deal? "Are you having boyfriend problems or something? You're being a bitch." Alma grabbed large chunks of her hair and looked ready to pull them out. Her patiently annoyed face vanished as the veins in her neck and forehead bulged.

"I can't even believe how awful you're being!"

"Okay, I get it. Everything's my fault. Whatever."

"No, you don't get it! You always think you're so smart but you never comprehend the most basic things. You don't get family. You get family all wrong. What the fuck does my boyfriend have to do with anything, you moron? All I wanted to do was help you!"

That's all JD *had* wanted. Help. Alma was good with cars. The old man took her on odd jobs when she was little, showing her how to work on them and then, for whatever reason, he never did the same with JD. But instead all

Alma wanted to do was mom him up and make him feel shitty, when all he ever felt was shitty. He wanted her to say she could fix it, but looking at the Escort again—the mismatched quarter panels, the cardboard taped to the window, the buckled front bumper, the butterflied front wheels—he knew the heap was a loss. He kicked the passenger door. Watched as the metal creased. He kicked again, the dent growing bigger. He glared at his sister.

"I don't need any more help. I'm good, thanks."

"What are you doing? Stop it! Don't make it worse. You're always making everything worse."

"That's what I do." JD kept kicking, now busting up the back passenger-side door. His body became slick with sweat as he repeatedly drove his heel into the metal.

"What is wrong with you?!" Alma stepped back, away.

"Fuck you!"

"Goddamn it, JD! You're the worst."

JD stopped kicking, turned, and walked away from Alma and his car. He stared at the ground, trying to control his breathing. He wanted to scream—not really at Alma, but just inhale deeply and let out a long exhaust of noise. JD needed away from his sister.

"¿Y dónde vas? You can't walk home from here, Juan Diego. Don't be so stupid. Get in the car." He could hear the exasperation in her voice. How tired of him she was. He was tired of himself too. Looking up, JD realized there was no place to go but the air force recruiting office—he'd gone right up to the front window. He looked back at

Alma, where she stood, hands on hips, head cocked, like she expected him to turn around like a scared little kid realizing he'd wandered too far from his mommy. *Nope.* JD turned back, pulled the Plexiglas door to the recruiting office open, and went inside.

Last Christmas Eve they'd been sitting in the living room watching Christmas shows on television. Rudolph and Frosty. JD, sitting on the floor, had wanted to get the Kinoflex Pro 8mm he'd lifted from the weekly Anaya family yard sale—open for business even on Christmas Eve! After looking the camera up and watching videos on YouTube, it seemed reasonable to think a camera like this could be the place for JD to start making movies. It looked like an actual movie camera, just smaller. A black case, silver trim with a protruding lens, a sleek handle for handheld shots that was easily removed for placement on a tripod. It didn't look like the other cameras JD had acquired over the years, cameras made for taping birthday parties and high school graduations. After all, if the Russians made the Kinoflex, then it had to be serious; from what JD could tell from the little Russian cinema and the parade of dashcam videos he'd seen online, they only seemed to be funny by accident.

Amá had been tired from making tamales with his tías and getting ready for the next day at Nana's, where the entire family gathered every year after Mass, and was falling asleep with her head on the old man's shoulder. Alma had been at her boyfriend's, which had pissed the old man off. He'd complained about this being family time, that he always worked, and when he didn't, everyone should be home. Of course, that was nonsense. Who ever knew when he'd be home? JD had wanted to shoot hoops with Juan or maybe go to some party Danny was talking about, but with his old man grumping around, he knew better than to leave. Besides, he had the camera.

The camera drive motor was manual, a windup, but it wouldn't rotate. With no rattling sounds, there was probably nothing broken, just a misaligned or jammed gear. There had to be an adjustment JD could make to get the camera running and start filming. Something easy. Unable to focus on Rudolph and his convenient deformity, JD asked his old man if he could borrow some tools.

"For what?" Pops kept his eyes on the TV, his arm around Amá; Tomásito was sitting by his feet. Unlike JD, the family was absorbed by Rudolph. Everyone liked their misfits better on television.

"I wanna take my camera apart. See what's wrong with it."

"What camera?"

"I got it at a yard sale."

"You bought a broken camera at a yard sale? How much you pay?" JD had his old man's unwanted attention now. Pops leaned forward to look at him as Amá sat up.

"What did you do?" she asked, the question automatic, like a greeting. *Good morning. Buenas tardes. You have the right to remain silent.*

"I got a camera at a yard sale today."

"He got ripped off is what he did," his old man said disgustedly. "Whose yard sale was it? Was it the Anayas? I told you not to go there. Ladrones."

"It doesn't matter."

"Bullshit. If they sold you something that doesn't work, then they should give you your money back."

"He's right, mijo," Amá said. "Don't protect them."

"I'll fight them," Tomásito said, jumping to his feet, striking a pseudo kung-fu pose, and kicking his leg into the air. "Ya!"

"That's enough," Amá said, pulling Tomásito into her lap. "Watch Rudolph."

"At least this one wouldn't let himself get ripped off." Letting out a long sigh, JD's father slumped back into the couch and rubbed his hand across his face, as if he just heard JD confess to trading the family cow for magic beans.

"I knew it was broken. I think I can fix it."

"Bring me this camera," his father had said.

The Anayas had wanted twenty dollars for the camera, probably a good price, but he still needed gifts for Amá and Alma, for his old man and Tomásito, too. He probably overpaid for the football he bought for Tomásito, the La Virgen statue for Amá, and the sunglasses for Alma. The *It's Beer Thirty Somewhere* clock for the old man. So JD didn't feel all that guilty slipping the broken camera into the waistband of his pants and leaving with a gift for himself. It was Christmas, after all.

“Here,” JD said, after grabbing the camera from his room.

His father held it flat in the palm of his hand, as if his hand were a scale determining the camera’s worth. “How much did you pay?”

“A buck,” JD said, guessing his old man wouldn’t care about a dollar.

“Well, at least it wasn’t more than that. I mean, even if you get this running, where are you gonna get film? Get it developed? This thing was ancient when I was a kid. Your tata used to have one. Nobody uses these, mijo. Even for a dollar, you got ripped off.”

“But it’s like a real movie camera. Look at it,” JD insisted.

“N’ombre, these were for home movies. ¿Verdad, mi amor?” He waited for Amá to agree with him, but she was falling asleep again, her eyes blinking closed. “Like I said, your tata had one. Used to record all sorts of unwatchable BS. It doesn’t even record sound.”

JD’s face must have crumbled, because his father added, “But if you wanna try to fix it, I got some small screwdrivers in the glove compartment of my truck that should work. Have at it.”

The screwdrivers weren’t in the glove compartment, but there were always loose tools on the seat and floor. So JD fished around the floor and underneath the seats. The condoms were tucked inside a brown paper bag that JD’s searching fingers had scraped across. He retrieved the bag, and thinking the screwdrivers might be in there, unfurled the worn paper. And discovered the box. It was carelessly ripped open, half left from a dozen. JD sat back with the condoms spilled in his lap, head tingling and body heavy, stunned, like he'd just been in a car accident. One he hadn't seen coming.

And now, sitting in the recruiting office, he felt that exact dazed feeling. And even though what had happened wasn't exactly the same as being twisted up in a metal box, the confused feeling—his head tingling like all the blood had rushed out and pooled at the bottoms of his feet, his urge to flee the scene—was. Alma had driven off and texted him seconds later:

GROW UP!!!!!!

Technical Sergeant Bullard's office, the name stencilled on the glass door, was plastered with some nerdy shit. Posters with fighter jets zooming through clouds, words like INSPIRATION and DETERMINATION printed in bold underneath. JD walked the seemingly empty office, the cheap furniture and carpet as unimpressive as the images of smiling airmen marshaling airplanes and holding M16s. The posters of groups of mechanics looking into the camera while standing beside bombs or surrounded by tools in maintenance bays all seemed to have a white guy, a black dude, and some brown person of unknown ethnicity. The vatos could've been Indian, Native American, Latino, or Muslim. It was the air force's way of saying, *Hey, Brown Dudes, this shit's for everyone.* Behind Bullard's desk were plaques, laminated newspaper articles, and neatly folded American flags inside triangular wooden frames. JD stood behind the recruiter's desk, reading. Curious. Three different citations were for service in wars, the dates spanning JD's entire life.

"Sorry about that." The voice obviously belonged to the recruiter and was friendly, but it made JD nervous anyway. JD quickly moved from behind the desk. The man was dressed in his blues, the stripes on his sleeves creased neatly down the middle. He wore a perfectly tied blue tie. "I was in the latrine. I'm Technical Sergeant Bullard."

"JD . . . and I'm sorry for being back there," JD said, not knowing what else to say.

"That's okay, JD. You looking to join the greatest air force in the world?" Bullard folded his arms across his chest and smiled like an overeager fitness instructor.

"Not really," JD said. "I was just leaving."

"Why so fast? Did I scare you?" Bullard walked to a chair by the front door and sat down. "Because if it's not me scaring you, it's something. You look freaked out, dude."

JD couldn't help but look out the window at his broken-down Escort. How was he getting home? No way would Danny come for him again. Alma was also out. The bus?

Bullard eyed the parking lot. "That yours? I bet that has a story." He pointed right at JD's hooptie. Lucky guess.

"You don't wanna know."

"Probably a fun night that ended not so fun. You're not

the first person that's happened to." Bullard turned his attention from the car to JD. "You worried about it?"

"No shit," JD said.

"You want something to drink? There is a mini-fridge by my desk." Bullard nodded right where JD had just been standing. JD was thirsty and tired. He reached for a soda and took a seat next to Bullard.

"How extreme," JD said, holding a can of Mountain Dew.

Bullard raised an eyebrow. "Are you making fun of a free soda?"

"Sorry," JD said, immediately feeling bad. *Damn.* "I'm sure this comes in handy when you recruit bros." He took a drink. The fizzy sugar water was fantastic.

"Gamers like it too." Bullard smiled. "Can I ask you a question?"

"I guess." Here it came. The pitch.

"Are the police involved?"

"No." JD avoided looking at the recruiter, who was trying his hardest to make eye contact. "It was just me and the post. Nobody really even knows about it."

"Were you drunk?"

"Yes." Honest. Why not?

"So, what are you going to do about it?" Bullard leaned back in his chair, wanting an answer JD wasn't sure he had. "You have an obvious problem with that junked-out car. You have to do something about it. Tell me your plan."

"I don't know. Fix it?"

"That would be way too expensive. You can't really

afford that. What's your next plan?" Bullard jumped from his seat and skipped over to his desk, then spun around and faced JD. "Go! Tell me!"

"Just leave it?" JD slumped down in his seat, now sure he didn't have the answers.

"Terrible idea. Eventually someone would report the car abandoned. You would get cited, multiple times. Then the car would get towed and you'd end up in court owing thousands of dollars for a car worth nothing. What's option three? Go!"

"What's the point of this?" JD suddenly wanted to go home. He wished he'd gotten in the car with Alma and hadn't talked crazy to her. Why did he always do that?

"The point is when people like you walk into this office they think they're looking for a job or college money, but what they need is problem-solving skills. The air force can teach you that, kid. Trust me. I've been in some tight spots."

Bullard leaned on his desk. He was muscular, his hair cropped short and perfectly combed, his chest stacked with medals. He seemed like a movie star. If Bullard had been their basketball coach, they might have won two, maybe three games, just on style alone.

"So what would *you* do?" JD thought about the camera he left plugged in to his computer, downloading all the footage he'd captured so far. Was he crazy to think he should've been filming this moment?

"Have it towed to a junkyard." *What? Yes, definitely out of his mind.*

"That's it?"

"Listen. If you have it towed to a junkyard, you can sell it to them for whatever they want to pay, and then the problem is solved. You didn't throw good money away, you didn't ignore the problem—making it worse—and you got a tiny bit to start over with. Isn't better problem-solving a skill you should have?"

"I can learn to think like that in the air force?"

"If you're smart, and you seem like you might be."

JD pulled out his phone, swiped at the screen. "So, what about jobs? I want to be a filmmaker. Is that an air force job? Maybe go to college."

"The air force has its own production team. We make our own promotion material and have access to the best equipment next to Hollywood. And, of course, there is the GI Bill for college. Plus all sorts of other benefits. But why talk about any of that right now? You look tired. How about I give you a ride home?"

JD knew full well that accepting the offer meant he would owe the recruiter. That Bullard would start calling and looking for him at school. JD had never seen Bullard before, but he noticed other recruiters trolling the cafeteria and popping up on career day. Looking for suckers.

"All right. But I'm not joining."

"Take my card. You may want to call me one day."

JD decided the dude wasn't *that* bad and took it. To be nice.

* * *

Later that night, when Tomásito was asleep, JD watched the footage as quietly as he could. He went over the images he shot: random moments of Juan and Danny talking, flashes of neighborhood houses and cars, lots of sky and clouds. The sound of a gunshot and the inside of his jacket pocket, the muffled conversation between him and Pops—all of the audio was terrible and unlistenable. JD realized his footage could be better edited into a nightmare than a documentary. He needed to learn the basics of filmmaking, because none of the important things that had been happening had made it onto film. He was missing everything; even his family footage was terrible.

He felt bad for what he'd said to Alma, for still avoiding Amá, and for being a bully to his brother. JD loved his family, but he could feel himself fading away from all of them—not just Amá. They would give him the boot, just like Pops, if they knew what he really thought and felt, if they spent time in his head. He was sure of it. He was about to text Juan and tell him about his car, but Juan had been on a self-imposed lockdown, studying nonstop for his basic-as-hell algebra test. The dude was freaking out over nothing, even getting Danny's prima to agree to come tutor him.

It was time for JD to do the same. JD grabbed his phone and began searching for a way to be a better filmmaker, a better anything, when a new idea suddenly bloomed in his head. One that would help him and also keep his promise to Juan.

Documentary Filmmaking
Documentary Filmmaking tips
Documentary Filmmaking techniques
Documentary Filmmaking courses
Documentary Filmmaking equipment
Documentary Filmmaking workshops
Documentary Filmmaking schools

Death Row
Death Row records
Death Row inmates
Death Row last meals
Death Row records shirt
Death Row stories
Death Row last words

BASIC ALGEBRA

Identity is an equality relation, $x = y$, meaning x and y contain some variables and x and y yield the same values regardless of what values are substituted for those variables. Or $x = y$ is an identity if x and y express the same functions.

It's Saturday afternoon and Roxanne is over to study, like she promised. You've been working on algebra for an entire week now, studying like crazy on your own while rehabbing your ankle, knowing you gotta focus. Má and Grampá are pissed at you. They don't say shit, but you can tell, getting side-eye from both of them.

You've taken Roxanne to your new room. She smells good, wearing a light perfume that's making you dizzy. You're both sitting on your bed, along with your algebra book, notebook, backpack, and Danny's graphing calculator. She's hugging your pillow. Your má has been in her room with the door closed all day. You thought about studying in the kitchen, to keep her from getting more pissed, but Grampá was in there rebuilding a carburetor. You're glad Roxanne never saw the inside of your old apartment and wish she never knew you lived there.

Roxanne starts with what she calls the basics, and explains that information about arithmetic operations on fractions can be extrapolated to all real numbers. She tells you to pretend that x will always be rational, that you could be sure the result would be valid for all numbers x. She takes your pencil and scribbles across the open notebook.

$$\frac{x+9}{12} + \frac{x-12}{9} = \frac{(x+9)(9)+(12)(x-12)}{(12)(9)}$$

Identities, she explains, are symbolic expressions that are true for all real numbers.

$$(x-y)(x+y) = x^2 - y^2$$

Roxanne is way too smart for you. That's on top of being too pretty. Too badass. She tells you that factoring is the decomposition of a mathematical object, reducing something to its most basic terms. You think of numbers dying—all the points and rebounds, all the assists and steals you hustled for, marked down in pencil inside green score books, slowly fading away. Roxanne keeps writing.

$$10x^2 + 51x - 180 = (2x + 15)(5x - 12)$$

She looks at you and smiles. "See." She's factoring now.

As Roxanne effortlessly writes symbols and expressions, you smile back at her, showing your crooked teeth that shame the shit out of you, and realize *this* is another thing that is out of your reach. You feel like Eddie, who will never really *get* basketball; like JD, who can't feel God.

That you are an *x* and your friends are *y*'s, all three of you different variables but equally fucked.

"Are you following this?" Roxanne puts the pencil down. "Am I going too fast?"

"Nah," you say, answering her first question. "And *x* can be anything I want, any number?" You can't help but think if *x* can be anything, then why does it matter what *x* even is? *X* is completely meaningless.

"Just not anything irrational, like pi. . . . See, you're getting it."

You need to know enough to pass Mrs. Hill's test, but you're stupid and there's no helping that. You inch closer to Roxanne, your leg touching hers.

Roxanne is still smiling, but she puts the notebook on her lap, reaches for your algebra book, and playfully slaps it across your chest. "Look, you're kinda cute, but we gotta keep working. We have a lot to cover."

"I'm sorry," you say. "My bad." You inch back, respecting her space but realizing you would gladly fail every math test for the chance to put your lips on hers, because you're irrational, in fact borderline fucking ridiculous, just like π.

LONG LIVE THE QUEEN (CHAPTER ELEVEN)

It took a few days before Juan felt comfortable with the idea of taking Fabi's old room, she could tell; usually he took the couch during visits. It looked nothing like it had when Fabi shared it with Gladi. The fluorescent stars Gladi had glued to the ceiling had long been scraped off, and the walls were painted, the bright pink now a clean white. The Strawberry Shortcake curtains were replaced with a set of blinds, and the cheap, blue shag carpet was now a rough brown Berber. Fabi barely recognized the room, which she was glad for. In fact the entire house seemed new. How hadn't she noticed, over the years of dropping Juan off, that her father had slowly redone the entire home? She peeked into her father's bedroom. It could be part vintage barbershop, part army museum. He slept on a neatly made twin bed tucked away in the corner of the room. A recliner sat in the middle before a coffee table littered with magazines and newspapers. The walls were peppered with awards and decorations from his time in the army; yellowed newspaper articles from the Vietnam War, where he did two tours, were framed and hung. In the opposite corner of the room was the mannequin. She remembered how Mamá used to call him Manny the mannequin; he was still dressed in her father's old greens—olive drab pants and shirt, web belt and canteen, jungle boots and the piss-pot helmet that had a dent where her father claimed a bullet had hit and knocked him clean out. He'd woken in a MASH unit and was later discharged on a medical. Except for Manny, there was no trace of Mamá anywhere in the room.

Fabi took the old sewing room. The room was really a bedroom, but never got used for that—though it never really got used for sewing, either. Sewing was something her mamá had always said she wanted to do but never did much of, the expensive Singer that Papá bought a forever trump card he played whenever she wanted something new for the house or herself.

We could use a new stove. The legs are broken. My cakes keep coming out lopsided.

Try making cakes with that sewing machine you made me buy. It cost enough money; it should be able to make cakes.

We need a new washer. It won't spin.

No pues. Just make us new clothes with the Singer.

The sewing room was where her mamá spent her last months, the room becoming a makeshift hospice. Where she died. Now it was a tidy bedroom with a queen bed, two end tables, and a sewing table at the opposite end, the Singer mounted inside the heavy wooden table and loaded with thread, ready to go if only someone would turn it on. Fabi wondered if her father had made the room nice for her. He'd always been better with his hands than with words.

Now leaving for work, Fabi rushed down the hallway but stopped short when she heard laughter coming from Juan's bedroom. That was weird. Curious, she slowly opened the door and peeked inside. A girl was sitting on the bed beside him, a book on her lap. She wasn't doing anything wrong, other than laughing, but the sight of her next to her son filled Fabi with panic. She could hear her father: *My house, my rules.* Fabi hadn't made her list of places to move yet. Had no money saved up. No plan. Juan froze when he saw her. He'd never had a girl over before, at least not that she knew of.

"So, what's going on in here?" Fabi asked, trying to sound like she wasn't there to bust them, though maybe she was.

"Nothing, just studying," Juan said, moving away from the girl. "I gotta pass a math test next week or I'm off the team."

"What? You don't expect me to buy that." *Wow.* Fabi couldn't believe how much she sounded like her father. She recognized Juan's friend, the same one with the new car. Were her and Juanito a thing?

"C'mon, Má. You don't act all weird when my other friends are here. You're embarrassing me."

He was right, of course. The poor girl looked like she wanted to vanish, pulling her knees to her chest and hugging them. Fabi instantly regretted shaming the girl again. Regretted the way she treated her and Juan at the mailbox the other day.

"Why didn't you ask *me* for help?" Fabi had struggled in high school too. Though, like her father, her trouble was in English, with words. "I'm not stupid, you know?"

"Well, I am, má. I *am* stupid," Juan said. "And if I don't pass this test next week, like I said, I'm gonna get kicked off the basketball team."

"You're not stupid," Fabi said, wanting to rush to her son. To hold him like she did when he was little, when him being scared meant needing her.

"I'm Roxanne," the girl said, standing up. Good manners, Fabi thought, relaxing a bit. "Juan invited me over. I'm sorry to cause all this trouble, and I'm sorry I drove off the other day without introducing myself."

"That's okay, Roxanne," Fabi said. "Juan caused the trouble. He's the one who never tells me what's going on." She leaned over and extended her hand, her armful of bangles jingling. She was aware of how short her skirt was, how low-cut her tank top was. Even though she pretty much ran the bar, she still needed to waitress; without tips she made shit. "And would you two please study in the kitchen? There is a no-boys-and-girls-alone-in-the-bedroom rule in this house."

"Since when?" Juan said, looking up at Fabi.

"Since *you*," Fabi said. "And it's taken Grampá almost eighteen years to get over it."

With Juan and Roxanne safely in the kitchen, Fabi jumped in her truck. She pulled the pistol from her purse. She wasn't about to break her father's rules either, so she'd decided she would sell the stupid thing or give it away—maybe back to a pawnshop? Until then, she'd stash it under the driver's seat, so if Papá did another room check, he'd find zip.

The .22 fit perfectly into the groove behind the lever that moved the seat back and forth, making her wonder if that was the intent of the space, if every truck had a space ready for a gun, and if most of the trucks on the road already had them nestled inside and she had no idea. *Crazy.* Maybe she would ask Ruben. *Ruben.* Man oh man oh man. She had to decide when to tell Ruben about being pregnant. Even with everything going on with Juan, she kept thinking about it. Honestly, almost everything reminded her. TV commercials with families who, for some reason, did laundry together. Her unpaid stack of bills. Juan. She dug through her purse and pulled out the sonogram. It had been almost two weeks since her visit to Project Vida.

At the clinic, she had managed to avoid looking at the sonogram screen. She'd been almost mute, answering the doctor's questions with one-word answers. No, she didn't abuse drugs or alcohol. No, she didn't have insurance. It had probably been a mistake to take the roll of paper when he offered her the photo, her hand reaching for it of its own accord. Because now she found herself looking at it practically every free moment. The image seemed to change each time she looked at it. At first the little white smudge seemed so lonely against the blackness, like a lost satellite floating in outer space, destined to always be so. At least that's what she'd thought until she began to think of her body as the outer space, her name, Fabiola Ramos, printed alongside the sonogram. Her being an infinite universe, expanding and endless. Possibility unexplored.

Paradise was down in Five Points, where the clientele had changed over the years even if the name didn't. When she first started working there, the place served mostly old neighborhood drunks. Then came gente fom Juárez, crowds of displaced men and women who'd come to escape the drug-war horror show, but they were eventually chased out by the current hipster crowd, who liked to ironically enjoy the dumb tropical-themed decor and cheap beer. Fabi pulled into the parking lot and saw Ruben's lime-green Hummer, the KING OF THE DEAL decal emblazoned on the back. Now, Ruben was a guy who never seemed to fit no matter the crowd. Not a drunk, not a refugee looking for community, and for sure no hipster, Ruben had one day wandered into Paradise, telling her he'd done so because paradise was exactly what he was looking for. So corny. He'd returned the following night, this time with a friend, and the two spent the night at the bar, chatting with each other but obviously there to see her. He became a regular, striking up conversations, telling her all about his dealership and the secrets to closing a deal. Ruben's talk had been a buildup to asking her out. Fabi said no to a night of dancing, then to dinner and a movie. Just not that interested. When he asked if she would go for coffee, just for an hour, she tiredly agreed, deciding Ruben was somewhat cute and at least harmless.

"Why don't you return my calls or texts?" Ruben now said as soon as Fabi walked inside the bar. The first rush of the dank air, the smell of stale booze and harsh cleaner, took her breath. The plastic pink flamingos normally perched at the corners of the bar had been knocked over and not put back; the inflatable palm trees, centerpieces for the booths, had gone flat. She had no idea where the pump could be.

"I did," Fabi said. "I told you I was busy moving."

"And I told you to let me help." He paused as if unsure, then added, "That you could even move in with me."

"Ay Dios. I thought I was being nice by not asking," Fabi lied. The bar was mostly empty, which was a bad sign. While the hipsters tipped okay, they usually started partying late and drank the cheapest booze. The owners hated them and were thinking of turning Paradise into a sports bar or worse, a strip joint, but their dummy son Chuchi loved them. They were his drinking buddies most nights.

"How's that nice, you ignoring me all the pinche time?"

"I gotta get to work." And that was the truth. And not just here. She still had unpacking to do. She had Juan to deal with. Not to mention a pregnancy.

“Then get me a beer, since all you wanna do is work.”

“What?”

“Get me a beer. That’s your job, qué no?”

Fabi sighed. So this was what she was going to have to deal with now. “Yes, fine . . . what kind?”

“Un PBR.” Ruben straightened his suit jacket, tipped his cowboy hat, and winked the same cocky wink he did at the end of his commercials. She’d never really noticed his ads before meeting him but now saw them all the time, playing during the local news and during sports. She could recite all of his cheesy jokes and knew the shoddy camera work and effects, the lens zooming in and out on his face, arrows pointing at the cheap cars as the words LOW LOW PRICES flashed across the screen.

“Whatever you say.” Fabi disappeared behind the bar to grab him a beer and start her shift, wishing the night were already over.

Ruben was still at the bar when the hipsters eventually showed. They ordered their PBRs and IPAs. A few made fun of Ruben while waiting for their drinks, talking shit about his clothes and Hummer. One called him the King of Neon. He gave them a thumbs-up as he kept trying to get Fabi to talk to him, while she served him beers and eventually shots. She expected him to leave at some point, but he stayed instead and got drunk. Why was it that men like Ruben, the “nice” ones, were just as relentless as the so-called bad boys and machos and bros at not taking no for an answer?

"Otra," Ruben said, shaking his empty can of beer at her. Someone had popped cornball surf music on the jukebox, the guitar fretting loudly, making it hard to hear. A group that had taken the table behind Ruben pounded shots and played with the underinflated palm tree.

"I'm cutting you off," Fabi said, arms crossed.

"Again? You can do that here, too?" Ruben laughed, slamming the open palm of his hand against the bar.

"Stop it, Ruben," Fabi said, noticing the crowd at the table beginning to turn their attention their way. "You're drunk, cabrón."

"No shit, cabrona. I've been drinking. What's wrong with you? Or, es más, what's *not* wrong with you?"

"Right now, you're what's wrong with me." Fabi turned and noticed a dude sitting at the table with black plastic glasses and a patchy beard whip out his phone. He started recording them.

"What did I do? I did everything you wanted." Ruben wasn't even looking at her, talking instead to the camera phone.

"You didn't do anything." Fabi knew reasoning with drunk men was a mistake, a rookie mistake, yet here she was.

"Mentirosa!" He looked back at her. "Why don't you love me? Tell me! Why do you think you're too good for me? You're a fucking waitress."

There was a pause of silence. The patrons at the bar turned to Fabi, waiting for her to say something. Ruben's eyes were red and glassy, the cowboy hat now sitting crooked on his head, his fists balled in anger. She realized the ongoing cost of saying yes to Ruben. That having that first cup of coffee meant one day moving into his house and having his babies; it meant slowly changing herself into whatever *thing* he imagined her to be that first day he walked into Paradise. Saying yes meant being part of some *deal*.

"I don't know," Fabi said, looking directly at Ruben, her eyes steely. "I'm just a fucking waitress."

"Whatta bitch," Patchy Beard yelled, holding the camera phone steady on them. Ruben stood up from his stool at the bar and immediately fell to the ground. The table laughed. "All the king wanted was his queen!" Patchy Beard called out.

"The waitress must have good credit," someone yelled to a roar of laughter. "Long live the queen."

Crawling on the ground, Ruben reached for his cowboy hat. Fabi crouched down and tried to help him up, but he shoved her, knocking her backward into the table. The half-empty bottles of beer and shot glasses rained down on her. Her clothes were soaking and instantly reeking of booze as she struggled to her feet. Bottles clanked around her. The zippy guitar played on the jukebox as a sea of hipsters gawked.

"That's what you get," Patchy Beard said, shoving his phone in her face. "Just wait until Chuchi sees this; his bar is like a novela!"

"Fuck Chuchi," Fabi said, pushing the camera away. The

drunken hipster idiots erupted into cheers. She scanned the room and realized she was surrounded by men. All of them were drunk, their swollen faces sneering. Shoving her way through the crowd, she ran outside. The whole incident was going to be uploaded onto some Twitter feed or other Internet bullshit. And that was the best-case scenario. She didn't want to imagine the worst case. It was time to go.

Outside, the tiny parking lot was dark, the only light coming from a city street lamp on a faraway corner. She heard footsteps crunching on the gravel for a moment, then nothing. Ruben's vehicle was still there, parked feet away from hers. She cautiously approached her truck, her heart beating fast. Where had Ruben gone? As Fabi hopped inside her truck she noticed the Hummer's driver's side door was partly open. Ruben was passed out in the driver's seat. She turned her headlights on and buckled her seat belt, her head throbbing, when she paused for a moment. She knew she should drive away. But the thought came again, the thought about being pregnant, about the possibility of *another* baby of hers growing up without a father. Fabi took a deep breath and slowly exited her truck. She cautiously approached the Hummer.

Ruben was slumped over, his keys still pressed in his hand. Fabi delicately took the keys and tossed them into the darkness. Muffled music seeped from inside Paradise as though nothing had happened. Business as usual. Fabi's phone buzzed in her pocket. She paused for a moment before pulling it out, already knowing who the text message was from. It was Chuchi, the boy boss who stayed hidden in his back office and only came out to party. She flipped open her phone.

YOU'RE FIRED!!!!!

Juan watched as Grampá sat in the driver's seat of his 1965 Imperial Crown listening to oldies. The sedan needed work—the leather interior was rotted from the sun and splitting along the seams, the dashboard cracked, and most of the wood paneling missing. The body needed paint, too. The midnight black had blotched and faded to a dull purple, and the chrome trim around the fenders and the trunk had stripped away. The music sounded muffled, hissing like songs played on a record player. Los Lobos sang: *"Here I am on the short side of nothing / Can't find my way home / No escape in sight . . .*

The Imperial sat in the backyard and had been there for as long as Juan could remember. Sometimes the hood was popped open, Grampá messing around underneath it. The car seemed to be the one thing in the house that never got completely fixed. Just last month Grampá had installed a new main after the pipe burst in the front yard. When Má asked why he didn't just patch the old one, he said he didn't want to risk another hundred-year freeze bursting it again. Grampá was crazy.

"Does it run?" Juan called out, standing in the kitchen doorway. He didn't know if he should go into the backyard; the swelling on his ankle finally was down, but it still felt sore. Walking in the dark through Grampá's junky backyard seemed like a sure way to retwist it. Grampá liked making Juan his helper when he visited—usually when Juan was in trouble for something—the old man explaining the importance of being a good wrench, of being able to fix things. *Not having to depend on no one but having people need you isn't a bad place to be,* he once explained while the two installed a fuel pump on a neighbor's Chevy Impala. Juan didn't mind helping, but Grampá didn't seem to be turning wrenches on the Imperial.

When Juan and Roxanne had finished studying—he was surprisingly getting the hang of quadratic equations and moving on to probability—Roxanne booked, saying she wouldn't hang out with him until he passed his test, and then only if he quit acting so stupid, now that she knew he *wasn't* actually stupid.

"She runs better than you, Juanito," Grampá said. "Get out here. I've been wanting to talk to you. That girl gone? Your má?"

"Yeah. It's just us."

"Good. Good."

Juan took shotgun. He hadn't noticed Grampá had been drinking. In fact, his abuelo was probably more than a little fucked up, a tallboy resting between his legs and a couple of empties tossed on the passenger floor. Juan had never seen Grampá like this before. He'd never thought of how much time the old man spent alone, whether this was normal for him.

"Are you drunk, Grampá?"

"Nah," Grampá said. He gripped and pulled at the steering wheel, as if correcting from a slow veering off. "I just closed my eyes for a second, officer. I'm fine."

"I'm gonna have to take you in," Juan said, joking. "Even though this car don't run, you're obviously a danger to society."

"Speaking of the law, let me tell you something, Juanito." Grampá turned and put his hand on Juan's shoulder, squeezed tightly. "You're not gonna get nowheres making all the mistakes you've been making, doing all the same pendejadas every other cabrón out here does. Mexicans don't get second chances."

"Whoa. I was just joking, Grampá. Take it easy. I know what you're saying."

"What do you know?"

"About what?"

"About what I'm saying."

"That I'm Mexican?" Juan had no idea what Grampá was trying to say.

"Don't be a smartass." Grampá let go of Juan, gripped the wheel of the Imperial again, and stared out the windshield. *Grampá's house, Grampá's rules, Grampá's crazy-ass words.* Juan didn't how long he should stay inside the car. If he was allowed to leave.

Then Grampá started up again. "Look, gringos, especially the rich ones, they get to fuck up. ¿Tú sabes? They still get good lives. Shit, great lives. They go to private schools and colleges and get lawyers on the spot—that's why none of them got drafted to the war with me. Mira, when they get arrested for whatever bullshit you got arrested for, or worse, they get a second chance. They are boys being boys. Or whatever bullshit the judge says about them. 'They don't know any better. They'll grow out of it. They're good guys.' Well, not you. If you wanna have shit in life then you can't be fucking up. Es más, you have to do a whole lot better than not fucking up. You gotta be perfect. You gotta be better than everyone around you just to prove you're not a piece of shit. Trust me, I know."

"Is that right?" Juan could see the windup for Grampá's been-there-done-that speech, but now he wanted to hear it anyway. He wanted a beer, too.

"Look. Before I got drafted and went to Vietnam, before they shot me in the head and left me for crazy, I was gonna be an engineer. I had the best grades in school. The best! But I didn't know I needed to apply to the university before going. To be *accepted* first. ¿Me entiendes? I thought I could just show up, fill out some papers, and go inside. Nobody ever told me how it was supposed to go. On the first day I showed up and they told me I couldn't get in until the next year. Maybe. I tried to argue, told them how smart I was, pero ni modo. I got drafted a month later. I went to the war. Infantry." He sucked down the rest of his tallboy and this time tossed the empty on the ground.

"That's fucked up, Grampá." Juan knew the story of Grampá's final mission, maneuvering through the jungle in an attempt to take some hill when a sniper's bullet swiped the top of his helmet, knocking him unconscious. Juan had always thought Grampá had been lucky to still be alive. He also realized that *he* hadn't applied to any school and didn't know how the whole thing worked, either. *Shit*. Was it already too late? He wondered if the coach from Arizona actually offering him a scholarship was enough to get him admitted. What if it wasn't? He thought of the draft, the country seeming to have been at war his entire life. Shit, what if they brought *that* back?

"Don't use those words around me, malcriado. That's first. Show some respect. And it's not too late for you. Not yet, but almost. You're wasting your time with basketball. That's for the blacks."

"Ay, Grampá. Don't say stuff like that. It's racist."

Grampá studied Juan, his face pinched with confusion, and Juan was sure he seemed ridiculous to him. Like a designer puppy or a robot created to play the trumpet. "Don't 'Ay, Grampá' me. You could still get on with the city in some way. Or try being a mailman. Federal has way better pay and insurance. You're gonna need that if you ever want a family. It's too late for you to be an engineer."

For a moment Juan imagined himself sitting in an office, wearing a blue short-sleeved button-down, matching blue shorts that didn't fit well, and black Velcro shoes. Surrounded by stacks of coupons for fast-food joints and envelopes with bills ready to be endlessly stuffed inside mailboxes. "I *was* just studying algebra. I could be an engineer if I wanted."

"With that girl in your room? You were studying?"

"Yes."

"No mames. You two were making babies, or trying to. Maybe you got lucky and couldn't figure it out. Stay away from that girl before you ruin her like your father ruined your má."

"Now that's fucked up, Grampá." He liked bullshitting with the old man, talking like he imagined other men talked. But on second thought, he added, "Sorry."

On the radio, José Feliciano sang Bill Withers's "Ain't No Sunshine." The sound was muffled and full of static, but Grampá surrendered to the sound. An engineer. Juan wished he actually believed he could be one. He felt stupid for not really knowing what an engineer actually did. *"Ain't no sunshine when she's gone / Anytime she goes away / And I know, I know, I know . . ."*

Grampá lightly pounded his fist against his thigh at each *"I know."* "I still miss your Grammá, Juanito. Her being gone is still a punch to the heart. A punch every pinche day."

"I'm sorry," Juan said, wishing the damn song were over. As the evening turned to night, Juan could see his breath. There wasn't a cloud in the sky, just black with a scatter of stars. He looked for the moon and thought of heaven, about praying. He'd asked God to give him a sign that shit was going to work out. That he'd be able to play, to get that scholarship. If not that, then maybe, finally, he could meet his dad. It was the least *He* could do. "At least Grammá is in heaven, waiting for you. You can see her again, right?"

Grampá pulled another tallboy from a cooler Juan hadn't even noticed on the ground outside the Imperial; he looked over at Juan and handed him the beer before reaching for another. Juan tried not to look surprised, just popped the tab, and took a long drink. It felt good going down. He wanted his head to become light and for the buzzing feeling to come quickly.

"No one is waiting for me. I always tell people that she is, but that's to make *them* feel better."

"So what, you think she's in hell?" Juan chugged again, not looking at Grampá after asking.

"Cállate. What I'm saying is that I don't think she's in heaven or hell. What she is, is dead. There is no such thing as Santa Claus, mijo. Didn't your mother tell you?"

Juan shifted uncomfortably in his seat, *now* really not wanting to look at Grampá. "Do you believe that because Grammá died?" Juan had heard his má say that before.

That after her mamá died she'd quit believing, at least for a while. She asked how God could do that to a person, slowly waste them away, even after all the time they'd spent praying. Begging. Wasn't that what Juan had just done? Begged for a scholarship?

"No, your grammá dying has nothing to do with it."

"Then why?" Juan never went to church, wasn't sure what religion he belonged to, if he belonged to one at all. He was certain he'd been baptized—he was Mexican, after all. But he knew for a fact that he'd never made his first Holy Communion, and he didn't know what came after that. JD complained all the time how his mother made him go to church every Sunday and on saints' days, how he had to go to catechism every year. JD liked to pretend he didn't believe, always pointing out contradictions or references to slavery in the Bible, but Juan suspected JD liked belonging somewhere. Having a tribe. Juan didn't have that luxury. Religion and faith were just two more things Juan was born without.

"Because of Noah's ark," Grampá said. "That is why."

"Oh, because no way did all those animals fit on one boat?" Juan guessed, taking another drink. "And how come no one has found the boat? And if we all came from Noah, then how come we're not all white people? Or Middle Eastern or whatever Noah was? I saw some shit about it on the History Channel. It does sound like bullshit."

"What are you talking about?" Grampá said, now eyeballing Juan. "If you can believe in God, then you can believe all that. That's easy. That's just faith."

"What, then? Because he forgot the dinosaurs?"

"No seas pendejo, Juan. Why don't you take anything serious?"

"C'mon, Grampá. You're asking me to take a kid story serious."

"That is no kid story. That cuento is about a God who murdered every man, woman, kid, and baby in the whole world." Grampá took a long pull from his beer and scooted closer to Juan; his eyes were bloodshot, droopy. "Imagine the never-ending piles of drowned bodies left to rot when the sun dried everything up. And just one family, forced to live through a planet being completely annihilated."

"That would suck," Juan interrupted, hoping to stop the conversation, but Grampá wasn't having it. He poked his finger into the middle of Juan's chest.

"In the Bible, mijo, it says God flooded the world because mankind is *wicked*. But if a man drowned his wife and all his kids because they were no good, but saved all their pets for his next not-wicked family, we wouldn't be worshipping the dude. No mames."

Grampá slid back to his side of the car and studied Juan, looking irritated. "Mira, if we're wicked, it's because God's wicked. That's what I'm saying. If God's real, then sooner or later *we're* gonna flood the world. *We're* gonna destroy everything. *We* are made to be monsters."

"Holy fuck, Grampá," Juan said, feeling drunk himself and wondering if he was made to be a monster. If he was at least part murderer.

Grampá reached over, put him in a headlock, and pulled Juan toward him, his hot breath radiating on Juan's face as he rested his head against Juan's. "God has to be a big fake because I just don't buy that. . . . And besides, you're right about the stupid boat. No way could all the animals fit on that shit."

Coach Paul left the back doors to the practice gym open this time. Eddie had beaten Juan to the court again and was already inside shooting jumpers. Racing back and forth after misses and makes. Juan had just finished exercising his ankle and popping ibuprofen, both to keep the swelling down and to help with the hangover he hadn't anticipated having from hanging out with his *grandfather*. Má had come home from work early and gone straight to her room, and Grampá had passed out in the Imperial—Juan had taken him some blankets during the night after he'd refused to go inside. He'd walked to the school and examined his ankle, which finally looked like an ankle, the bruising still there but fading, discoloring from deep purple into orange and dingy yellow around his toes. He'd been on it way too much, but there was nothing he could really do about that; he had no car. Now, from the bleachers, Juan eased his foot into his basketball shoes and gently laced them. He didn't plan on playing, but he wanted to shoot. To keep from losing his jumper. To put the ball in the hole. He was aching to put the ball in the basket.

Eddie had a good-looking jumper, fluid, with a high release. He followed through without staring down the shot, looking to rebound instead of waiting for the ball to whip through the net. He was taller than Juan. Bigger and probably stronger. Juan wanted to hate the motherfucker and his game but couldn't. It would be stupid not to want him on your team after watching him shoot and dribble and move on an empty court. But if the floor was clogged with nine other players, the game gummed up with plays and tactics and shit talk, Eddie's game would jam. Coach Paul had it wrong: Eddie wasn't too dumb to learn the plays. His problem was lack of vision. Eddie knew all the assignments, where everyone needed to be, in every set. What Eddie couldn't see was the game itself. When a defense they hadn't practiced for appeared, when JD or anyone else missed an assignment and there was no place to pass the ball, or when the opposing point guard called him a scrub-ass bitch, Eddie froze. These were the moments Juan loved, and he knew that's what separated him from players like Eddie. If a set broke down, Juan didn't panic, didn't pick up his dribble or rush to call time; he improvised. Sometimes he called for a screen, wanting a pick and roll or a pick and pop, but mostly he drove into the teeth of the defense and let them know he'd be in their grill all night.

"What time you get here?" Juan said, walking toward the court.

"Six," Eddie said.

“Shit, why so early? I thought we said eight. That’s early. I’m early. Hungover but early.”

“You’re hungover again? Do you and JD get drunk every night?”

“No. I got drunk with my abuelo.” Eddie quit shooting. The echo of the bouncing ball stopped, the gym now an eerie quiet.

“You drink with your grandfather?”

“You don’t gotta say it like *that*. ‘You drink with your grandfather? You have a porcelain doll collection?’ The shit ain’t *that* fucked up.”

“That shit’s pretty fucked up.”

“Well, at least I’m too old for dolls.”

“But you’re not old enough to drink. . . . Just saying.”

If only Eddie knew the shit Grampá was talking the night before, he’d flip out. Juan had already been having nightmares about the dudes in the Cutlass; the last thing he’d needed was the image of drowned bodies in his head. Last night he’d dreamt he was floating beside them, awake but unable to move as they drifted submerged among car parts and crushed beer cans.

He snatched the ball from Eddie’s hands and dribbled around the court. He took it slow, crossing the ball over and going behind his back, his body remembering how it was done. He pulled up around the elbow and floated a jumper, the rotation of the ball lifeless, the arc flat and hard. The ball thudded against the side of the rim.

“You need to square up,” Eddie said, retrieving the ball.

"You never said why you got here at six," Juan said, wanting the attention off his terrible shot. Maybe they could go back to talking about drinking with Grampá. "You don't suck that bad."

"It's Sunday. I have church at noon, and I'm better than you, at least for right now."

"Oh. Well, let's get started with the practice, then. I don't want to make you late. And we gotta work on your shit talk."

Eddie bounced the ball between his legs like he wanted to take Juan off the dribble.

"You can come if you want, to church. You can show me more of Coach's offense on the way."

"I don't think so," Juan said. "I'm not really into that."

Eddie tossed him the ball. "So, what are you into, besides basketball?"

The whole scene depressed Juan, how cliché it was setting up to be. He knew, depending on his answer, a list of inevitable questions would follow: Did he want something more out of life? Did he feel trapped or unloved or hopeless or pathetic or stupid or motherfucking worthless? Did everything he did, no matter what, always seem to turn out bad, so why not give this a try? *Fuck,* he was recruiting himself. And, of course, the answers to those questions were all yes.

"Drinking," Juan said at last. "Haven't you been paying attention?"

"That's probably why you suck so bad at basketball."

Juan raised his arms in the air, gesturing toward the empty bleachers. "Eddie's got jokes, everyone!"

Standing at the free-throw line, he decided he would shoot for two. If he made them both, he would go to whatever church Eddie went to. If he made one of two, he would stay at the gym after they practiced, work on his free throws and jumpers, and try to rebuild his game before the one chance he had passed him by. There was no way he was missing both. He purposely tried not to think about Arizona. A scholarship. He shot the first ball. It felt awkward but dropped right through the net. Eddie tossed the ball back to Juan. He didn't ask Juan any more questions, seeming to sense that Juan was working something out. Juan spun the ball in his hand; he'd missed the feel of the waxy skin, and realized he'd never gone more than a week without playing since, like, forever. Without the game he'd been unraveling. He squared his shoulders, extended his arms, and released.

BELIEVE BELIEVE BELIEVE (CHAPTER THIRTEEN)

Eddie was the oldest of five: him and three sisters, each about a year apart, and a baby brother still in diapers. His parents smiled welcomingly as Juan jumped inside the busted minivan, helping make him, oddly, not feel like he was in the way as he took Eddie's seat and Eddie rode in the narrow trunk. They asked about his ankle, how it was healing. Thanked him for helping their son. Eddie's mother wore a dress that flowed all the way down to her ankles. Eddie's sisters were dressed exactly the same and looked like those little egg-shaped dolls that fit inside each other from smallest to biggest.

Eddie's old man drove, jumping on the freeway. He was dressed sharp in a white shirt and tie, his face serious. "Michael or Kobe?" he asked, seemingly to no one.

"Kobe!" Eddie shouted from the trunk.

Juan felt cheap compared to Eddie's family, still wearing his basketball clothes, smelling like sweat and booze. Eddie had changed into black slacks and a white polo shirt at the gym.

"Not you," Eddie's father said. He glanced at Juan in the rearview mirror. Cars zipped out from behind them to escape the van's black exhaust, then cut sharply in front of them, the van putting along. "I already know *you're* wrong. I'm asking Juan."

"Jordan," Juan said. Of course he'd never seen Jordan play, only watched old clips on YouTube. But everyone knew *that* answer. "Kobe's great, but all his moves are stolen Jordan moves."

"I like this kid," Eddie's father declared. "And Magic is greater than both of them." He turned back to look at Juan, momentarily taking his eyes off the road. "He's the greatest player of all time." They were only going forty miles an hour but the engine was revving hard, all sorts of warning lights illuminating on the dash.

"Whatever, Dad." Eddie's voice came from the trunk. "*LeBron* is the best ever."

"Diablo." Eddie's father crossed himself. A semi truck roared past, shaking the van. "LeBron James is good, pero he's not even better than Kobe. Who was not better than Bird. Who was not better than Dr. J." They kept driving, the van's engine sounding ready to seize—or even explode—the vehicle making noises he was sure not even Grampá could explain. He pictured Eddie squeezed in the trunk, bouncing around and seeing the cars zooming up behind them from the big back window. No one seemed to notice the crazy amount of traffic but Juan.

"Are we getting close?" Juan asked. A pair of SUVs pulled up beside them, both crowding into their lane. Eddie's mother smiled at Juan, probably thinking he was eager for church. The sisters squirmed in their seats, and Juan wondered if maybe they thought they were moments from crashing too.

"You should be more like this kid!" Eddie's father hollered to his son. Thankfully they pulled off at the next exit. Juan's back was slicked with sweat, his legs tired from thumping up and down the entire ride. He was done with freaking out about crashing, worrying about Eddie in the trunk getting smashed and dying.

"So, who do *you* think is the greatest?" Eddie's father asked, turning to Juan. *"Magic?"*

"For sure," Juan said, not really caring and just glad to be off the freeway. He focused on the church in the distance, trying to calm down. The building could've been a multiplex, a new stadium for some minor league soccer team, or a fancy museum, if anyone in El Paso had ever cared enough to build fancy museums.

Inside "the Center," beyond the huge front hallway and the extending corridors lined with closed doors, was a theater. And this was an actual theater, with stadium seating broken into three huge sections before a stage with three no-shit movie screens suspended in midair. All of them flashed inspirational quotes and churchy memes like †HRIVE and GOD IS ON YOUR SIDE and ☛ † ☚ THIS WAY TO HEAVEN.

Sitting in the middle section and surrounded by people dressed almost exactly like Eddie and his family, Juan felt ridiculous in his basketball shorts and NO BLOOD, NO FOUL T-shirt. While he'd always thought JD bitched too much about church, it had always sounded kind of nice to him, a quiet place. But the Center seemed to be something else entirely. Like maybe a smoke machine would be involved. There was no art on the walls inside the theater, no confessional booths or burning candles. Juan liked those things.

Not long after they sat, the lights dimmed and music blared seemingly from everywhere, even under their seats. Behind them a guy on a soundboard was busy turning knobs, getting the rock music—not the good kind, something like 3 Doors Down, only *downier*—to sync with flashing lights and the new images now racing across the three screens from left to right: BELIEVE! BELIEVE! BELIEVE! †= ♥ † = ♥ † = ♥

The pastor came on stage. He was an old white dude dressed in a polo shirt and blazer, a pair of jeans. The vato seemed pretty casual, even in the way he walked toward the podium, a bounce in his step, head bobbing. The motherfucker definitely had swag and probably went by Pastor Ricky or Pastor Bobby. Everyone clapped and cheered as he approached the mic, and Juan was sure no one at Our

Lady of Guadalupe gave it up when Father Mumbles took the pulpit. Eddie's family clapped right along, all except for Eddie, who seemed preoccupied. Juan had ended up next to Eddie's father, and he was somewhat glad, able to avoid Eddie and not have to pretend one way or another about what he thought was happening.

Pastor Cool wasted no time getting started. "What do you do when life doesn't play nice? When all the things you want to have happen to you, don't? Where do you turn?" Now this seemed like some convenient bullshit, a message designed specifically for Juan. Juan couldn't help but look over at Eddie, who wasn't paying attention at all, instead sneaking peeks at his phone. Eddie's father noticed his son too and snagged it, the image on his screen a headshot of Magic Johnson and what looked like career stats.

The pastor went on, quoting from the Bible, interpreting the quote—even explaining the Hebrew translation. He told stories about his life and the lives of his friends, about people who had turned to him when things had gone shitty. Juan thought this was illegal or maybe should've been; JD had once told him that anything said during a confession was totally confidential. Point for the Catholics. The pastor then explained how shitty the Apostle Paul had had it following Jesus. "In Corinthians the Apostle Paul tells us: 'Five times I received at the hands of the Jews the forty lashes less one. Three times I was beaten with rods. Once I was stoned. Three times I was shipwrecked; a night and a day I was adrift at sea; on frequent journeys, in danger from rivers, danger from robbers, danger from my own people, danger from Gentiles, danger in the city, danger in the wilderness, danger at sea, danger from false brothers; in toil and hardship, through many a sleepless night, in hunger and thirst, often without food, in cold and exposure. And, apart from other things, there is the daily pressure on me of my anxiety for all the churches.'

"Now," the pastor said, as if nodding at Juan. "If all this can happen to the Apostle Paul and he can still keep the faith, he can still feel the love of our Heavenly Father, then why can't we? No matter how trying our lives become?"

But hearing how shitty Paul had it made Juan feel worse about the world. Pastor Cool seemed to have it wrong. The apostle never mentioned love, only anxiety about the future. Juan thought about Grampá and his Noah story. About monsters. About his father.

"Can I get an amen for that? An amen for the love of our Heavenly Father?"

"Amen! Amen! Amen!"

Juan knew his má had at least two letters from his father. He wanted to read them, to know how Armando ended up on death row. What did it mean to have a murderer for a father? As your God?

Pastor Cool continued prowling the stage, selling everyone on being just like Paul, on suffering their way to heaven.

"Amen! Amen! Amen!"

• • •

"Do you think I can have a Bible? If you have an extra or something?" Juan asked Eddie's father as the minivan stopped in front of Danny's house, engine running. By the sermon's end everyone had been gently swaying copies over their heads, singing along to some pumped-in gospel music. "I want to read about the flood." After hearing Grampá's mass murder story and Pastor Cool's series of unfortunate events, Juan wanted to read the verses for himself.

"That's one of my favorites," Eddie's father said, turning around in the driver's seat. "You don't have a Bible at home?" He seemed more puzzled than judgmental. Like Juan told him his house didn't have windows.

Juan squeezed his way from the van and hopped onto the sidewalk. "I don't think so." Eddie's mom and sisters were staring at him, Eddie was looking away, and Juan realized *they* were ashamed for him. "Never mind. Bye, thanks." Juan booked it for Danny's front door.

Eddie's father shut off the minivan and followed him. "Hold up, Juan."

Juan paused. "This is my friend's place," he told him. "It's cool for me to be here." The sun was in Juan's face, forcing him to squint. He looked down the street and could see the development where he'd been arrested.

"I know this house," Eddie's father said. "It's Daniel Villanueva's. He's in our congregation."

"You mean the Sarge?" Juan had no idea Danny was a junior. "I didn't want you guys to have to drive me all the way home. You've been cool enough." The truth was, Juan was horrified they might catch Grampá passed out in the Imperial or Má walking out in her work clothes. He also didn't want to go back in that van, to make Eddie go back in that trunk.

"Where do you live, Juan?"

"In Central."

"We live right in Five Points. That's real close. Are your parents there now? I can still drive you."

"My má is, but she works late so she's probably sleeping. My father . . ." Juan paused again, then out of his mouth came "My father is on death row." Juan felt weird enough saying "my father"; being fatherless was who he'd been for so long. But the death row part—the unexpected, unwanted part—was an unbelievable relief. He no longer had to wonder about the other half of himself—the parts he didn't recognize—even if those parts could be part murderer. Part monster. He was whole for the first time.

Then, to Juan's total surprise, Eddie's father hugged him, a strong, no-escape, nothing-bad-could-possibly-happen-to-you kind of hug. He was taller than Juan, like Eddie, and muscular in the arms and shoulders, in great shape except for a soft belly. Juan sucked air through his mouth, his nose suddenly clogged with snot; he was sobbing. Sobbing! He couldn't stop. The clean white shirt and tie Eddie's father wore was turning into a wet mess, and Juan felt himself going limp, his head light. Eddie's father held him up, telling him the Holy Spirit was with him and everything was going to be fine from now on.

DATABASE OF SHIT (CHAPTER FOURTEEN)

The Sarge wasn't home and neither was Danny's mom. Juan was no longer sobbing but in a daze as Danny, wearing, oddly, a pair of work gloves, walked him upstairs. Juan needed to sleep, for the pounding in his head to stop. Danny dropped him on the top of his bed and grabbed a blanket from his closet. Juan wondered vaguely if Danny's gun was in there, next to his blankets and clothes, the image of it, the crisp sound of the pop, suddenly floating in from his memory. Danny cracked open a bottle of Gatorade and left it on the nightstand, not saying a word. He was a good friend, and that was Juan's last thought before drifting off to sleep. When he awoke, head still pounding, eyes and mouth dry, embarrassed from crying, there was JD, laptop open, staring at him, the look on his face screaming: *Finally!*

"Listen to this," JD said, not even waiting a second for Juan to fully come to. "'You clown police. You gonna stop with all that killing all these kids. You're gonna stop killing innocent kids, murdering young kids. When I kill one or pop one, y'all want to kill me. God has a plan for everything. You hear? I love everyone that loves me. I ain't got no love for anyone that don't love me.' That dude's name was Jeffrey D. Williams. Now listen to this one. 'Life is death, death is life. I hope that someday this absurdity that humanity has come to will come to an end. Life is too short. I hope that anyone that has negative energy toward me will resolve that. Life is too short to harbor feelings of hatred and anger. That's it.' He was Richard Cobb. Listen, this next motherfucker, Jesse Hernandez, was crazy. 'Tell my son I love him very much. God bless everybody. Continue to walk with God. Go Cowboys! Love y'all man. Don't forget the T-ball. Ms. Mary, thank you for everything that you've done. You too, Brad, thank you. I can feel it, taste it, not bad.' What the fuck? 'Go Cowboys'? Who the fuck gives a shout-out to a football team right before getting put to death?"

Juan struggled to sit up. He grabbed the bottle of Gatorade and took a long drink, his dry mouth feeling instantly better. His splitting head was another story. "What the fuck are you reading? What are you even doing here?"

JD shrugged. "Danny texted that you were here. That Eddie's cult family dumped you off. I had to *borrow* my sister's hooptie to drive over. Mine is a little banged up, if you remember."

Juan downed the rest of the sports drink. "Thanks for coming?" The walls of Danny's room were covered with drawings—not mural style, but comic book art, panels freshly painted. Juan tried to follow the action as it spread across the room, but it wasn't finished and there were few words. He looked at the carpet and noticed paint stains everywhere. The neat vacuumed lines and new smell was already gone.

"The Sarge is gonna be pissed," Juan said, pointing at the stains. How could Danny have ruined this already?

"Oh yeah. He's completely fucked when his jefe walks in here." JD scanned the room like he'd just noticed the paintings. "But I like the work. 'The Rip' is a good title. I guess Danny *is* an artist. But back to business. Dude, I found your father! And what the fuck I was reading were the last words of dudes who've been executed by the state. It's all online. The state tracks everything. E-V-E-R-Y-T-H-I-N-G. What the dudes did. When they're scheduled to die. Their last words. Their race. Where they're from. What they ate. It's a whole database of shit."

"Really?" Juan sat the rest of the way up. He knew all sorts of information could be found online, but Texas keeping all that data in one spot seemed crazy.

"I know what you're thinking: 'That shit's crazy.'" Of course JD got right in his head.

"I *was* thinking that, but how do you know you found my father? I didn't tell you his name."

JD had a cocky look on his face, the same one he had whenever he scored a bucket during garbage time. "You told me when he was scheduled to be executed. He's the only one set for Valentine's Day."

JD turned the laptop toward Juan. The brightness was blinding, but as his eyes adjusted Juan saw the old form that had been filled out on a typewriter and eventually scanned for the Internet. That's how long his father had been locked away. A last-century killer.

NAME: Armando Aranda
DOB: December 9 **DR:** 999178
RACE: Hispanic **HEIGHT:** 5'8"
WEIGHT: 130 **EYES:** Brown
HAIR: Black
COUNTY: El Paso **STATE:** Texas
PRIOR OCCUPATION: None
EDUCATION LEVEL: 11
PRIOR PRISON RECORD: None
SUMMARY: Convicted in the shooting death of 60-year-old Sheriff Clark Jones. Aranda and two accomplices attempted to rob a diner when the victim was shot, once, fatally through the head by Aranda.
CODEFENDANTS: Fernando Mendez and Carlo Rubio
RACE OF VICTIM: White male

The picture of Armando Aranda was in black and white, the photocopy no good, blurry and darkened and making it hard for Juan to recognize anything but the information underneath. Hispanic. 5'8". Brown eyes and black hair. Highest level of school completed: eleventh grade. Juan struggled to breathe; those details could easily be his own. He wished JD would close the laptop, suddenly not wanting to know any more about Armando Aranda.

"I got all the info I could on him," JD explained. "More than just what's on this site. Gotta tell you, it's not great."

Juan rubbed his head; it was still throbbing. "Maybe I don't need to know all the specifics." Juan hadn't been ready for this JD, for go-getter JD who had all the details that put his father on death row. The letter Armando had written to his má had been mostly sweet, thoughtful. It couldn't have been written by a monster, right?

JD was staring at him, his face as confused as Eddie's dad's had been earlier that morning. "It's too late for all that. If we are gonna make the trip, you need to know what you're getting into. You can't wait until you get there to find out the shitty details. We're going to a prison, dude. Maximum security. Death row. It's gonna be fucked up."

Juan couldn't concentrate. The pounding in his head and the comics Danny had drawn were distracting him. On the wall near the bed, the Rip—a teenage girl who looked a lot like Roxanne, except she had wild blue hair and was dressed like a Goth Selena—sat in one panel squeezing her head; the next showed a close-up of her face grimacing between the palms of her hands. In the final, incomplete panel, she was someplace totally different and dressed as a general, leading a platoon of half-painted soldaderas. The caption below read: *The Rip—Master of the Multiverse!* All four walls were the same. Each with the Rip partially drawn and painted, going from one unfinished to another barely there universe. Juan wondered what was happening on Danny's walls, but more than that, he wondered what would happen to himself once he knew what Armando had done. If, after knowing, he would be like the Rip, going to another universe. One where he no longer recognized himself. After all, he'd only read the one letter, where Armando seemed more sad than dangerous.

"Man, where are you?" JD said.

"Sorry," Juan said. "These drawings are fucking me up. I didn't notice them when I came in."

"Danny smokes too much weed."

"Yeah," Juan agreed, at the same time wishing he had some weed right now. "You mind if I read what my old man did for myself?"

JD handed him the laptop. "Sure, man."

Juan read about the diner and the robbery, about the murder of Clark Jones. The knot in his gut he was getting while reading the short article was probably the same one that twisted in Má's when he used to ask about his father. Did she wonder, like he was wondering now, if death row was his birthright? Juan now understood why Má always turned squirmy when talking about his father, why she insisted on waiting until he was "older" to tell him the truth, because the subject was "complicated."

"I wonder how it happened," Juan said, handing the computer back to JD. "Like, maybe it wasn't all his fault. Sometimes shit happens. You know?"

"I don't know how you accidentally shoot a dude in the face, but the articles don't say, really," JD said. "But you're right about shit happening. I don't know." JD was being a good friend, just like Danny was earlier. Looking up the information. Coming to get him. Lying to him. "I looked up the rules for visiting. We have to be on his list, otherwise we can't get in."

Juan began to sweat. "So we can't visit. We're fucked." He couldn't tell if he was upset or relieved.

"We're not fucked yet. I dropped a letter at the post office that should go out tomorrow."

Juan sprang to his feet. The shit getting real. "You did *what*?"

"Cálmate. I just did a little lying. I said you're a blogger—that's the lying part—and I'm a filmmaker, and that we're interested in telling his story and hope he would put us on his visitor's list. Okay, a few more lies. But if my letter takes three days to get to him, another couple for the guards to read it and then give it to him, and then say one more day to put us on the list, we should be good. We can leave Friday or Saturday and be there by Sunday for visiting hours."

Juan began pacing the room. He caught a glimpse of Danny through the window. He was in the backyard, shoveling peat gravel into a wheelbarrow from a huge pile in the corner. Was the Sarge making him landscape the yard by himself? Juan turned to JD. "What if he doesn't want to be in a movie or a blog?"

"What if he doesn't want a son? If you were about to die, finding out you had a kid would be kinda fucked up, no? You might not want to deal with it. I think it's better if we don't give him the chance to say no." JD clenched his fists as he spoke, obviously excited. And probably right.

"You don't think it's still kinda fucked up? We're not bloggers or whatever." Going back to the window, Juan watched Danny wheelbarrowing and dumping mounds of gravel over the naked desert ground, smoothing the piles he'd made with a rake.

"Dude, I'm at least trying to make a movie, so that's true. And any asshole can be a blogger. Open a Tumblr if you're so worried about lying. We can do it for real; I don't care. . . . One more thing."

"What?" Juan returned his full attention to JD, though he suddenly wondered if Danny's life wasn't as great as he'd originally thought. They didn't hang as much since he'd moved and the Sarge had retired from the army. He'd help him shovel gravel right after talking with JD—would make JD landscape too.

"We need a vehicle. Mine's busted. Let's ask Danny to come. His parents wouldn't notice if he was gone all weekend."

All of a sudden everything was happening too fast. But

JD was waiting for an answer. "True. Let's do that," Juan told him.

But there was this: the plan was good. And it felt crazy, unreal. He'd gone so long barely saying a word about his father to anyone. And he'd never told anyone how blank he'd always felt, like a character in a story who'd been bonked on the head and was unable to remember who he'd been before; but instead of trying to help him recover his memory, everyone seemed to wish he'd just be cool with being an amnesiac. He thought he'd always be alone with his "daddy issue." But everything was suddenly changing. And now, just after mentioning the letter once, asking one time for help, JD—sometimes annoying-as-fuck JD—was going to take him to meet his father. Juan felt tears rolling down his face for the second time in a day, happy to hear his best friend in the world calling him "the biggest pussy on the fucking planet."

FABI AND GLADI (CHAPTER FIFTEEN)

Fabi sat on the sofa and read through the letter. She had to argue with Jabba to let her into the building the day before; the demented woman at first refused to let her inside so she could ask the new tenant if they were stockpiling any of her mail. The renter, a twentysomething girl, had been keeping a stack of it in her kitchen, not sure what else to do with it. Frustrated, Fabi had snatched the loose heap of junk mail and bills and left without going through it. She hadn't noticed the slim letter from the El Paso County Clerk's office until now.

Juan's arraignment was set—the letter a single page with all the particulars. Building location and case number, day and time. In a week Fabi and Juanito would be in front of a judge, and now she knew what "evading arrest" meant. It was a Class A misdemeanor, meaning it was the most serious and could land her Juanito up to a year in jail. Ay Dios. *Ay Dios*. On top of that, she still had no idea what she was going to do about the pregnancy. She needed a new job, and to make shit worse, Gladi was in town.

Gladi had arrived unannounced that morning from McAllen, Texas, with her bags, her gringo husband, and two small Yorkies that hadn't stopped barking. They were in the kitchen with Papá, talking quietly about how they'd planned to spend a week at the house but didn't know Fabi and Juanito had moved in. They didn't mind getting a hotel. Didn't want to be an "intrusion." Gladi was a clinical psychologist with the VA. Fabi could never remember what her gringo husband did. Something in an office, by the looks of him. Tall, doughy, and bearded. Geeky with glasses. They'd been married a couple of years; Fabi skipped the wedding.

"Hey, Fabi," Gladi said, walking into the living room with Papá and her husband. "I didn't know you were awake."

"Why wouldn't I be awake?" Fabi said. "It's the morning. I'm an adult." She held up the stack of mail she'd been going through for Gladi to see, minus the arraignment letter. She'd been hoping for another letter from Mando—though now she wondered what to write back. *What could I possibly say?*

Her sister looked like she wanted to come in for a hug, but Fabi stayed on the couch. She and her sister rarely spoke. It wasn't like they'd had some big blowout, an overly dramatic reason not to. Their battle lines were simple. Gladi was the good girl, the one who never made mistakes, and Fabi was . . . well, not that.

"Let me take you to breakfast. How about Marie's?"

"It's an Asian-burger fusion joint now," Fabi said. "And I'm not hungry."

"*What*? And *what*? Besides you're always hungry. What changed?"

"I've changed," Fabi said, scooting away from her sister.

"No, she hasn't," Papá said, joining the conversation. "Your sister's still rude like usual."

"How about L&J? They have killer chilaquiles."

Papá smiled at Gladi, always so giddy whenever she was around. "She'd love a free meal. She doesn't have a job." He looked at Fabi with his usual frown.

"That's not nice, Papá," Gladi said. "If she doesn't want to go she doesn't have to."

"No," Fabi said, standing up. The Yorkies were really yapping now; Gladi, Papá, and gringo husband were all looking at her. She could feel her anger building, rising from the bottoms of her feet and surging up through her body. "He's right. Nothing I had planned for this morning matters. At least not now that *you're* here. Not looking for a job. Not my *abortion*. Let's go get those chilaquiles."

"Abortion?!" Her father looked ready to faint. "¿Qué dijo ella?" He looked at Gladi and then her husband, who were both staring hard at the ground. He wouldn't look at Fabi. "What did she say?"

"That I'm pregnant. What else could I be saying?" Fabi grabbed her purse off the table and looked defiantly at her sister. "Are we going or not?"

Now Papá and Gladi were eyeballing her, trying to guess if she was serious or not. Fabi hated how quickly she said the craziest thing that came to her head. This, she supposed, was the real reason she never talked to Gladi. She hated the person she became with her sister around. Self-conscious and easily flustered. And *stupid*. A teenager all over again.

The chilaquiles *were* good. *Gladi wins again.* On the drive to L&J Cafe, she and Gladi had pretended like the scene in the living room hadn't happened. That Fabi hadn't turned down the invite. That Grampá hadn't insulted the shit out of Fabi. That no one said "abortion." Instead they had chit-chatted about the summer weather in McAllen—humid, hot. Fabi had reminded her of El Paso's—dry, hot. Papá and hubby had stayed behind, leaving Fabi and Gladi to themselves, something Mamá would have loved to see. The names Fabiola and Gladiola had been her idea. A flower lover, that was how she thought of her two girls: as a springtime she would enjoy even in the winter.

"So, an abortion," Gladi said, quickly shoving a forkful of chilaquiles into her mouth.

Fabi guessed talking about the weather was getting too boring for her psychologist sister. "I don't know," Fabi said, glancing around uneasily, as if Ruben could be in the booth behind theirs. "I'm thinking about it, not that I have one scheduled or anything. But maybe. Soon." Gladi swallowed hard and looked at Fabi in the way Fabi guessed she did with her clients—not a blank look, but a not-quite-smile-not-quite-frown look, an *I'm listening* expression she probably learned in a classroom.

"I didn't even know you were pregnant—" Gladi began.

"You and Papá are the first people I've told," Fabi said, wondering if dropping the news at the end of her second letter to Mando counted. "I'm not really happy about it."

"So . . . this wasn't planned? It doesn't sound like it." Gladi took a sip of her coffee, then another bite of her breakfast. From a distance they probably looked like they were enjoying each other's company.

"No shit, Gladi. Who plans on getting pregnant just to get an abortion?"

Gladi motioned for Fabi to stop, her hand up like a crossing guard's. "Cálmate. I just want to help . . . if I can."

Of course she did. The great Gladi back in town to save her fuckup of a sister who was stuck in the exact same boat she was in back in high school. Only now that boat also had an eighteen-year-old facing a year in jail. A *year*. And for what? For being scared? For running? Fabi suddenly couldn't eat. She dropped her fork and rubbed her face with the palms of her hands, enjoying their smooth cool relief for a moment. Juanito. She needed to find a lawyer. Had no idea where to even start looking. How could she even pay for one?

"Do you need me to pay for it?" Gladi asked. "I can do that. It's no problem."

Gladi was in her head now. Her sister must've had a time share in there. "How different would our lives have been if Mamá never got cancer? If she were alive?" Fabi said quietly, then glanced out the window. Cars steadily drove up and down Stevens Street, commuters making their way back and forth to the gateway and onto the interstate, past old Concordia Cemetery, with its hard dirt ground and scattered tombstones.

"What are you talking about?"

Fabi looked back at her sister. "Nothing." Mando's letter had been turning over in her mind. His idea of small truths—Mando's overly complicated way of saying that the past mattered. That everything that had happened to her, every choice she'd made, was being passed on to Juan in some way, and would be passed on again.

Gladi pushed her plate to the middle of the table, looking frustrated, her shoulders slumping. "I don't know what you're talking about. I don't live in that head of yours, Fabi."

"Back in the day you could have helped me, but you didn't. It could've changed my life. Juan's life too."

Gladi let out a long sigh. "What *exactly* could I have done, back in the day?"

"I don't know, *exactly*." Fabi looked back out the window. "I just got abandoned by everyone back then. By you. Papá. Mamá."

“Mamá *died*!” Gladi picked up her fork, dug at her now-cold chilaquiles. “You always act like you were the only one who was going through shit . . . the only one whose mother died. I took care of Mamá pretty much alone until her last day. Do you ever think of that? That *I* needed *you* too? It was my senior year! And everything *would* be different if Mamá were alive, but she’s not.”

Gladi tossed the fork and it clanked against the plate. The truth was, Fabi didn’t know what she wanted or expected from Gladi. She’d been angry and scared all those years ago. Alone. She was still those things. What she wanted, more than anything, was for her mother to be alive. “You’re right,” Fabi said. “My life just turned out so . . . hard. I should have done everything different.”

Gladi took a sip of coffee, and as if searching for the right response, jumped right back inside Fabi’s head. “Fabi, what’s happening to Juan?”

“He’s taking an algebra test today. He’s been worried about it.”

“You know that’s not what I mean.”

Fabi nodded, wondering if this was what therapy was like, having no clue why anyone would willingly do it. But she said, “He’s got court next week. He could face up to a year in jail.”

“Ay Dios. What happened?”

Fabi ran her hands through her hair. “That’s the thing. I don’t even know what he really did. He was at a party, doing what everybody does at a party. Stupid shit. Then the cops came. He ran away. Of course, they caught him, and I think they beat him because he was limping and had to go to urgent care afterward, and now . . . he could be in jail for a year. I don't get it. He was just being a kid. I don't have the money to pay for any of this, either."

"Kids do stupid things," Gladi said, reaching to hold Fabi's hand.

Fabi's hand went limp inside her sister's. "I remember. Juan is the result of stupid things."

"That's not true," Gladi insisted. "Juan wouldn't be here unless he was meant to be."

"You sound like a greeting card." Fabi patted Gladi's hand before pulling hers away.

"And you sound defensive," Gladi replied. "Look, Juan is going to be okay. Living back with Grampá is a good thing. He graduates this year, right? He can still go to college. I can help you with that. And I have a lawyer friend who lives in town. We can give her a call. I'll pay for it—Juan is my nephew, after all."

Híjole, Gladi made everything sound so easy. Fabi knew her sister wasn't rich, but she had money and seemed happy and maybe not evil (abortions and lawyers weren't the best things in life, for sure not free, but people needed them and Gladi could afford both). Hell, the cabrona was even aging well, had Mamá's smooth skin and soft face, her make-everything-better smile. And Fabi wanted her son to have a life like Gladi's. If not the life he hung up for himself on his bedroom walls.

“Can I ask you a question? And don’t get too mad?” The waiter was refilling their coffee.

“Sure,” Fabi answered.

Gladi patted her belly. “What’s up with the father?”

Fabi took a sip of her fresh coffee as Gladi dumped pink packets of sweetener in hers. “We broke up. If you watch any TV while you’re here, you’ll see one of his stupid commercials. He owns a used-car dealership, EZ Motors. He’s Ruben ‘King of the Deal’ Gonzalez.”

“So *that* was never going to work out.” Gladi leaned in close, elbows on the table, her head resting on the palms of her hands. *Is this therapy or girl talk?*

Fabi slipped her hands around her cup, enjoying the warmth on her palms. “I didn’t love him. Plus, his dumb ass got me fired. You can watch it on YouTube.”

Gladi’s eyes widened. “Oh! That’s terrible.”

“Yeah, well. Shit happens. Let me ask *you* something,” Fabi said, motioning at the nearby waiter for the check, then turning back to Gladi. “What’s up with marrying Seth? I thought you always wanted to marry Antonio Banderas. I remembered wearing *Desperado* out with you back in the day.”

Gladi sheepishly smiled. “I always *did* want an Antonio Banderas type.”

“So why didn’t you go and get one?”

“They aren’t around. There were hardly any Mexicans at my college and none at my job. At least none working where I work, and I spend most of my time there. It’s

where I met Seth. We just talked at first and then dated. The normal thing. It wasn't what I dreamed of when I was sixteen, but it's been good. He's a good guy. And yeah, I love him." She laughed. "Even if he looks weird in leather pants."

"And now you have Yorkies."

"True." Gladi laughed again. "They were my idea. He wanted Chihuahuas, but I wasn't sure if he was being racist or not." Now Fabi laughed, a real laugh, and it felt good. She hadn't noticed that L&J had become crowded; outside, people trudged up and down the sidewalks, going to work in the nearby printshops and convenience stores, the barely-hanging-by-a-thread antique shop. Everyone was getting on with their morning. It was amazing the way life pushed onward no matter what could be happening in any one person's life. This used to bother the hell out of her, but maybe it wasn't such a bad thing after all. Everyone pulling everybody else in one forward direction simply by continuing to live.

"You know Antonio Banderas is Spanish, right? Not a Mexican," Fabi said, reaching for the bill as the waiter placed it beside Gladi. Fabi wanted badly to rewire how she thought of herself, to stop hating the person she was, the girl she used to be.

"Well, shit, my whole life's been a total lie," Gladi said, allowing her sister to take the tab, them both laughing, *actually* laughing. "And everything is going to be fine, Juan especially. Even with his algebra test. I just know it."

A TEST OF ALGEBRA

Probability is an area of mathematics that uses experiments to yield chance results; however, the results over time do produce patterns that enable us to predict future outcomes with notable accuracy.

Questions of Permutations and Combinations:

Because of a mistake in packaging, 5 pairs of defective basketball shoes were packed with 15 good ones. All the pairs of basketball shoes look the same and have an equal probability of being chosen. Three pairs are selected.

a) What is the probability that all three pairs are defective?
b) What is the probability that exactly two pairs are defective?
c) What is the probability that at least two pairs are defective?

Answers:

a) E=3 pairs of defective shoes, $n(S) = c(20,3) = \frac{20!}{17 \bullet 3!} = \frac{20 \bullet 19 \bullet 18}{6} = 1140$,
$P(E) = \frac{n(E)}{n(S)} = \frac{10}{1140} = 0.0088$

b) F=2 defective pairs, $c(5,2)c(15,1) = \frac{5!}{3! \bullet 2!} \bullet \frac{15!}{14! \bullet 1!} = 10 \bullet 15 = 150$,
$P(F) \frac{n(F)}{n(S)} = \frac{150}{1140} = 0.1316$

c) G = at least two paris are shitty, $G = E \cup F$, $P(G)$
$= P(E) + P(F) = 0.0088 + 0.1316 = 0.1404$

Extra Credit:

What are the odds your má buys a pair of these reject kicks, them destroying your ankle and fucking everything up?

FUCK YOU FOR EVEN THINKING IT.

An **exponential function** is a function whose value is a constant raised to the power of the argument. $f(x) = a^x$

Questions of What Is Real:

Hey, asshole, did you know the concentration of alcohol in a person's blood is measurable? The risk R (given as a percent) can be modeled by the equation $R=6e^{kx}$ where *x* is the variable concentration of booze in the blood and *k* is the constant. You got that, stupid?

a) Suppose that the concentration 0.04 results in a 10% risk (R=10) of an accident. Find *k* in the equation.
b) Using *k*, what is the risk if the concentration is 0.17?
c) If the law asserts that anyone with a risk of having an accident of 20% or more shouldn't drive, how fucked up were you and JD when you wrecked? How lucky were you that the cops weren't there to bust you again? How long do you think your luck will hold out? I bet you don't even think you're lucky, do you?

Answers:

a) $x = 0.04$ and $R = 10$, $R = 6e^{kx}$

$$10 = 6e^{6k(0.04)}$$

$$\frac{10}{6} = e^{0.04k}$$

$$0.04k = \frac{10}{6} = 0.5108256$$

$$k = 12.77$$

b) using $K = 12.77$ and $x = 0.17$, $R = 6e^{kx}$

$6e^{(12.77X.17)} = 52.6$ A good chance you're gonna run into a pole in an empty parking lot.

c) No, I don't feel lucky. Is there some dumb formula to solve for bad luck, to at least cancel that shit out?

Extra Credit:

Graph the exponential function of your sorry-ass life.

THE CONSTANT IS BEING FUCKED. THE ARGUMENTS FUCKING ME ARE NUMEROUS.

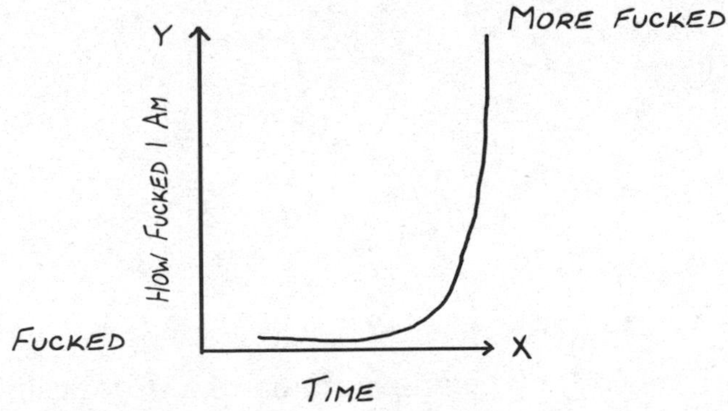

A **hyperbola** is the set of points in a plane whose

distances to two fixed points in the plane is a constant.

Question of Applications:

Suppose a gun is fired from an unknown source, S. An observer at O_1 hears that shit 1 second after another at O_2. Since sound travels at 1,100 feet per second, it means that the point S must be 1,100 feet closer to O_2 than O_1. So, motherfucker, S lies on one branch of a hyperbola with a center at O_1 and O_2. Tell me you got that shit? That you know the difference of the distance from S to O_1 and S to O_2 is the constant 1,100? If a third not-doing-shit-but-watching observer hears the same shot 2 seconds after O_1 hears it, the S will lie on a branch of a second hyperbola with a center at O_1 and O_3. The intersection of the two hyperbolas will tell you the location of S, of the motherfucker shooting. That's really what you want to know, right? Who the fuck is shooting at you? Or you could just run and say fuck the math. Hear those pops and fucking run. That's the only answer, pendejo.

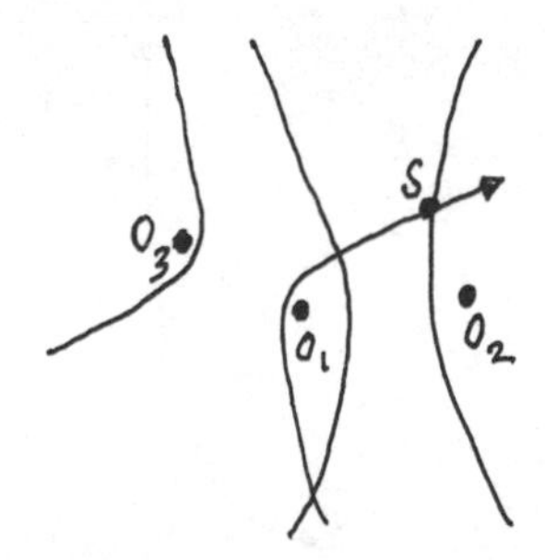

a) Are you still having nightmares? Are you still underwater? Still being chased? Shot?

b) Have you been watching the clock this whole time? You're running out of time.

c) You're gonna fail.

Answers:

I DON'T HAVE THE ANSWERS.

Extra Credit:

Remember when you told Grampá you could be an engineer? You never believed you could, not for a second. What about going to some community college in Arizona after graduation to play basketball? What about balling out in front of some college coach that may not even exist because your current coach is a shady motherfucker and probably lying to you? You have a court date coming. There's also that, don't forget. What's the probability all that shit works out for you? Also, isn't your dad a murderer?

Extra Extra Credit:

Are you more likely to play pro basketball or follow your daddy straight to death row? What's more in your bones? Remember to show your work.

Oh, by the way, your má's here. She's standing at the door looking in. Man, she's pretty fine, for an old lady.

WHEN WE WERE FEARLESS (CHAPTER SIXTEEN)

Fabi had the name of Gladi's lawyer friend, Vanessa Peña. She remembered Vanessa. She was like Gladi—straight As, in all the nerdy clubs, and even beat out Gladi for valedictorian (Gladi would've had her if not for Mamá dying, resulting in a B in AP English). Fabi searched through Grampá's old phonebook, wanting to see if she had an ad, but the thing was ten years old. She thought of Googling her, but of course her father didn't have Internet and Fabi still had a flip phone. The one good thing about living in her old apartment had been that Flor never password-protected her Wi-Fi.

After spending the morning talking with Gladi, she realized just how shitty the last few weeks had been for Juanito. She imagined his night in jail. How awful it must've been. How injuring his ankle and stressing about school were probably freaking him out. Even moving into a new house had to be hard. She hadn't really talked to him about any of this; she'd been too busy dealing with her own shit. Fabi decided she could wait to call Vanessa. She wanted to spend the day with her son, to do for him what Gladi had just done for her.

It had been years since Fabi walked the halls of Austin High. The inside of the building was essentially the same, which at first she found comforting, then sad: The ceramic green tile along the walls and the black-and-white checkered flooring straight from the forties. The classroom doors heavy and wooden, with greening brass knobs. Her high heels echoed down the empty hallway as she made her way to Mrs. Hill's room, Juan's algebra classroom. Fabi had told the secretary at the attendance office that Juan had a doctor's appointment for his ankle, though she wasn't sure why she'd lied. It wasn't like there was anyone for her to get in trouble with. Fabi strolled the halls, not wanting to sit and wait for the student escort to return with her son—too excited about the day she envisioned with Juanito. Posters lined the doors to classrooms and were taped above water fountains. The say-no-to-drugs and beware-of-gangs posters that hung on the walls and classroom doors when she'd been a student were replaced by social media and cyber-bullying warnings, some with hashtags along the bottoms: #bekindonline and #sextingisforever. She wondered if the kids actually found the posters helpful, or, like when she was young, they were more for the adults, hanging posters much easier than actually having to talk about any of that stuff.

Juan's class appeared to be taking a test, everyone with their heads peering down at their desks, scribbling away. *Shit*. The test was still going. Juan was blankly staring at the clock. Fabi had also hated algebra; she remembered how nervous she used to get taking tests. She often knew the answer but got nervous about having to show all the right steps. Her work. Still, as she continued to watch through the small window in the door, she found herself wanting Juan to be like all the other kids and get to work.

Before leaving the house Fabi had folded the notice for the arraignment, stuffed it back in the envelope, and tucked it in her purse along with the sonogram and her letters from Mando. She planned to talk to Juan about it and the lawyer they would get. She knew Juan had no faith in her, like she'd once had no faith in Grampá. But that's what today was about. Fixing the past.

"What are you doing here?" Juan hissed, closing the door to Mrs. Hill's classroom behind him. He'd caught her peeking inside the classroom, bolted from his seat to the door. "You're not supposed to be standing alone in the hallway, you psycho."

"What? I'm your mom . . . and I need to pull you from class. We need to go shopping," Fabi said. Hearing her words out loud made her cringe. How wrong they sounded. "And quit talking to me like that." *Wrong again*.

Juan's face was pure confusion. "Shopping? What are you even talking about? I gotta pass this test. It's only my future, Má!"

"Well go back and finish then. I'll wait. But we gotta talk right after."

"Talk about what? About *shopping*? You never make any sense."

Fabi dug through her purse, grabbed Juan's arraignment letter. "You got court *next week*, malcriado. You're facing a year in jail; you need a suit to keep you from that future. Let's talk about *that*! Let's talk about *that* future." She knew the afternoon she'd been wishing for, the shopping and talking and making things right with Juanito, had just blown up. That she'd blown it up.

"Fuck," Juan said, moving toward the classroom and then stopping with his hand on the doorknob, looking like a spaceship losing signal from its home planet. His face blank and expressionless. Fabi realized he wouldn't be able to concentrate on what was left of his test. That he would probably fail. That *she* couldn't stop failing, either.

"Let me tell your teacher we have to leave for an emergency. It's not a lie. You can't finish the test later?" Juan didn't move, still frozen.

Then, as if regaining signal, he shook his head. "Nope. I'm turning my test in. I'm done." Juan quickly disappeared back inside the classroom.

What had she done? She stood, frozen in the hallway, not sure what to say or do. She had no business being there.

Juan stormed out of the classroom, his backpack slung over his shoulder, and bolted down the hallway, making his way past a security guard and toward the main exit. At least he no longer seemed to be limping.

Trees lined the front of the school, their naked, weather-beaten branches splintered and gnarled, looking ready to snap in the wind. Dust swirled. Fabi hoped to find Juan waiting by her truck. Hoped that he hadn't run home or who knew where else. That he wasn't lost to her. She wanted to make up for what just happened, to still make up for everything.

Kiki's had been her father's idea. He loved the hamburger steak, smothered with chile con queso and served with a side of french fries and beans. With a pitcher of beer. Especially if he wasn't paying. And Gladi and Seth were treating. Fabi had wanted to take Juanito out alone, but she guessed this was okay—she could wait for the weekend, once Gladi was gone, to really start fixing everything. They had time; she could share him. After Juanito had stormed out of the school, he *had* waited for her by the truck. They'd gone to Penney's and bought a suit, a real nice one that was just the right price to fit on her card. She tried talking to him at the store, as she pressed pairs of pants against his legs, made him try on jackets and loop on ties over different style dress shirts, but Juan barely said a word, still pissed. She got it.

Now they all sat at a table by the bar, trying to make small talk. The restaurant was unusually crowded for a weekday. On weekends there was always a long wait, sometimes out the door. The walls were lined with old photographs, celebrity autographs documenting long-ago meals, and yellowing reviews from the local paper. The wood paneling on the walls needed to be replaced, as did the matching tables and booths. "I love coming back home just to eat," Gladi said. "The Mexican food in McAllen isn't as good."

"I like it," Seth said, surveying the restaurant.

"What do you know?" Juan said, not even bothering to look at Seth.

"You ever been to McAllen?" Seth asked.

"Why would I go there?" Juan shoved a tostada with salsa verde into his mouth and glared at his uncle. He had the same annoyed look on his face he had whenever Fabi made the mistake of introducing him to a boyfriend.

"Well, point for me," Seth said, drumming the table. "One day you'll leave this place. Maybe after college you can even travel the world."

"Travel the world? Sure. I'll go book my flight."

"Well, after college," Seth said. "Lots of kids do it. Take a year to find themselves."

Juan shoved another tostada into his mouth, avoiding eye contact with Fabi. She wanted him to stop talking and wondered if he wanted to, too, but couldn't help himself. Wondered if, like her, he sometimes felt words burning in him like a fire, growing from small to raging and eventually scorching everyone he talked to.

Seth scooped a chip with salsa into his mouth and turned to Gladi, who'd been silently watching. "Babe, this *is* fantastic!"

"It's from a jar, and I'm not going to college, pendejo," Juan interrupted. "I'll probably have to join the army. I bet I can see Afghanistan. I hear it's lovely in spring."

Papá abruptly banged his fist against the table. "You're not joining the pinche army. No goddamn way."

"Papá," Gladi said. "No one's joining the army. Calm down."

Juan slowly rolled his eyes. "But how else am I going to find myself?"

Fabi reached across the table and tried to hold Juan's hand, but he pulled away. "Por favor, Juanito," she murmured. "That's enough."

"Enough what? Enough of the truth?" Juan said. "We're poor. The only time we even get to eat in this dumpy restaurant is when someone else pays." Juan wasn't avoiding looking at her now, his eyes laser beams burning a hole into her. "What's *enough* was you ruining my last shot at getting into a college, to buy a *suit*."

"Callaté," Papá said, again banging his fist against the table. Fabi noticed his pitcher of beer was almost empty, and no one had been helping him polish it off. She should have noticed. She'd seen guys like him at work for years, quiet but angry men, seemingly okay until they lost their shit without warning. Her father, she was realizing, was a drunk.

Seth picked up another chip. "What's so wrong with the army?" he asked her father. "I thought, being a vet, you'd actually be pushing him toward something like that."

"Ay Dios," Gladi said. "Please stop talking, Seth. Papá, it's okay. No one is joining anything. Juan is going to college. Everything is going to be okay."

Huh. Fabi thought Papá would be pro army too. He'd been around Juan's age when he was shipped off to war—just a boy, now that she thought about it. Just like Martín Juan Morales, the boy she met while Mamá was sick in the hospital, had been. He'd already graduated from El Paso High and enlisted in the army, was waiting to leave for basic training; his father was dying of prostate cancer at the same time as Mamá was dying of colon cancer. He was quiet. Nice. He played basketball. He was a guy Fabi wouldn't have gone for if not for the situation. They grieved together, spent weeks together, just the two of them, after both their parents died; it was a relationship that had complicated her life more than any other. It was a relationship that— Her thoughts were interrupted by her father, who was now going off big-time.

"Let me tell you both something. When I was Juanito's age, I got drafted. I didn't have no choice. I had to go to the army, and off to the war, where I got shot in the head—on my *second* tour. If I didn't go, I would have been taken to jail. To *jail*! ¿Me entiendes? And back then, only poor people got drafted. Rich kids got to go to college. Today, it's the same. Poor people still fight the pinche wars and the college kids don't have to do nothing. The only difference is now the poor kids get tricked into joining instead of being told—"

"Hold on there. Nobody is getting tricked," Seth interrupted. "Nobody is taking anyone to jail for not joining. It's completely different."

"Seth! Why are you still talking?" Gladi exclaimed, tugging at his arm. "Stop talking."

"Mira. That means 'look,' Seth. You probably think I'm some drunk old man. And that's because I am. But that doesn't mean I'm wrong."

Juan seemed fixated on his Grampá—and not in a sarcastic looking-to-make-a-joke kind of way. Fabi wondered—oh no—if he was now seriously thinking of joining the army. And like her father, she would be against it.

"I never said that," Seth said, suddenly looking around nervously.

"I'm going to divorce you," Gladi said, shaking her head in disapproval. "I'm calling a lawyer as soon as we get home."

"You know the reason they took the draft away?" Papá paused, taking a chug from his beer. "The draft turned everyone into something. A draft-dodger. A prisoner. A protester. Or a soldier. The war got everyone, one way or another. Now, no one even notices the war. Because no one notices poor people."

Martín died in Iraq. She read about it in the paper, his funeral at Fort Bliss. Juan was barely in school at the time.

She remembered dropping him off and sneaking into the church the morning of the funeral. Remembered Martín's wife, a tall blonde woman, standing in the front pew as Martín's casket was wheeled to the front of the church. She was holding a baby; another was tucked inside a car seat at her feet. Twins who would grow up without their father.

Gladi moved the pitcher of beer away from her father, but it was too late to keep him from talking crazy. "I could've been a great engineer, but I got shot in the head. My brain's a mess now. Before that, when I was Juan's age, me and your mamá were in love. That's when we were fearless. When we were our best. I've been sick since the war, since the bullet. When your mom got sick, it was the war all over again. And when she died, I never came back."

Across the table Gladi was crying; Seth rubbed her back. Juan, who'd been listening to her father intently, was now looking at Fabi. She recognized the look on his face. Guilt. Guilt for blowing up dinner the way she'd blown up his algebra test. Fabi felt her eyes watering. She turned to Papá. He was munching his hamburger steak, and she wondered what kind of man he might've been if he'd never been drafted. Fabi didn't want bullets for Juan. She didn't want war. She wanted her son to be fearless.

THE BADJUANS (CHAPTER SEVENTEEN)

After dinner, when Juan was sure Má and Grampá were asleep, he took the suit from his closet. He'd tried it on at JCPenney but had been too pissed to take a good look. To enjoy it. The pants and jacket were navy blue, the long-sleeved shirt a crisp white. The tie was thin and red and matched a new pair of socks. His má had found them. He knew her coming in the middle of his test hadn't really fucked him up any worse than the actual algebra, but blaming her came easy. It always had.

The thing was, he had always secretly wanted a suit. Knew that looking good meant feeling good, and was the reason he hung magazine cutouts of perfectly cut Tom Ford suits and oil-black Chrysler 300s in his room. To feel bulletproof. He imagined himself one day being drafted into the NBA. Standing on a stage under bright lights, television cameras fixed on him, dressed exactly like this. Smiling and knowing that everything was going to be okay. Finally and for the first time.

Putting on a clean T-shirt first, Juan slipped on the crisp dress shirt and fastened the buttons. He had no idea how to tie a tie; he would have to ask Grampá or jump on YouTube when he found a place with Internet. The dark blue pants felt thin—probably how all expensive things felt. Delicate, fragile. Juan tucked the shirt in and fastened his new black leather belt, centering the buckle along his zipper. His dress socks were even thinner than the pants, but he didn't try on his new dress shoes next. Didn't want to crease the new leather, not yet. Instead he popped on the new pair of basketball shoes his má had also gotten him. *A little something extra,* she had said with a wink. He looked at the shoes, bright white, simple and clean. New. Why couldn't he have been grateful at the time, when she obviously needed him to be? He was always fucking shit up with her, and his trip across Texas to meet the man she never wanted him to know was going to be another fuckup. How could it not be?

He stared down at those new shoes. His ankle felt good, maybe healed, but Juan probably wouldn't really know until game day—no way would he practice hard enough to risk reinjuring his wheel before that. He slid on the jacket—the final touch—and looked at himself in the mirror above his dresser. His single-breasted jacket fitted; he looked taller and felt stronger than normal, not unlike he did on the basketball court. He wished he could wear it all the time. He imagined wearing suits to school, replacing his torn-up backpack with a shiny black briefcase. He would straighten his tie and unfasten his jacket button before taking a seat in each class, take out big sheets of yellow legal paper for notes. Let everyone know that from now on he meant business. *Ha.* Of course, what he really needed to learn was how to tie a tie. He imagined this was something a father should teach a son, but since his was on death row and Grampá was asleep, YouTube would have to do. If anything, he should be grateful to be a fatherless kid in the Internet age. He grabbed his phone and hoped he hadn't already gone over on data.

Hey, Papá Google:

how do you t
how do you tie a tie
how do you tweet
how do you twerk
how do you turn a fraction into a decimal
how do you talk to a girl
how do you talk to an angel

Juan thought about texting JD, having him meet him at his old apartment with his laptop to help with the whole blog thing, but instead he grabbed his Má's piece-of-shit Dell and started to walk, still wearing his new suit. If JD could become a filmmaker, then Juan could be a blogger—or at least he could open a Tumblr. He thought back to his night in jail, the concrete room full of drunks and junkies. The Monster, who scared the shit out of Juan, and the tattoo across his neck. He'd been arrested for beating his wife, his knuckles swollen and bloodied. He'd laughed as he explained to one of the guards how the bitch hit him first and *she* should be the one locked up. Getting arrested had been worse, though: the swarm of cops had rushed him, their knees, elbows, and fists driving his body and head into the ground before twisting his arms into cuffs. Them laughing before he pissed himself in the back of their patrol car. JD was right to want to record what was happening to them. Why not make a movie about their lives? How else would anyone know the kind of shit that happened to them?

Armando Aranda had been in prison longer than Juan had been alive; Juan wondered how comfortable he'd become living in a prison, alongside the worst kind of murderers, and decided that would be a question he'd ask. Along with if he ever had a good night's sleep. Facing a year of jail himself, Juan not only wanted to know who his father was, but also *what* his father was. *Who* he might end up becoming. The thought scared him.

Since it was only about a mile away, it didn't take long to get to the old apartment. He wondered if Jabba could be watching, the old bitch probably itching to call the cops. But her apartment was dark. He settled on his old milk crate, being careful not to dirty his new pants or jacket.

He should have felt right at home, except he couldn't recognize the landscape. The black sky drowned the silhouettes of trees and bushes, and any outlines of surrounding houses, in darkness. The moon, like the sounds of the neighborhood, all seemingly swallowed by deep space. Juan thought of the day he'd fought JD, and Danny's gun had gone off. At the time, Juan had been more focused on the fight, but now, knowing how his father killed a man, he couldn't help but think of Danny's gun. The bullet. Not one of them had wondered where the bullet had landed. How the bullet, after soaring through the air, could've ripped back to earth and hammered through someone's skull or chest, maybe a kid's or some old person's. Shit, Jabba had a reason to call the cops.

Signing up for a Tumblr account was easy, and so was choosing a name to blog under: thebadjuans. (JD would absolutely hate that!) Not sure where to start, Juan looked up his father. He read about his crime on the Texas Department of Criminal Justice website, but couldn't find anything more on him besides other articles about the crime, a botched robbery that was only sort of like a Tarantino movie in that it took place in a diner. The articles made fun of him for copying *Pulp Fiction*, making him more of a character than a person. JD had made Juan watch an online bootleg of *Pulp Fiction* a long time ago, and though he'd liked it at the time, he knew he could never watch, or like, the movie again. To the world, Armando Aranda was a piece-of-shit cop killer getting exactly what he deserved.

He was also Juan's father, but who knew if he deserved anything for that. With the screen glowing, lighting his face, Juan typed: *Armando Aranda is my father.*

Suddenly, Juan sensed a new glow behind him; the light in Jabba's apartment kitchen window flicked on, and he saw her standing, looking out to where Juan sat. He slammed the laptop shut and crouched down. There would be no posting tonight. He didn't know if Jabba had actually seen him, but if she had, she would have already called the cops. They would be on their way.

The wall separating the backyard from the alleyway had long since fallen, the cement and flagstone just pieces of rubble. He could run toward the alley, past some mesquite trees with thorny branches, and then down the alley. If his ankle had been 100 percent, this would be a no-brainer, there being a slight chance the old metiche wouldn't see him. But even if Juan made it, there was still the chance the cops would pop up at Grampá's anyway and he would have to deny being at the apartment in the first place. Lie to Grampá and Má. *Shit.* He was always lying.

He bet the cops were already on the way, so he bolted for the alley, where Jabba must have caught a glimpse of him because she lit his ass up, turning on a series of spotlights newly mounted to the building's brick wall and blinding Juan as they popped on in unison. Juan could no longer see Jabba in her apartment window. He ran blindly, only this time Juan wasn't in unfamiliar territory, and like a bat, he radared himself out of trouble. And unlike that night at Danny's, his ankle held up as he raced down the alley. With his má's Dell securely in his hand, Juan pumped his arms and legs as fast as he could, feeling the night air against his face and burning in his chest. He didn't hear a single siren as he ran through stoplights but then froze dead in his tracks. The Cutlass, that *fucking* Cutlass, was stopped at an intersection, at a red light. Juan quickly hid the laptop inside his suit jacket.

"Look at this vato," the driver called out. Juan remembered him, the tattoos on his neck and arms looking more like scars than art. He remembered the shotgun, too. The blackness of the inside of the barrels. "He's already dressed for his own funeral." The light turned green but the car didn't move. "Why are you running? And what are you hiding in your jacket?"

"The cops are after me," Juan gasped, gripping the laptop. "They're right behind me."

"I don't see no cops," the driver said, waving him over. "Show me what you're hiding."

"I don't got nothing. Man, the cops are coming." Juan looked behind him and then down the street. The cholos had probably already seen the laptop. He was fucked.

"What crimes could you be doing dressed like that, with a laptop, in the middle of the night? This ain't Wall Street, motherfucker!" The driver leaned out the window just as sirens moaned in the distance, the sound slowly becoming louder.

"I told you," Juan said, relieved for the first time ever to hear the cops, then ready to get away from them.

A voice came from inside the Cutlass. "Fuck this banker. Let's go!"

"Next time, Banker," the driver said, keeping his eyes locked on Juan as he sped off.

Back in his room, Juan was a mess, but at least the suit wasn't, just a little sweaty, his kicks a little dusty. He hung everything back in his nearly empty closet, carefully placing the jacket and pants inside the thin plastic covering that came from the store. The shoes went back in their box. As he slid them onto a closet shelf, they bumped against something. He reached behind the box and pulled out a Bible. A Bible? The cover was brown, made of leather. The corners curled upward like they'd been rubbed a zillion times. He found his má's name neatly written on the front page: Fabiola Ramos.

Juan opened his window and lay down on his unmade bed. He closed his eyes, the Bible in his hand. The night air was cool. A car horn blared outside, a man now yelling; music was thumping from a nearby house. A party was just getting started. The sound, Juan knew, would go on for hours, ending with police sirens and the sound of the ghetto bird chopping overhead. Over the years Juan had learned to ignore the commotion, but tonight he felt the uproar buzz in his chest. How long had Los Fatherless, those fuckers in the Cutlass, been out for him? Why wouldn't they just leave him alone?

He sat up and thumbed through the thin pages of the

Bible, looking for the flood story Grampá had told him. He found it in Genesis. In the beginning.

> *Yahweh saw that human wickedness was great on earth and that human hearts contrived nothing but wicked schemes all day long.*
>
> *Yahweh regretted having made human beings on earth and was grieved at heart.*
>
> *And Yahweh said, "I shall rid the surface of the earth of the human beings whom I created—human and animal, the creeping things and the birds of heaven—for I regret having made them."*

As he read, Juan realized Grampá had it wrong, believing God was a fake. God had to be real, and he was as terrifying as all the monsters he'd made.

OVER THE HILL AND FAR AWAY (CHAPTER EIGHTEEN)

Juan's ankle was sore from last night's sprint, but it wasn't reinjured. He'd gotten all sorts of lucky. A first! He walked to school alone, like he'd done ever since he'd moved to Grampá's and JD had wrecked his car. It was a new ritual he actually enjoyed. It was Tuesday, his day to practice with Eddie, and he wondered when *he* should get back to the gym, what with Senior Day only a week away. The entire week was going to be big. He had the game and then the arraignment. A college coach and then a judge, both judging him on totally different kinds of courts. As he got closer to the front steps of the school, Juan suddenly remembered everything hinged on the results of yesterday's algebra test.

"Danny's throwing another party on Friday. That's the day we're planning to go," JD said as Juan plopped down beside him on the front steps of Austin. "I just saw that shit on his Instagram." The wind blew hard around them. Whistled. Juan was glad he'd worn a long-sleeved shirt.

Juan's phone buzzed in his pocket. It was Roxanne.

How'd the test go? ☺

Juan had missed her. The scent from her lotion stayed on his pillow for a few days, making him crazy. He totally now understood the word "crush." His brain went to pieces whenever she was around. Even when he thought about her. He'd wanted to call her for days. But he wanted to prove he took her seriously, and instead holed up in his room studying, afraid he would embarrass himself by failing the test. To this point, all he had done was embarrass himself in front of her. He was done doing that.

IDK my ma came in the middle of it to buy me a suit!!!

Or maybe he wasn't.

WTF!?!?! CALL ME LATER!!

as long as im not shopping 4 briefcases

JD playfully slapped at Juan's phone. "Wipe that stupid smile off your face. It's disgusting. Seriously, what are we gonna do about a car? For the trip?"

Juan didn't want to think about that now. For once things were just working out without going to shit. "I thought you were going to ask Danny to come with us? You said we could go in his car." Juan couldn't help but feel pissed at JD, even if Danny throwing a party was totally out of his control.

JD shook his head. "Danny's been . . . weird lately. I was going to ask him, but he hasn't been answering texts and hasn't left the house in days. Then yesterday, boom, a party announcement."

Juan didn't find this so weird—Danny sometimes did this. Took a few days of alone time. Wouldn't answer his phone—no texts, no PMs. Wouldn't open the door if you came by the house. Then, like a caterpillar busting from its cocoon, he would butterfly out and want to party. Juan never did go back and help him shovel rock; damn, how could he space on *that*?

"There's only one option," JD was saying. "Borrow your mom's truck."

What?! No way. That was another thing Juan didn't want to think about: borrowing Má's truck. No *way* would she lend it to him. He barely knew how to drive. So he passed on answering. "Let's go grab something from the vending machine. I'm hungry."

But walking into school and down the hallway, he felt increasingly anxious. Had Mrs. Hill graded the algebra exams? The test was hard, but he'd answered most of the questions. He'd studied. Now, at the vending machines, he decided he should talk to her, ask her to grade his test. *Beg* her to let him do extra credit after explaining how Má had come by during the exam, to buy him a suit for court, and distracted him. That he was facing a year in jail. And that his father was on death row and about to die. And that a college recruiter was coming to watch him play, *if he passed*. And all he needed was to pass.

JD shoved his shoulder. "So, can we use your má's truck or not? This is kind of a big problem."

"I don't know," Juan said truthfully. "I've never asked her to borrow it before. Can't you borrow, like, Alma's car? Or your old man's?"

"Everyone in my family hates me right now. So . . . no."

"Okay, let me think about asking my má." But Juan knew there was no way. And he couldn't take his mind off that test. "Let's go find Hill. I need to check on my algebra test. Like, right now."

JD stopped short and looked ready to fight, his whole body tense. Like a really pissed-off giraffe. "For real? Who gives a *fuck* about algebra?" The halls were completely empty, long and narrow. Juan liked them this way. Quiet, before all the noise and confusion of people.

"Look, if I didn't pass this test, all this, my entire future, is for shit anyways."

"If you didn't pass a test, meeting your dad is for shit? What are you talking about?"

Juan spun around. "Look, if I didn't pass this test, I don't get to play on Senior Day. If I don't ball out on

Senior Day, then I don't get a scholarship. Then shit could get real fucked up. A judge could decide I'm a total fucking loser and sentence me to jail time. Maybe a year. So, yeah, I'm pretty serious about algebra right now."

"All right," JD said after a moment. "But I'm going to record you. Since this is such serious shit."

"Whatever." Juan turned and hurried toward Mrs. Hill's classroom. Fuck. He didn't really want JD to record anything, but arguing with him was a waste of time. JD trailed a few yards behind as he reached Mrs. Hill's door. It was closed, but she was inside. Juan pressed his forehead against the window like a psycho, like his má had, hoping to get his teacher's attention. It was just before zero period.

"Try knocking," JD said, keeping his distance. "It's, like, a custom."

Without his having to knock, Mrs. Hill looked up and waved Juan inside. He quickly opened the door and closed it behind him. He didn't need anyone else to follow him in. Not even JD. The room looked the same without students, but it smelled different. Gone was the smell of bodies, of sweat and plastics and stale air. The room smelled like coffee. The air warm. Sweet.

"What do you need, Juan?" Mrs. Hill asked him with a smile.

"Have you, uh, graded the tests yet?"

"No. The test was barely yesterday."

Juan stood over her, suddenly unsure what to say next.

"Is that all?"

"I guess so." But that wasn't all. Juan wanted her to grade the test. Mrs. Hill looked at him patiently, waiting for him to say something. "I just need to pass the test so I can play in Senior Day. I studied pretty hard."

"Your coach was telling me that. He said you had a tutor. Is that true?"

"Yes. From a private school." Juan had no idea why he thought that would impress her.

"Are you here to ask me to grade it? Because, honestly, you just standing there is getting a bit weird."

"Please!"

Mrs. Hill let out a sigh. "Okay, let's take a look." She dug through a pile of papers until she found Juan's and whipped out her pen. Out of the corner of his eye Juan could see JD holding his camera to the door's window. His stomach was a jar of angry bugs, desperately crawling along the sides to escape and pulling one another down to the glass bottom. Hissing. Mrs. Hill marked his exam, shaking her head. Eventually, she looked up. Juan wanted to puke.

"This happens every year, Juan. Every year someone like you walks in here, wants me to grade their test, either at the end of the semester or when they need to be eligible for whatever the case may be, and tells me how much they need to pass, and almost every time the same thing happens. You can't believe how frustrating this is for me."

"I'm sorry," Juan said, and he actually meant it. "I really

studied this time. I promise." He felt like an idiot. An idiot for thinking he could pass in the first place. An idiot for bothering Mrs. Hill, who probably now thought he was an even bigger idiot than before he came in. Coach Paul was right. He was a rock breaker. A yard raker at best. Mrs. Hill handed Juan back the test: 75%.

Juan held the test in both hands, making sure the score was real. It was a win. A classroom win, no less. Another first! "Not pretty, but you passed," Mrs. Hill said. "All it took was a little effort. What is it about you kids? Why can't you just do this from the start? Just care about your own education as much as you care about basketball or running around in the streets?"

Her voice was like crowd noise. "Thank you," Juan said.

"Are you even listening to me?"

Juan rushed over and hugged Mrs. Hill in her chair, pinning her arms to her sides.

Then, still in the middle of a bear hug, Mrs. Hill noticed JD filming in the window. "I don't understand you kids. Not one bit."

WE GET TO BE TERRIBLE (CHAPTER NINETEEN)

Finally, it was Friday. The plan was to head to Danny's party and then hit the road from there. JD packed a gym bag of clothes, a toothbrush, and deodorant. A charger for his phone and camera. He'd already wiped the memory cards clean and packed a notebook and pens. He tossed the old Kinoflex in the bag, even though he never actually got it running. Then he sat anxiously in his room and waited for Juan to show with his má's truck—he'd finally been cornered into borrowing it, and he'd only agreed to after JD promised to do the driving. He thought of the hours of road ahead, of what they would see at Polunsky—plain grayish buildings wrapped in fencing, the tops coiled in razor wire. Guards in a tower with sniper rifles. Juan's old man locked inside. Juan had to be nervous too, because *he* fucking was. JD decided to shoot some B-roll to keep calm.

Flipping on his camera, he panned across the room. As usual he'd made his bed; his side of the room was neat like always. His laptop and shoes were neatly tucked under the bed, the bootlegs now re-alphabetized and grouped by country of origin. He hadn't seen Alma since that day at the recruiting office almost two weeks ago. Turned out she worked all the time, just like Pops, like Amá, which made avoiding her easy. She'd had his car towed to a junkyard just like the recruiter had suggested. Made a cool hundred bucks. Maybe *she* should join the air force. JD kept Technical Sergeant Bullard's card in his pocket. He didn't want to leave it out where anyone could see, but for some reason he didn't want to hide it either.

Gliding down the hallway, he passed the camera along the wall. Pictures of him as a toddler with Alma as a little girl, her squeezed in Pops's arms in most of them, smiling big. He zoomed in on her face, hoping to rip off the Ken Burns effect he'd read about on Wikipedia. There were photos of Amá pregnant with Tomásito and then of her holding a squealing baby. Throughout the house, their childhoods had been documented in pictures—not the kind done at studios, where everyone wore matching clothes and stood in front of black or gray backdrops with fake cheesy smiles, but in snapshots. Some set up—sure, with fake cheesy smiles—but others caught in random moments playing in the backyard or family cookouts. JD liked these best; they were how he remembered those days. When things were good.

As he recorded, he thought about how much his parents must've loved babies. There were so many baby pictures! But the camera seemed to have been whipped out a lot less often the older he and his brother and sister got. Suddenly there were only sporadic photos from Christmas mornings or birthdays. As JD filmed, it dawned on him there were fewer and fewer photographs once he hit middle school. Then there were none, as if the family suddenly vanished. *Shit. What happened?* He shut the camera down. Off to the side there was a picture of Pops from before he and Amá were married, him in his army service dress. His expression was serious, unsmiling. Maybe a little scared. In the photo, he couldn't have been much older than JD. He remembered a similar portrait of his abuelo hanging in the living room of his abuela's house, his old man's old man, who died before JD had been born, uniformed in his army service dress, his face the mirror image of Pops.

He wondered how long Amá would keep pictures like this up now that Pops was gone. He wandered into the dining room; they used to eat meals together when he was little, but after Tomásito was born, Amá took a gig at the State Center and jobbed long hours there, mostly on swing shifts and sometimes overnights. Without her around they mostly ate in front of the TV. Turning the camera back on, it didn't take long for him to finish going through the two-bedroom house. He moved slowly toward Amá's room. The door was closed, which it had mostly been since the day she kicked Pops out. JD had no idea if she was inside.

“Anyone in there?” JD said, knocking. He waited, thinking maybe he would turn off the camera, but decided against it, and instead turned the lens on himself. He spoke into the camera. “Tomorrow it will be three weeks since Amá found the condoms. Since then, I’ve gotten into a fight with my best friend. I’ve been kicked off the basketball team. And I totaled my car. I also haven’t talked to my own mom since that day—not that we really talked all the time before that. I did follow my old man driving to his mistress’s house, so I’m up to date on him. Me and my sister aren’t really talking either. And my little brother hates me. So things are *cooool*.”

Amá swung open the door. “Who are you talking to?”

JD quickly lowered the camera. “Myself,” he said, feeling his face flush. “I’m making a movie.” He held up the camera for her to see. She was getting ready for work, dressed in a pair of brown scrubs and white tennis shoes, her hair pulled back in a tight ponytail.

Her eyes narrowed. “What do you know about making movies?”

“Nothing, believe me.”

“Is this for school? Tell me you’re still in school.”

“I still *go* to school,” JD said, the camera still recording.

“Shouldn’t you be there *right now*?”

JD stood there for a moment, not knowing what to say or do. “Maybe,” he finally tried.

Amá disappeared back inside her room, leaving JD in the doorway. “I can’t believe you’re ditching right now,” she called out. "This *movie* thing has nothing to do with school. I just know it. Turn that camera off."

"I'm sorry, Amá," JD said. "I'm really sorry." He wanted to tell her what he was up to. That he'd skipped the second half of school today to get ready for a road trip straight through the middle of Texas and to death row. To help Juan. But she wasn't going to be cool with any of that. No way. He left the camera running.

"So what do you want? I need to go to work." Uninvited, JD cautiously went inside his mother's bedroom and panned the camera around the room. The walls had been stripped bare. Her and Pops's wedding pictures had been taken down, which answered JD's earlier question. He peeked inside the closet. Most of his old man's clothes were still there, as if at any moment he could come and take his life back like nothing had happened. JD wondered where he'd been without his stuff. If he'd been staying in the Northeast with his side piece or keeping a bachelor pad loaded with new shit. "I told you to turn that thing off!" Amá's hands were on her hips, her voice annoyed. "Why don't you ever listen?!"

"Sorry. I thought you wanted to talk to me," JD said.

"Weeks ago."

"I know. I'm sorry."

"And I know you crashed your car," she said, sitting on the corner of her bed. "That you've been out partying and acting crazy. I don't know what to do with you." She looked tired. Not from work but of JD, of his bullshit. "I'm glad you're okay, mijo, but I'm . . . worried about the kind of person you're turning out to be. You're never here. You're never with us. It's like you're a ghost. Like you're dead to this family."

JD took a step back. "That's not true, Amá." That wasn't right. Was it?

"I think it is, mijo. We've all come together after what happened. We've all cried and been close. Everyone but you. Even your apá has shown remorse. But you, you still party. Still hang out with your friends, over us. You ignore your family. You wouldn't even come and talk to me. Ignored me for weeks. ¿Por qué?"

JD moved beside her, wanting to be close, wanting to talk. But she kept going, not letting him answer. "You see all this stuff in this room? I can't bring myself to touch any of it. I wanted your help, Juan Diego. To box this all up. To count on you. But I can't. The family can't." Amá sat stiff and straight; her words, the expression on her face, were matter of fact. Her dark brown eyes lasered in on him.

"The family *can* count on me." But JD knew the *family* really couldn't. It wasn't that he was a ghost, or couldn't be counted on, but he now understood—as Amá tried to burn a hole through him with her eyes—that his family was the thing that was dead. And it had died long before he found the condoms. His family had been killed off by work, by hours of night shifts and side gigs. By everyday life. JD realized his little camera, his new desire to collect stories, could never keep up. The proof was on the walls of the house, in picture after missing picture.

"If I can count on you, then box up your apá's stuff. He's never putting another foot in this house again. You can do that for me. Right?"

JD's phone erupted in his pocket, buzzing and static bass, indecipherable lyrics looping from inside his pants pocket.

"Ay Dios," Amá said. "What is that?"

"It's Run the Jewels. They're my favorite."

"Run the what? Never mind . . . Are you going to help me, be part of the family, or not?"

At any moment Juan would be at the front door. The call was probably him wanting to know how to drive stick and hoping to make the short distance between his grampá's house and JD's. JD needed to answer the phone. He needed to answer it even if it meant becoming a ghost to Amá. He could make it up to her. Make things right with Alma and Tomásito, too. JD answered the phone, and Amá reached over to the nightstand and snatched her purse, stuffing her keys and wallet inside before pushing past him, now not bothering to even look at him as she stormed from the room. The front door slammed behind her as she left for work.

Bullard. *Shit. Not Juan. Shit.* JD wasn't sure how Bullard had gotten his number, but the recruiter was quick with the questions: How was it going? How was school? How'd the car thing go? Cops get involved? JD answered: eh, eh, junkyard, and nah. That's when Bullard told him about the production journalist gig. Writing scripts, producing videos, telling stories. It was perfect and also rare—those kinds of jobs get snatched up quickly and never really open up in the first place. So they had to move quick. If JD could come down to the recruiting office and take a test, he could slide him right in. It was perfect.

"The truck looked like a cat about to puke." JD was jerking his body back and forth, mimicking the halting way Juan had approached the house. "This motherfucker was driving with his chest pinned to the steering wheel."

"I couldn't move the seat back! Má is short," Juan said. "Shit, I did the best I could."

"Couldn't . . . or didn't know how?" Danny asked before chugging from his forty. JD was glad to see Danny acting like his normal self. Clowning. Laughing. This party wasn't crazy like the last one. Instead, two couples hung out in the kitchen talking, and a pocket of people in the darkened living room watched a movie. Everyone else was in the backyard, maybe fifteen people total. JD only knew Juan and Danny, and now Roxanne—who had suddenly joined them. They stood by the same wall JD leapt the last time.

"*I* moved the seat just fine," JD said, taking a sip from his bottle of water.

"I knocked whatever was blocking the piece-of-shit seat loose right before I got to your house. I heard it sliding around right before you got in," Juan argued.

"Yeah, right," JD said. "I didn't hear shit."

"You don't have to be cool all the time, Juanito," Danny

said. "I already told my cousin whatta big loser you are. I told her not to let you hit it."

Roxanne lifted her chin, like she was ready to fight. "I'm in charge of what I do, primo," she said. "And we're only texting right now, so *relax*. Besides, you can have *that* Juan, if you want." She nodded toward JD.

"You mean Juan Diego?" Danny asked. "No one wants *that* Juan."

"That seems to be true," JD said, thinking he could call the air force recruiter in the morning. Schedule the test for when he got back. What harm woud it do?

They all laughed. Roxanne and Juan stood close to each other, their shoulders close enough to touch but not. Were sneaking each other lovey-dovey looks. They made JD want to barf. When they'd first met Roxanne, JD thought that maybe he had a shot with her. She was the kind of girl he was all about, smart and sarcastic, and he was sure they hated the exact same things. But as JD pulled out his camera and fixed the lens on Juan, he realized why he never had a chance: Juan would never be called a ghost. He didn't fade into the background. Not the way JD always seemed to.

JD filmed across the backyard. It was evening going into night, the sun setting and the cloud-filled sky a blast of orange and purple. No one looked familiar until he spotted Melinda Camacho sitting alone in the corner of the yard. *Melinda?* It was . . . it was just the way he'd first seen her, years ago, the summers at his abuela's, no one wanting to play with her, sitting alone. And, still, she looked banging, like she did that day at the bakery, and even though JD wanted to hate on her, what he wanted even more was a reason to talk to her.

"Stalk much?" Roxanne said.

"Not as much as I used to," JD said, turning the camera to Roxanne. "It's just so hard to find the time. You know?"

"You had the camera on her for like five minutes," Roxanne said. "It was kinda creepy."

"Who are you looking at?" Danny said, looking in Melinda's direction.

"Nobody," JD said, knowing he was about to be clowned. He wondered if leaping the backyard wall and running away again was an option. Juan would forgive him a second time, right? Humiliation was way worse than not seeing your father for the first and last time.

Juan punched JD in the arm. "No fucking way! Dude, it's Melinda Camacho," he whispered.

"You guys know her?" Roxanne said. "She's, like, the class everything."

"I thought *you* were the class everything," Juan said.

"Roxanne's the class fuckup," Danny laughed. "She lives with me and wants to hook up with *you*, but quit changing the subject."

"Shut up," Roxanne said, scowling. "And this isn't about me. How do you guys know her?"

"Her grandparents live next to my abuela," JD explained. "And her fancy parents moved her back to the neighborhood to live with us poors and maybe teach us yoga."

"Wow, you *are* a stalker," Roxanne said.

"And don't forget how you used to make out with her when you were, like, in sixth grade?" Danny teased. "I remember hearing all about it. Juan said you've been all in love with her since."

"Eighth grade," JD corrected as Danny and Roxanne laughed. Juan put his arm on JD's shoulder. JD wasn't "all in love" with her, but yeah, he still thought of her—even though those thoughts were now turning bitter.

"Those two years make a *big* difference?" Juan joked. Danny and Roxanne laughed harder. Music came on from inside the house, some obscure EDM. Danny usually liked his music that way—unlistenable—but JD liked the mix of accordion and trumpet over hard basslines. It seemed ready to provide a soundtrack to what was coming: him being humiliated.

"I'm detail oriented," JD said, keeping his camera rolling.

"I never wondered about *that* orientation," Danny said with a smile.

"A gay joke, really?" Roxanne said. "No seas pendejo." No one seemed to notice the camera was recording anymore. JD kept it going, determined not to miss any more moments—even if that moment sucked for him. He looked over at Melinda. And he realized for the first time that her old man had been right to keep her away. Look how JD had treated his mother, his sister. It was amazing how shitty he could be.

He focused the camera on Juan and Roxanne. They

looked happy, like one day they could be a thing. Shit was turning around for Juan; JD was glad for that. He really was. Juan had passed his test. His ankle felt good, and if he balled out—no reason he wouldn't—then he would get his ride at a junior college. Danny, like he'd been telling everyone all year, was already hooked up, his college paid for by his old man's GI Bill benefits. But JD couldn't hold that against him. Danny was smart and could actually graduate college. He was actually a good dude. JD kept filming. By this time next year, he was sure he wouldn't see either of his two friends again. He'd be alone. He would lose his second family.

JD went to replay his footage on the camera, wanting to see what he'd just shot. The images were dark and grainy, the footage completely useless. Of course it was. JD turned the camera off. It didn't matter. All around the party JD could see people who were, from a distance, just like him. Except soon they wouldn't be. The stupid camera couldn't capture these differences anyway, the differences that mattered, and even if there were a way to make the camera do a trick like that, he didn't know it. He knew he was dreaming with filmmaking, and that kind of dream shit was for motherfuckers who came from money—not him. And soon the dream-having motherfuckers would disappear to college and not have to be happy or braggy about working something union with the city. They certainly wouldn't get stuck as waitresses or cashiers or doing something in sales, which is just another way of saying cashier. And they definitely wouldn't waste their bodies in construction or landscaping or as mechanics, not cleaning houses or hotels or chasing around kids that weren't their own. Juan and Danny, as long as they didn't fuck up along the way, could join them, but JD had no shot. Zip, zero, shit.

Then, seemingly from out of nowhere, he heard, "Hey, Juan Diego." It was . . . Melinda. She had come over to stand next to Roxanne. "I thought I saw you over here."

"What up," JD said, immediately feeling like an asshole. "I was gonna say hi, but you looked busy."

"Busy being all by herself?" Roxanne smirked. "You're smooth, JD."

Melinda smiled. A small and perfect smile. "Smoother than the bro who spent twenty minutes trying to hook up by quoting Will Ferrell movie lines. He was pretty drunk."

"His movies aren't *that* funny," JD said seriously. "At least, not pick-up-girls funny."

"Here we go," Danny said. "JD is our group's movie critic. He basically thinks the book or foreign version of any movie is better than any adaptation or remake. Even when he's never read the book or seen the other version."

Melinda laughed, studying JD. His stomach churned nervously.

"Is that true?"

"Mostly," JD said with a shrug, trying to be cool. He couldn't believe he was here, talking to Melinda, and he wondered what she was thinking. If she could tell his pants were slightly high-water or that his socks didn't match.

Did she think he was a hood rat? He looked at Danny and Juan; both grinning like idiots. Being around them always made him comfortable, but now they were making him nervous . . . *more* nervous.

"Who has time to watch two versions of every movie anyway?" Roxanne chimed in. "But Will Ferrell movies *are* funny."

"Like, pick-up-girls funny?" Juan slipped his hand inside Roxanne's. "I can quote those to you, like, all day."

Roxanne playfully pulled her hand away. "Okay, maybe not *that* funny."

"What kind of comedies do you like?" Melinda asked, turning to JD. "What's your favorite?" Melinda was being cool, making small talk with a boy she used to know from the neighborhood. Giving herself something to do at a party that she probably found boring anyway. Still, JD couldn't help but be psyched. He wouldn't have been able to walk up to her and just start talking, and no way would he be able to sit at a party alone without feeling like a sucker, without wanting to leave. She had cojones, for sure. The only thing JD had going for him was that he was funny. *Maybe.*

"*The Passion of the Christ*," JD deadpanned. "Hands down."

"What the fuck?!" Danny yowled.

"Not everyone likes slapstick," JD explained. "I get it. Plus, the end sets up for a sequel. Still, it's not as over the top as *Home Alone*." Melinda cupped both her hands around her mouth, and JD wasn't sure if she was going to laugh or puke.

"That is the second most fucked-up thing to happen in this backyard," Juan hooted.

Melinda had probably heard about the raid. Those kinds of stories spread through high school hallways like the flu. The nervousness in JD's stomach now felt like miniature horses galloping in circles in his gut, corralled with nowhere to go. Who knew if cops raiding a high school party was even a bad thing to Melinda? Maybe blasphemy was the worst thing in the world to her, and he'd just blown his chance, like the Will Ferrell guy. Did making fun of a Mel Gibson movie even count as blasphemy?

"I thought *Home Alone* was preachy," Melinda said, smiling.

"I watch that shit every Christmas," Danny said, still laughing. "And that pinche *Die Hard*."

At that the horses in JD's belly clomped away, and for the first time in a long time JD didn't feel on edge. Standing there with his friends, watching them laugh, he realized that he'd been feeling like shit almost all the time. Like shit could always turn bad. Shit at home, shit at school, shit on the way home from basketball games, shit while cruising with his boys, shit while at a party—shit going to shit all the fucking time. The only time JD wasn't on guard was when he was making jokes.

"We gotta get going," Juan said, pulling out his phone and checking the time. JD had, for a moment, forgotten about the trip. About everything.

"Where you guys going?" Melinda asked.

"They're making a movie," Danny said, nodding toward Juan. "Going to find this one's long-lost death-row daddy."

"Jesus," Roxanne snapped at Danny. "Why do you always say the wrong thing? The most terrible thing you can think to say?"

"Because these are my boys," Danny snapped back. "We get to be terrible." Danny hopped over to JD and flung his arm around his neck. "Spielberg over here is gonna film that shit. If I'd known they were going today, I would never have thrown this party. I would be going with them. But I can't leave all these fuckers in my house. They would destroy everything, and the Sarge would finally lose it on me."

"I can't believe you called me Spielberg," JD said. "He hasn't done anything good since he executive produced *SeaQuest 2032*."

"That's not true!" Melinda interrupted. "I thought his producing *Real Steel* was a brave choice."

"I love you?" JD blurted out. *What? Why?* His head suddenly felt light and disconnected from his body, like a stray balloon drifting away from an outside birthday party—and probably toward power lines.

"Oh shit," Danny said, laughing and letting go of JD. "Let's turn this party into a wedding."

"What?" JD yelped. Could Melinda want to disappear as badly as he did? He hoped not. Hoped he hadn't weirded her away before anything even started again. Because . . .

was something . . . no. *Moron*. No. "Shit, Danny. Chill."

"Where are you guys going?" Melinda said, acting as if dudes at parties told her they loved her all the time, *not* like he was a moron.

"We're driving to Livingston, Texas. To the death-row facility. So Juan can meet his father," JD explained. "We have to get going if we're going to make the visiting hours."

"That sounds intense," Melinda said, her face full of concern. Then she seemed to wait for JD to say something else, but without any jokes, JD had nothing.

Juan and Roxanne huddled off by themselves; JD guessed they were saying their goodbyes. Danny slapped him across the back, their *See ya*. But now JD worried how he should say goodbye to Melinda. If he should offer a hug? A handshake? He never knew what the fuck to do in situations like these, so he did what he always did and shoved his hands inside his pockets along with his camera. He nodded at Melinda and Roxanne—who'd come back from hugging Juan—and walked off, feeling himself vanishing, like maybe he *was* a ghost. Juan ran up behind him.

"That went pretty well," Juan said supportively. "Except for that awkward-as-fuck goodbye and the 'I love you' part."

JD spat on the ground. "I'm pretty much a player."

"With mad pegué."

JD cranked the truck's engine, which gave a couple of encouraging revs. He'd never been outside of El Paso, him sick his one chance to travel with his basketball team. And he didn't think Juan had either. And for the first time JD wondered what everything would look like outside the city limits, once they were no longer in the desert. How different would the air be? The landscape? The look of the sky? Would he be able to breathe the difference or feel it somehow? Would *he* be different? Could he be?

Fabi,

I got a letter from a couple of vatos saying they want to come down and interview me. Said they were filmmakers and bloggers (not sure what that is) and want to tell my side of the story. Put it on the Internet. One guy's name is JD Sanchez, but the reason I'm telling you this is that the other name is Juan Ramos. This has to be your Juan? Your son? I'm thinking you probably don't know anything about him coming here and that you never told him about me. I can guess why he is coming—he's found one of my letters and is coming for the truth. I guess you never told him everything. They asked to be on my visitor's list. I put them both on, in case they do come.

I'm running out of time, and I know you're not coming. I feel like the first days after getting here. Lonely. Wanting to die all the time. At the same time wanting to appeal, to fight and keep from being put down like a dog. Both things true at the same time.

I understand why you won't come. It's better to forget I am here. To think I died a long time ago, on that day in the diner with Clark Jones. Or the day I was sentenced guilty. Did you already imagine my funeral? Did you cry, say something nice about me? You probably didn't do any of that. I'm not mad. I can't stop writing. Not until this is over. They are going to bury me with "EX" on my grave.

They are going to record my last words. What I say will be written down and put on the Internet, where it will live forever. You will be able to read it one day. I like this idea, or I used to. Now it scares me because what if I say something stupid because I'm scared? And what if I'm too scared to say anything? I'm practicing. The last thing I'm ever going to do is speak, but I've never been good at talking. Do I apologize again? I already did that in court. And in letters. I'm done with that. What's left?

Most of the guys in here are holy rollers. They went that way after so much time. I can't say I blame them. I never went that way, but I see why people do it. The outside world no longer exists when you're on the row. You need another world. This one is nasty. But if our world is so fucked up, then how can the one responsible for creating it be any better? I don't know.

Nothing ever changes in here either. So we never change, or at least it's hard to. So guys arrested at eighteen are forever eighteen, think like they're eighteen, unless they force themselves to change. I read a lot of books. Tried to change that way, not worrying about the next world but instead going into different worlds, at least for a little while. I tried to change my life by seeing how other people lived. What they saw and what they did. That's all life is, right? How you feel, what you say and do? I was the characters in all these books and had all these different lives. I don't know if that's right, if that is any way of living at all, but it was all I had in here. How I survived. I'm not that kid anymore. Not the one who shot that sheriff. Not even the one who loved you in the way I loved you. I'm working on my last words. If I see Juan, I will tell him all the mistakes I've made and how, from in here, there was no way to make up for them. I could never fix what had happened locked away in here. Still, I found a way to change. To be better than I was, if not the best person I could've been. When he asks me if I'm his father I will tell him the truth. That I am not. That his father was a better man than me. At least he was, all those years ago.

FLOATING AWAY
(CHAPTER TWENTY)

Fabi dropped Mando's letter in her lap after reading it. Her small victory of arranging that her mail finally be forwarded began to float away. She looked up from the porch, wondering how long Juan would be at Danny's.

"Papá, where's my truck?" she called out. "Are you working on it?" It wasn't parked in her usual spot in front of the house. Come to think of it, she wasn't sure she noticed it there when she and Gladi got back from Vanessa Peña's office, but maybe her father was tinkering with it in the backyard. Fabi searched her purse for her keys. Also gone. *Huh.* She reached for her phone.

To: Juanito

Maybe make it an early night and come home. We need to talk. :)

"No sé," Papá said, joining her on the porch. "It was here earlier. I think." She began to pace back and forth, looking at the empty space where her truck should be.

"You talk to Juan at all today? He told me he was going to Danny's. Did he tell you something different?"

"No, the little criminal didn't tell me nothing all day."

"Quit calling him that," Fabi scolded. "What's wrong with you?" She gripped Mando's letter and reread the beginning.

> I got a letter from a couple of vatos saying they want to come down and interview me. . . . One guy's name is JD Sanchez . . . the other name is Juan Ramos. This has to be your Juan? Your son? . . . I can guess why he is coming . . . for the truth.

Your Juan.

Your son.

Is coming . . . for the truth.

Fabi crumpled the letter into a ball and looked at her phone. No answer. Juanito wouldn't swipe her truck and drive across the state. Would he? Her brain began to churn. He was just arrested a few weeks ago; he had court coming. Juanito didn't even have a driver's license! *Your Juan, your son, is coming for the truth.*

She suddenly had a vision of Juan on the road, the black

Mazda zooming down the highway, nothing but darkness ahead of him. She'd been gone with Gladi all afternoon. Juan could be hours away, and at any time her piece-of-shit truck could break down on the side of the road, leaving him stranded. The rest of Texas wasn't Chuco. A Mexican kid, especially one who looked like Juan, could find trouble, both with the locals and the cops.

"I know he's not a criminal, mija," her father was saying. "I like to joke around."

Fabi forced herself to refocus. She folded her arms tightly and glowered at Papá. "Well, you're not funny!"

Grampá looked at her foggily, propping himself up against the open doorframe, a tallboy in his hand. Wow—until they'd moved back in, Fabi really had no idea just how much time he spent alone crawling down cans of beer. Still, he could tell something was wrong because he asked, "What's happening, Fabiola?"

Gladi squeezed by their father and joined them on the porch. She swung her arm around Fabi. "Everything okay?"

Fabi winced as her sister hugged her. "I'm pretty sure Juan took my truck and is driving it to the middle of Texas to meet Armando."

"*Armando?* Your old boyfriend? The one in prison?" Papá said incredulously.

"Why would he do *that*?" Gladi asked, slowly pulling her arm back.

Fabi tilted her chin upward, trying to look at them both. "He thinks . . . he thinks Armando is his father."

"Well, isn't he?" Her father tossed his tallboy into the yard, the remaining beer glugging into the dirt, beading into mud.

"No. He's not, Papá," Fabi said.

"Good." Grampá grasped the doorframe to keep from falling. "I'm glad my grandson's got a different father. That Mando was bad news."

"That doesn't even matter. Not anymore," Fabi said, now pacing back and forth. "All that matters is finding Juan." The sun had vanished behind the mountains. Night scared Fabi. Now more than ever. There seemed to be no gravity in the dark, *everything* in danger of floating away. She called her son. No answer. She searched her phone contacts for JD's number. He *had* to be with Juanito. She called him. Nothing. She tried Danny next. Same. Fabi was sure she was being ignored. Juanito couldn't have gotten that far yet, could he? She tried texting again.

To: Juanito

I know why you are doing this. I'm sorry for never telling you about your father. It was a mistake. My mistake!!! I've made a lot of them. Too many. Turn around, come back. PLEASE!!!

Nothing.

To: Juanito

I'm not mad you read the letters. I know you are curious.

You have a right to be. I will tell you everything. PLEASE TURN AROUND NOW.

To: Juanito
COME HOME. YOU HAVE COURT NEXT WEEK. A BIG GAME. SCHOOL. A FUTURE!!!

Again, nothing.

To: Juanito
The man in the prison is not your father.

She waited for her phone to buzz in her hand. No response. *Damn.* She texted JD.

To: Juanito's Dumb Friend
ARE YOU WITH JUANITO? TELL HIM TO TURN THE TRUCK AROUND. HAVE HIM CHECK HIS PHONE. I KNOW YOU THINK YOU ARE HELPING HIM BUT THIS IS DANGEROUS. YOU BOYS COULD GET HURT.

To: Juanito's Dumb Friend
COME BACK NOW. PLEASE!!!!!

She texted Danny next.

To: Juanito's Dumber Friend
IF YOU'RE WITH JUANITO, COME BACK!!!!

Fabi quickly packed a bag for her and Gladi and soon they were on the road, heading down Piedras Street and toward the highway. Gladi punched the address of the prison into the GPS of the rental car, the pleasant voice stating that they would reach their destination in approximately twelve hours. Oldies played softly on the radio, the slow melodies reminding her of the tunes she'd heard with Gladi at L&J Cafe. Of life moving forward, only now it wasn't. Fear and traffic both paralyzed her.

"We have to find another way. We're losing time," Fabi said.

"On it." Gladi studied the traffic, calculating. That was her sister. Focused. Determined. Always good in a situation like this. Papá's favorite song came on the radio, the chorus drilling into her head: *"And I know, I know, I know, I know, I know, I know, I know."* What Fabi knew was that everyone believed Juan was Mando's baby, and they believed that because she never told them different. Martín Juan Morales was Juan's father. Back then she'd been ashamed of how she chased after Martín, for wanting and needing him as badly as she did while still being in love with Mando. The truth was, her grief and guilt had shamed her into keeping quiet.

"I fucked up," Fabi moaned. She looked over at Gladi, who was inching them through traffic, her eyes on the road ahead. "And I keep fucking up."

"I don't know what's going on exactly, but we'll figure things out."

Fabi leaned her head against the passenger window, letting the story unreel in her head, preparing for how she'd explain it all to Juanito. She'd discovered she was pregnant after Martín had gone to boot camp, and after Juanito was born she decided not to tell Martín, suddenly afraid that he could want custody, could steal her baby away to some army life at any time.

"I planned to tell Juanito about his dad when he was still little, but then Martín died. . . . I mean, how do you have that talk . . . after *that*?" Fabi turned to her sister, noticed the threads of wrinkles creased along her forehead. Strands of gray in her hair. She continued. "How do you tell your son that at first you never told him about his dad because you didn't want him, or anyone else, to find out that you were sleeping around while your mother was *dying*? That I was ashamed and then later, afraid he was going to hate me and I would lose him. I just couldn't lose him too."

Gladi reached for Fabi's hand. "I don't think that would happen, and I know Juan would never hate you." In the low light of the cabin, Gladi could've passed for Mamá. Even her voice. Soothing and sure. God, she missed her.

Fabi squeezed her sister's hand. "After Mamá died, *I* hated Papá for not saving her, for not taking her to the doctor sooner. I stayed mad at him, mad at all the mistakes. I took Juan's chance at a father and built his life out of my mistakes."

Traffic started moving and Gladi punched it, buzzing between cars before getting stuck behind a minivan with busted brake lights. "Let's just focus on finding Juan. Maybe JD is with him—he's the one you've been texting, right? I'm sure that kid has his license. He's the tall one? I remember meeting him at your old place last year. That poor dude is going to have to move your seat all the way back just to fit behind the wheel."

Fabi gaspd. "Oh shit. My gun! My gun is in there!"

"What?" Now Gladi looked rattled. "You have a *gun*?"

She had a gun. It was in the truck. In the truck with her son. And here *they* were. They were stuck in traffic, looking for a place to turn the car around. For a way to turn everything around.

From: Juanito's Dumb Friend
MEET ME AT THE OLD APARTMENT

The old apartment was only blocks away. Fabi jumped from Gladi's rental and ran down Piedras Street. A block away she realized she'd left her purse and bag, any second thoughts of what to do. She raced around the corner and saw a group of old neighbors, and people she didn't recognize, gathered behind streamers of bright yellow police tape at the back of the apartment. And there was her truck parked in the alley, boxed in by police cars. Red and blue lights flashed everywhere. A helicopter buzzed overhead. *Juan! Where is Juan?* She couldn't see him. Everything was so loud; a policeman barked gibberish over a bullhorn. She spotted Flor, talking with the police. Flor locked eyes with

Fabi, uncertainty in her face. Horror. Fabi had seen that look before, the day Flor had learned about her husband.

Fabi called out for Juan, pushed her way through the crowd. No one seemed to notice her except Flor. When her Juan didn't answer, she screamed for him again. Then again and again. She shrieked until people finally snapped awake, making a path for her to follow. Fabi's cries never stopped; they were as loud and coming from as deep inside as the day she had given birth to her son.

BARELY MISSED EVERYTHING (CHAPTER TWENTY-ONE)

"So we're the Bad Juans?" JD said as he drove toward Juan's old apartment. "I'm glad you went with a pun. It means we're serious."

"Perfect, right?" Juan said.

"Are you sure you want to go to the old apartment? Isn't Jabba, like, ready to call the national guard on us?"

"I just want to upload the Tumblr. I wanna be legit. Everything has been going *good* lately. I don't want to miss something." It was true. He'd been on a roll, for the first time ever. His ankle was ready. He'd passed his test. He gotten Má's truck to JD's without wrecking it. And of course there was Roxanne; he was pretty sure she was as into him as he was into her.

"So what, are you gonna break into your old room or something? We're gonna get busted before we even leave town."

"Nah, Jabba has Wi-Fi. We'll just cruise up the alley, upload the page, and then hit the road. We won't even have to leave the truck. Just park next door if you're worried."

"As long as we're quick, *Bad Juan*."

"I knew you'd hate it," Juan said, grinning. He booted up his má's Dell. He'd finished his first post, found the images he wanted to upload—a baby picture of himself to go alongside another he found online, and one of the gurney where his father would be executed. The thin mattress and pillow at the center of a sterilized room, thick leather straps fastened to metal-rail sides meant to hold an inmate still as the poisons flooded his body. The entire contraption rested on a thin pedestal, covered with white sheets. The room itself was painted a kind of turquoise green, lit with fluorescent lights, like a hospital, but not. The only baby picture Juan could find of himself was one with Má giving him a bath, him a wet, red, and angry ball of fists.

"Well, I like the name," JD said out of the blue. "It's hilarious."

"It's getting hard to tell when you're being sarcastic," Juan said.

"Not really," JD said. "It's only all the time. So what are you calling the first post?" JD raced down the highway, switching back and forth between lanes.

"Funny you should think of that," Juan said. "I called it 'First Words.'"

"But aren't we getting your old man's *last words*?"

Juan held up a hand. "You know how parents, at least on TV, are always waiting for babies to say their first words or whatever-the-fuck? They can't wait to hear *something*."

"I guess."

"Well, I can't wait to hear what Armando is gonna say. I've been thinking about his first words to me my entire life, and then what mine would be back to him. That's what I wrote."

"Well, that sounds better than my stupid idea," JD said, all sad. "I wanted to call it, like, 'The Row' or 'I'll See You Soon.' Something like that."

"Those are pretty terrible," Juan laughed. "But you're the filmmaker. You got that shit covered."

"You know it."

They got off on Piedras and were stopped at a red light below the underpass, when that pinche Cutlass crept to a stop beside them. Juan glanced over, and then quickly looked straight ahead.

"Shit, keep looking forward. Those fuckers from Los Fatherless are back."

JD stiffened, nervously adjusting his seat belt. "The ones with the shotgun?"

"Yes. Don't look."

"Fuck. What do we do?"

Juan glanced over and saw the back passenger had his shotgun pointed out his window; the driver was mad-dogging him, feet away in the lane beside them, his window down.

"Hey, Banker," the driver yelled, motioning for Juan to roll his window down too. "Why don't you tell your boyfriend to drive to your house so we can borrow that laptop you were hiding the other day? That truck looks pretty nice también. I think we wanna borrow that!"

Juan slowly slouched down in his seat, hoping to get the computer off his lap and onto the floor without them noticing. He whispered, "Don't drive by our houses. No matter what." He rolled down the passenger window.

"Why were you slouching, Banker? Don't tell me you got the computer with you. Why are you carrying it around with you all the time? Are you, like, a hacker? You stealing people's Bitcoins? Hand it over, Banker, and we'll let you keep your boyfriend's shitty truck."

Then, thank God, the light turned green and JD punched it, leaving the Cutlass behind. The Dell fell to the floor. Man, Juan was so glad JD was driving. He knew his way around Central; he zipped up Piedras Street and then turned down Wheeling toward Memorial Park, where he doubled back and lost them. Juan reached for the laptop. It was sliding around the cabin. He couldn't let it get busted; Má would kill him. But what his hand touched wasn't the laptop; it was the cool rubber handle of—a gun?

Juan wrapped his hand around it. A *gun*? He pulled it out from under the seat. The weapon felt like a natural part of his hand, light but somehow weighty. His thoughts instantly flickered to how easily this could solve their Cutlass problem. He became dizzy thinking about it: cruising up to those fuckers at the next red light and leaning out the passenger window, lighting them up. His finger traced the trigger, the smooth curve begging to be squeezed. He remembered the sound from Danny's gun, the crisp *pop* cutting through all the noise, making every other sound vanish. He wouldn't hear them calling him Banker or laughing at him before they realized what was happening, wouldn't hear them crying out in terror as he squeezed the trigger, only the sound of firing: *Pop, pop, pop.*

"What the fuck is that?" JD yelped as he pulled into an alleyway behind a dumpster, not far from Juan's old place.

"I guess . . . it must be my má's?" Juan said, now seething. "I had no idea she even had one." He hated how those dudes always had him running scared. But holding the gun had quickly erased that fear. It let him be *mad*. It was like magic, a bad magic. But now he wasn't fearing *them*.

"What do you wanna do?"

"I don't know. . . . What do you mean?" But Juan knew exactly what JD meant.

JD banged the steering wheel with his hands. "Should we go after those assholes? I bet they'd quit fucking with us if they knew we had this. . . . Is it loaded?"

"I don't know. I don't even know how to check."

"I bet it is, and that's twice those dudes rolled up on us."

"I know," Juan said, laying the gun down on the bench seat between them, not mentioning that it was the fourth time for him. Now JD was gripping the steering wheel, his legs fidgeting up and down, surging with angry current, a circuit about to blow.

"So?"

"So, my old man's about to get the death penalty. It's the whole reason we're here right now. Maybe we shouldn't fuck with this thing."

"Fuck, man! I hate this shit." JD slumped back in the driver's seat. But he kept glancing at the gun, like he wanted to hold it but needed Juan's permission first. Juan wanted to tell him that holding it would make him feel as powerful and as in control as being on the other side of the barrel had left him feeling weak and helpless. How could it not?

"So, you wanna hold it?" he said. They remained parked, engine idling. No sign of the Cutlass. JD's driving had done more than a gun could to get rid of the fuckers.

JD looked at the black metal between them. "No," he finally said. "But what are we gonna do with that thing? We can't take it with us. If we get pulled over, we're fucked. We gotta get rid of it." JD sat up, suddenly smiling as he pointed through the windshield. "There's a dumpster. Let's toss it in that dumpster and go."

"It's my ma's. And what if some kid finds it?"

"Again, fuck! Maybe we should call the trip off, then."

"We're not calling off nothing," Juan said. He couldn't take the gun home. By now his má would be all pissed about the truck and probably already blowing up his phone. JD's, too. Thing was, they'd both agreed to turn their phones off until they'd reached the halfway point to Livingston, to avoid chickening out and turning back when angry phone calls from home came rolling in. Because, honestly, he might chicken out if they did. Then Juan nodded as an idea came to him. "Can we leave it at your place?"

"I thought you said not to drive by our houses. What if those fuckers see us?"

"You're right, you're right." Juan rubbed his face, the cool palms of his hands a temporary relief. He had to think. The gun was going to fuck everything up, and of course those assholes in the Cutlass were still out there. All Juan needed was a break to still make it, a small bounce to go his way. A lucky call. Anything.

"Let's hide it at the apartment!" JD cried. "We were going there anyway. You can update the blog, and I'll find a place to stash it. We hit the road after. No big deal."

"I don't know," Juan said. Getting out of the truck was a bad idea, especially with Jabba on the lookout for him. It was desperate. But then, he didn't have a better option and there were plenty of hiding spots for the pistol. The never-used shed, or inside the flowerpots, buried in the potting soil. Tuck it into a hole along the eaves of the roof. He would have to be fast. He could be.

"How about you upload the blog, and I'll hide the gun," he said at last. "I know the perfect spot."

JD eyed him. "You sure?"

"Yeah, I got this."

• • •

As JD drove the few remaining blocks to the apartment, Juan kept an eye out for the Cutlass. JD shut off the headlights before cruising up the alleyway behind the apartment building and parking, then killing the engine. The backyard lights glowed dimly, and the windows inside the complex were dark. It *was* Friday, everyone probably out partying or at the movies. Doing *something* that didn't include guarding their backyard. Juan opened his doc with his blog post and his JPEGs, went over with JD which ones to use, the username and password for the account.

"You sure you didn't see those dudes on your way up here?" Juan said, holding the open laptop tightly. Not wanting to let go. Not wanting to pick up the gun.

"No, man," JD said. "How's the signal?"

"The Wi-Fi's good from here," Juan said. The screen was the only light in the cabin.

"Dude, who knows where those assholes went. . . . They probably hassle half of Central. C'mon, let's go. We need to get the fuck outta here." JD eased the laptop away from Juan.

"You're right. I'll be quick." Juan took a deep breath, grabbed the pistol, and stealthily moved toward the back of the apartment. It was hard to see; the dull lighting from the porch provided him cover, but it was making his options for hiding the gun hard to spot. He scanned the yard. The flowerpots by the sage bushes had been moved. And the door of the toolshed was secured with a chain-and-combo lock— Damn, when had Jabba done that? He spied an empty Chico's Tacos bag on the ground. Okay, he could wrap the pistol inside and then toss the bag on the roof of the toolshed, where no one would ever see. *Unless they happened to be on the second floor of the apartment building. Shit.* The hole in the eaves had to be there—no way was Jabba fixing *that*. Juan had wanted to avoid getting this close to the building, especially with the gun. The indestructible, badass feeling it had given him earlier was long gone; now he just felt crazy nervous, his whole body buzzing.

He could hear the sound of tires crunching rock and dirt in the distance, them coming to a stop, an engine idling. There were no headlights. Juan glanced back to see if JD had noticed, but he was plugging away on the laptop, oblivious. He'd fucked up, coming back to the apartment. Juan squeezed the gun's handle, ran his index finger over the trigger. It seemed obvious now, how his future was knotted with everyone's past. His old man's. His má's. Even Grampá's. His fuckups were all part of an ancestral knot of fuckups that was impossible to untangle. This was it. Juan hunkered down, kept still.

What if he turned and ran down the back of the alley, leaving JD behind?

What if he just started shooting?

Shit. Shit. Shit.

Juan chucked the firearm into a bush and bolted.

When floodlights lit up and the red and blue siren lights circled, the first thing that popped into Juan's head was the PAC. How the harsh fluorescent lights sometimes created the same disorienting effect on the basketball court. His arms and legs pumped as hard as they could.

"Stop! Put your hands where we can see them!"

Juan ran toward the truck. He could see JD, the absolute terror in his eyes as the floods exploded light into the cabin. He caught a glimpse of the laptop screen, it tumbling toward the passenger seat as JD jerked back. His baby picture next to the image of the gurney. What he'd never noticed before was the look on his má's face, her trying to dry him as he twisted angrily in her arms. She'd been afraid. Afraid she was doing it all wrong. Juan recognized that look—*his* look. Juan couldn't see the cop, or cops, or tell where the shots were coming from; he only heard the sounds echoing from all around. The bullets dropped Juan to the ground, to the rocks and dirt, as he reached for the truck's handle. He barely missed making it back inside. Barely missed everything.

PIEDRAS (CHAPTER TWENTY-TWO)

JD never saw Juan running toward the truck. Never saw his friend lost in the blinding whiteness of the floods. But he heard the gunshots. At least five of them, all popping off one after the other, the sound seeming different than that time with Danny.

JD didn't duck underneath the dash, or flee the cabin after hearing the first shot. Instead, he froze. In the driver's seat, he looked straight ahead and waited for the bullets to blast through the windshield and rip through him.

When the firing ended he heard yelling. A man calling to stay down, to get his hands up. Before JD could even do that—get his hands up, stay down—he was pulled from the inside of the truck and slammed chest-down to the dirt, his head colliding against a hunk of rock embedded in the alley ground. A knee dug into the middle of his back and another was against his head.

From underneath the truck, on the other side, he could see Juan. Still as a stone. A single cop, a shadow, knelt beside him, close, but not touching. Juan. JD couldn't breathe. His head was cut; he could feel the blood pooling around his face, his eyes burning. He sucked in dust trying to breathe. Coughed. Choked. There was so much weight on him. Someone yelled they'd found the gun. The bushes. That this was the same truck reported racing around earlier. He was yanked up as hands jammed down his pockets and waistband, racking him in the balls, searching, but for what? Another gun? They pushed him back down on his back, discarded. He knew Juan was dead.

A cop was talking about all the bullshit he was going to have to go through because of this piece-of-shit gangster. How everyone saw the perp pointing that fucking gun at him, that piece of shit probably an illegal. *Right? We all saw. We all saw, right?*

JD's phone had fallen underneath the truck. He glanced around, and with no one watching, he reached for the phone, not able to take his eyes off Juan, and grabbed it. He glanced around again, then, sitting back up, he wiped the dirt and blood from his face and turned the phone on. Juan's má had called. Had texted, too. He texted her back, telling her she needed to come. Next JD called his old man, his father being the only person, in that moment, he could think to call. JD was cuffed and hauled away before either of them showed.

* * *

His father picked him up from the station the next morning, where JD hadn't been under arrest but had been kept all night answering the same questions over and over, a medic even stitching his face as different sets of cops kept at him. *What, exactly, were you doing at the apartment?* "Uploading the blog. Dumping the gun." *Why were you "dumping" the gun?* "Because getting caught by the cops with a gun could get you killed. The gun belonged to Juan's mother." *Did you know Juan took the truck without telling his mom?* "I thought he had permission." *What were you going to do in Livingston, Texas?* "Juan was going to meet his father. I was going to film it. It's on the blog. Read the fucking blog." *Did you see Juan point the gun at the officers?* "No, but he didn't." *How do you know that for sure?* "Because fuck you. That's how I know for sure."

He and his father drove to his father's new apartment, stopping for McDonald's on the way. Turned out Pops still lived in Central, in an unfurnished one-bedroom on Piedras just north of Mobile. His bedroom had a mattress on a box spring in the middle of the room, a pair of blinds with bent and missing slats pulled halfway open, and a trash bag burping dirty clothes in the closet. The kitchen had hardly any food, the counters lined with crumpled bags of takeout. The living room had a futon, a small TV on top of a mini fridge, and a coffee table bubbled with water damage.

"Put this in your belly," his father said, tossing him a breakfast sandwich.

"I'm not hungry," JD said, crashing down on the futon.

"I know." Pops dropped his keys on the coffee table. "You need to eat anyway." Before they'd come inside, Pops had to jiggle his keys to get the lock to work, and JD heard the sound of his dog tags on the key ring knocking together. The clinking noise had always meant Pops was home. JD was surprised how much he missed that sound. He closed his eyes, wanting to conjure a warm memory, but instead his mind flashed to the image of Juan dead in the dirt, halfway underneath a truck. He reached for his father's keys, rubbed his thumbs over the raised lettering. *I am never going to see Juan again.*

SANCHEZ
TOMAS
012-80-4179
A POS
ROMAN CATHOLIC

"Can I have these? Please?"

His old man sat on the couch beside JD and took the keys, worked the tags from the key ring, and handed them to him. He turned on the TV. The Cowboys were playing. JD would remember the game for the rest of his life—not the score or even what happened, but how he and Pops didn't do anything but talk football, and how good it felt to not think about what was happening. At halftime his old man went out for tacos even though JD still wasn't hungry, and JD called the recruiter, knowing he was ready to vanish completely. Bullard answered, even on a Sunday, and JD explained how he didn't give a shit about the film production job. That all he wanted was to leave the day after he graduated high school.

LAST STATEMENT
Date of Execution:
February 14

Offender:
Armando Aranda #999178

Last Statement:
"After spending most of my life on the row, I'm not afraid of dying. I'm more afraid of saying something stupid, of being remembered as the worst thing I did or as the worst thing that happened to me. I don't want to turn into a scary story, but I don't want to be forgotten, either. For it to be like I never existed or even mattered. There is a boy who thought I was his dad. Who wanted to meet me, but he never made it to the prison. I know who his father could be, a good dude. The kind of man who can point a kid in the right direction. The one he took for himself and not the dead man's way."

20 June

Fabi,

I've been thinking of all the things that could've gone different. If I'd never run from the cops at Danny's party and got him busted, or put the idea of visiting Armando in his head. I should've been the one hiding the gun. I don't think he trusted me to do it. I should be dead. I know how bullshit that sounds. That it doesn't change anything.

Juan was running away when the cops shot him, not pointing the gun like the local news said. Like the cops kept saying. For a while I thought there would be some CNN or even Fox News coverage about the shooting, that the truth would come out. What a joke. Now I know black lives matter, but no one gives a fuck about brown lives, and when gringos shout "all lives matter" they're just throwing white shade on everything. I looked up his dad after you told me about him. All I could find was a tiny blurb: "Staff Sgt. Martin Morales died during his second deployment in Iraq, in a city called Baqubah. A bomb exploded inside a house he was attempting to clear."

I have footage of Juan—it's not very good—and I watched it almost every day before I left. I was making a movie when he died, and I've kept at it even though I have no idea what I'm doing. I took some B-roll at the cemetery where he's buried. I filmed my family. Got scenes as my parents split up for good, Ama packing up Apa's things and leaving them on the porch for him to get. All the pictures in the house coming down as Ama got ready to move. She and Tomasito are moving in with my Tia Monchi, Pops is staying in his terrible apartment, and Alma is moving in with her novio. Ama wasn't surprised when I told her I'd joined the air force, not that I meant joining to be a surprise. She finished a bite of pan dulce, nodded, and said, "I figured you'd abandon us completely one day." She was right. Pops took it different when I told him, said he was proud to be the father of a military man. Glad his son was following in his footsteps. His dog tags are the only thing I took with me.

I read the last words of Armando Aranda a week after the execution and wondered, *How the fuck did that guy end up there?* I wondered how Martin Morales ended up in Baqubah, Iraq. Did he ever wonder? No one recorded Martin's final words. Juan's last words to me were "I'll be quick." If he said anything after, to the police, to God, to anyone he thought may have been listening, I don't know.

Boot camp isn't hard but feels like it could be at any moment. There's a lot of waiting for something to happen, and everybody is freaked out all the time. At night I hear dudes sobbing. Crying that they want to go home. That they've made a mistake. I didn't cry after Juan died. Not the day he was killed. Not at the funeral. I haven't cried about my family either. Before I left for the air force I was hooking up with a girl I'd been stupid over ever since I was in eighth grade. I really liked her, but I left without saying goodbye. I barely talk to Danny. I'm the ghost my family said I was.

Juan was the person I would've told all this to. You're the only piece of him left.

Goodbye.

AB Sanchez, Juan D
322 TRS / FLT 462 / (Dorm A-9)
1320 Truemper St. Unit 369520
Lackland AFB, TX 78236-6095

SOLVING FOR WHAT'S UNKNOWN (CHAPTER TWENTY-THREE)

The storm over the Tucson Mountains—the multiple slashes of lightning, the grayish-black sheet of pounding rain cutting across the range toward Fabi's little casita—was a welcome sight. Fabi opened the small window over the kitchen sink and breathed the desert air, the smell of wet dirt and creosote. Blooming palo verde. She'd never experienced a monsoon like this. One that meant business. Hard-blowing winds and fat, relentless rain flooded the mountain almost every night, leaving the tiny backyard of her new place at the base of the mountain sloshed with mud and rock. Spiky weeds grew wild in the yard seemingly overnight—Grampá pulled them most mornings after spending nights hiding out in his room, not wanting anything to do with the storms.

Fabi had finished unpacking a week after moving in,

and finally developed the film she'd found when packing up her old apartment. Most were pictures of Juan as a newborn swaddled in blankets, his face pinched shut. Her favorite was of her holding him at a party, her smiling at the camera and Juan's eyes opened wide, watching her. Her Juanito, always the careful observer.

She placed the photos in frames, hung them in her bedroom and around the house. She'd also rescued old pictures of Mamá from Papá's drawers as they packed up his old house, and hung those, too. They sold the house a month after the funeral and used the money to buy this new place. Gladi had sent some photos she'd been holding on to as a housewarming gift. Fabi painted all the walls, and she and Papá took to working on the place. Replacing the bad plumbing. The rotting electrical. The collapsing roof. Fabi had a sewing room, the Singer set up by the window and overlooking a garden she planned on starting the following spring. Papá said he would frame out a flower bed, something for vegetables. He suggested maybe she should learn to sew—if she wanted. When Fabi came across items neither her or Papá thought they needed or wanted to look at again, jewelry or some old army memorabilia, she took them to a van she'd passed on her first drive into town, a multicolored VW just off I-10 with a plywood sign with the word DONATIONS spraypainted across it. A woman inside received those things gratefully.

A week after Juan's funeral, Coach Paul visited Fabi at Papá's and told her about the scholarship he'd hooked

Juan up with in Arizona. He explained how Juan had done a good job coaching another boy while he'd been injured, and what a shame it was her son had been caught up in "that life." He said he'd had no idea Juan had been into drugs or stolen a vehicle until he'd watched all that mess on the news; he knew about the arrest record, but who didn't have one on this side of town? The coach wanted Fabi to know he'd done everything to get Juan on the straight and narrow, and considered himself to be just as much at fault for what happened as she was. He cried.

While Fabi hated that Coach Paul bothered to stop by in the first place, she liked the idea of Arizona. Of starting over. There was nothing left for her in El Paso. She went to the library and found the school Juan would've gone to, pictures of the basketball gym, of science labs, of young faces in image after image looking happier than anyone at a community college probably ever looked. Fabi decided *she* would be the one to go to Pima Community College, and told Papá to pack his things the moment she returned home.

Like the coach, and JD, her father also blamed himself for everything. Blamed himself for not taking her and Juan into his home sooner. For not being a bigger part of their lives. For not teaching Juanito to be a man. As if Juan was killed for not being a man. That was *exactly* the reason her son was killed. For being a man. A brown one.

Fabi's pregnancy ended two days after Juan's funeral. She started cramping and then bleeding one morning, a supernova occurring inside her body, the universe captured in her sonogram suddenly collapsing. Because it was early in the pregnancy, a doctor from Project Vida later told her she'd be perfectly fine, able to have kids again if she ever wanted. Fabi thanked the doctor, not knowing what else to say, only knowing that nothing in her life would ever be perfectly fine again.

The next morning would be Fabi's first day of class. She'd registered at the West Campus of PCC after applying and taking her assessment tests all on the same day. She had even declared a major—electrical engineering—even though her adviser, a woman named Yvette who was younger than she was and had her degree from the University of Arizona hanging in her office, said she didn't need to pick right away. Fabi placed directly into College Algebra, MAT 151. She'd studied the algebra book she found in Juanito's room, worked on the same equations he'd done, going through his notebook and working out all the same problems. That afternoon she ate her lunch in the basketball gym. There was no team practicing inside, no smell of sweat or buzz in the air. Instead, long tables were set up to help students register for classes and sign up for different clubs. Fabi looked for a sewing club but only found crocheting.

The rain unloaded, and Fabi shut the window, the drops pelting the glass. The water started coming down so hard and fast that she could no longer see through it. Her first class would be College Algebra, and she was surprised by how much she already liked the subject. How much easier it was than she remembered from high school. She liked how answers could be reduced to their lowest terms. That the problems could be solved at all made algebra better than real life.

The rain continued, and the water in the backyard rose, seeping through the torn seal along the kitchen door. Fabi opened it; cold water rushed over her bare feet and flooded onto the linoleum. She walked into the storm. Lightning cracked across the purple sky. The rain slapped hard against her face, her body. Near the foot of the mountain, small avalanches of mud and rock slid toward her and her home. Threatened worse. The wind shrieked and thunder boomed as the thin branches of mesquite and palo verde in the yard flexed to the point of breaking. Fabi knew the storm would be over soon, everything calming to a stop. Only wreckage left behind.

At sunrise her father came out of his room and went to work cleaning up the fallen branches, cutting them into smaller pieces with a hand saw, and then he washed away the mud from the concrete walkway. He stacked fallen mountain rocks into a neat pile in the corner of the yard before repairing the seal under the back door to keep water from seeping back inside.

Fabi biked to school on her first day as a college student and navigated the hallways of the Santa Catalina building until she found her classroom. She took a desk right in front. A clean whiteboard bolted to a gray wall faced the room as students took their seats. Still sweating from the ride, Fabi took out her book, pencil, calculator, and her notebook—no, Juan's notebook. The first few pages were still alive with his handwriting, his name written on each one at the top right-hand corner. As the professor came into the classroom, Fabi turned to the first blank page and wrote her name exactly the way her son had. Without a word the professor grabbed a dry-erase marker and began to scribble an equation on the whiteboard, a long mix of letters and numbers. When he finished he set the marker down.

"If you cannot solve this equation, do yourself a favor and drop this class now."

Fabi and the rest of the class stared at one another, puzzled about what to do. Unlike the images she'd seen online, nobody was smiling. Some in the class took out pencils and paper and got to work, while others packed their belongings and left. The fluorescent lights of the room were bright and harsh, the window blinds closed, blocking any morning light from sneaking in. Fabi thought about Juan and knew exactly what he would do if he were sitting there instead of her. At that moment there was no other place Fabi wanted to be. Fabi carefully wrote the problem down and began solving for what was unknown.

ACKNOWLEDGMENTS

I'd like to thank Meg Files for believing in my work and inviting me to present at the Pima Writer's Workshop where I was lucky enough to meet Dara Hyde, my now agent and confidant.

Dara was the first person to read *Barely Missing Everything* and the one to point out that the audience for this novel was young adults, teens just like Juan and JD. I'll be forever grateful for her insights and her help in making this novel what it is.

And to Caitlyn Dlouhy, a superhero of a person and my editor. Thank you for being the champion Juan, JD, and Fabi needed. You have shaped and molded *Barely Missing Everything* with your careful brilliance. Without you I would not have been able to fully unlock this story. Thank you. Many thanks to the Atheneum team, who love books and readers.

Thank you to my family, to my má who is just like me but also way different, to my brother and sister who got my back. And to my father, who died two months after I signed the contract for this novel, and who I miss every day. This book is made from their sacrifices. I love you all.

Without Fernie Rubio and Carlo Passaseo, without our childhoods, this story could not have been written. We miss you Carlo.

Thank you Marlo, my wife of twenty years. I've been made better at life by your fearlessness and determination, by your generosity of spirit. I love you, and thank you, thank you, thank you. And a special thanks to our two daughters, Margie and Gabby, who were both born as *Barely Missing Everything* was being written. Their energy is on every page.

And finally, to each and every reader, thank you.